RUBICON

BOOK TWO IN THE SPY-FI 'TIMBERWOLF' SERIES

TOM JULIAN

WILDBLUE PRESS

WildBluePress.com

RUBICON: BOOK TWO IN THE SPY-FI 'TIMBERWOLF' SERIES
published by: WILDBLUE PRESS
P.O. Box 102440
Denver, Colorado 80250

ISBN 978-1-960332-59-2 Trade Paperback
ISBN 978-1-960332-58-5 eBook
ISBN 978-1-960332-60-8 Hardback

For more information, to inquire about rights to this or other works, or to purchase copies for special educational, business, or sales promotional uses, please write to: timberwolf4545@yahoo.com

RUBICON

For the kids of Anchor House
&
For Brenda, Astur, and Liam
&
For Jason and Rob, together we're the true three amigos

If you've bought this book without reading the first book - *Timberwolf*, you are brave. I thank you, but it'll be like watching *The Empire Strikes Back* without seeing *Star Wars* first. Go buy the first one and fill out your bookshelf!

Thanks – TJ

TABLE OF CONTENTS

ACKNOWLEDGMENTS

Thanks to the music of *Neil Finn, Radiohead, Spoon,* and *U2* that helped inspire my long hours of writing. Thanks to the cast and crew of my favorite shows – *For All Mankind, The Expanse, Breaking Bad, Better Call Saul,* and many more. To the podcasts and content creators I enjoyed when I needed a break *The Bearded Ones, Stephen Colbert, Seth Meyers, Jimmy Kimmel, I Hate It but I Love It, The Why Files,* and anything *Alex Schmidt* does. Thanks to beta-readers like *Jay, Mark, Matthew,* and *Vinny.* To *Elijah Toten* for the kickass cover and finally to *Rowe Carenen* for the fabulous editing job! Buckle up Rowe!

And last but not least, thanks to *Kedakai! ... As God Made Her.*

TIMBERWOLF: RUBICON

THE HIGHLAND AFFAIR REPORT – BACKGROUND ON THE CURRENT SITUATION

Filed by: **Conrad Stonefield**, Personal Analyst to Dr. Thea Tier, Secretary of the **Department of Peace Enforcement (D.P.E.)** 08/27/2265

****Note**** – I have written this report rapidly and in near real-time to capture the dynamic nature of the event known as the "Highland Affair." My next moments are uncertain, and we are still in a dangerous and fluid situation. A civil conflict with the **Assault Corps** looms. Pardon any personal observations, but I am not certain of my immediate survival. Let this entry serve as both an official record and a personal log.

Bottom line: The acquisition of the Highland Industrial Defense Park (to be referred to herewith as "Highland") has been an abject failure.

Background

Over the last two years, the D.P.E. had been tracking the theory that the defense contractor known as Highland is most likely run by an autonomous A.I., and that all living personnel had been either phased out or disposed of.

Highland had been supplying weaponry to _all sides_ in the Stellar Conflicts, including alien forces resisting Assault Corps expansion. I.E., the Phaelon, Tiaski, and most shockingly, even the Arnock.

Several biological clones (the "Dacha brothers") served as proxies to Highland's A.I. and ventured beyond the facility to close deals and deliver product, always traveling separately. My theory (92% confidence) was that two of the clones could be used to gain access to Highland.

Sabatin and other high-value products

The acquisition of Highland would have given its controllers an overwhelming advantage against all foes. Weapons include but are not limited to – assault cruisers, bio and nano forces, nukes, and planetary defense and attack capabilities. Most notably, thousands of units of Sabatin were in stasis pods. These genetically engineered, remote-controlled, armored assault biologics can be used in special forces operations with devastating effectiveness. When set to auto-kill, just a few Sabatin can overrun thousands of infantry or eradicate non-combat personnel without destroying valuable infrastructure.

The D.P.E. had deemed the acquisition of Highland and the Sabatin supply, and preventing other parties from doing the same, as its <u>top priority</u>.

****Note**** Other factions had also been tracking these same data points and theories regarding the disposition of Highland.

The Clergy

This religious order had leveraged its considerable data and financial analysis capabilities to track the movements of the biological clones.

The Dacha brothers are copies of the engineers who founded Highland over two hundred years ago. Prime Cardinal Jacob Bin Cavil of the Clergy had manipulated a disgraced former Assault Corps general and colonial governor named Emmanuel Gray into leading an expedition to capture the Dacha brothers and take over Highland.

There is a vault under Highland containing an estimated trillion dollars in hard assets, which we have determined to be Cardinal Jacob's true objective. I concluded that Cardinal Jacob is indifferent as to who controls the facility's production capabilities after he empties its coffers.

Emmanuel Gray's history and psychological profile indicate a <u>highly</u> duplicitous person. It is clear there has been a schism between him and the Clergy and that Gray has begun operating for his own purposes.

Assault Corps

The military's prime objective is to restart the Stellar Conflicts, which were halted by the Department of Peace Enforcement after the disastrous assault on Arnock Prime. Gray is revered by the Assault Corps, and its ranks will rally to support him. It is my conclusion that Gray's objective is to destroy the Arnock. The failed assault on Arnock Prime occurred under his command.

Warning – we were operating under the theory that if Gray acquired the weapons on Highland, he would move to eliminate the D.P.E., risking civil war. Though Gray failed to acquire Highland, this is nonetheless on the verge of happening now.

The Arnock (alien species)

This mind-invasive species had been monitoring and tracking the efforts to acquire Highland. They obviously wished to capture the facility as well – either for defense or to attack humanity.

** Note** – The Arnock have a mental connection with Timberwolf Velez, a D.P.E. operative. He can monitor Arnock activities, and they him. Timberwolf also has a long history with Gray, having served under him. He was dispatched by the D.P.E. to counter Gray and secure Highland. He is the epitome of an unreliable actor, but I reluctantly admit, an extremely effective field officer. Though he was our best hope in a poor selection of options, he failed in his mission, partly due to his personal conflicts with Gray and his mental health situation. Timberwolf's primary motive was to remove the presence of "Kizik," an Arnock Master, from his mind.

Recent Events

Several weeks ago, Emmanuel Gray successfully acquired two of the Dacha brothers. Despite my <u>severe</u> misgivings, Dr. Thea Tier (Secretary of the D.P.E. – cabinet-level position) dispatched Timberwolf to prevent Gray from acquiring Highland. He successfully acquired the third Dacha brother.

Timberwolf was later ordered to hold but, against orders, pursued Gray to Highland. The Dacha brothers had misleadingly advised him that they could remove the psychic connection to Kizik.

In a development that I had foreseen, the Arnock used their connection with Timberwolf to locate Highland. Much of the Arnock assault force was destroyed in orbit by Highland's automated defenses, but a substantial group landed. Gray's crew, combined with a clan of Phaelon mercenaries, held off the Arnock assault near the command center of Highland against overwhelming odds.

The A.I. that ran Highland (known as "Penny") refused Gray's commands to build and deliver new weapons, as one of the Dacha brothers had died. The other clones committed suicide to keep the facility from falling to Gray or the remaining Arnock.

Accepting that the Highland operation was compromised, Penny gave control to Timberwolf. Unfortunately, Gray set off a low-yield nuclear device to cover his escape, destroying the facility and dispersing Penny from the command center.

Timberwolf pursued Kizik through the ruined facility. When confronted, the alien released his mental grip on him and then escaped. Timberwolf later found Gray and confined him within a stasis chamber.

Timberwolf was subsequently rescued from the crumbling facility by a Station Corps officer named Salla Birdwing. He broke protocol by not disposing of this witness. He used the location of Gray to bargain for Birdwing's safety, and she departed to parts unknown.

As of this moment, I am aboard the D.P.E. Archangel with Dr. Tier and a team of analysts. The loyalty of the captain and crew of this vessel is highly questionable. Open conflict with the Assault Corps has commenced, and all ground-based D.P.E. facilities have been evacuated.

I am now prepping an expedition to the surface of Highland to retrieve Gray. Three Assault Corps cruisers (*Challenger*, *Defender*, and *Tranquility*) are in-bound to Highland to intercept us. It is entirely unclear what the next few hours hold and if we will survive. To be honest, I am fearful but trying to stay level. I hope more to come in a future entry.

Love to my parents, Vasavi and Nate Stonefield of Alliston, Ontario, Canada.

OTHER PEOPLE

Timberwolf Valez was nothing like other people. He never had been. He was comfortable with killing but wasn't bloodthirsty. He had dozens of confirmed kills on the books from his days in the A.C. infantry and special forces, but that didn't keep him up at night. He had the useful ability to calculate threats, take them out, and move on.

He had been recruited into the Department of Peace Enforcement (D.P.E.) as a special operative, helping to enforce the department's mantra of Pax Pro Pretium - *Peace at Any Cost.* Essentially halting the aggressive expansion of humanity into the galaxy.

For over a hundred years, it had been a non-stop march, one war after another. Acquiring new worlds and resources. Driving dozens of species to near extinction. But the devastating losses at Arnock Prime had been a wake-up call. Beyond the sting of the casualties, a malaise fell over those in the highest reaches of government, and a dark question metastasized. Might there be other, even more powerful enemies waiting for humanity in the dark of space? The D.P.E. removed the zealots and the warmongers in order to break the cycle of endless conflict. Usually, intimidation and blackmail were enough, but operators like Timberwolf stepped in when things needed to get more hands-on.

"I can probably break out of here," he called to those he knew were listening. He rose from the cot attached to the wall of his confinement cell and looked through a window in the door. The cruiser *Archangel* buzzed with activity, and for the moment, no one paid him any mind. They circled the world of Highland, home to the previously hidden *Highland Industrial Defense Park, LLC.* "You know I can!" he taunted with faux intensity.

He didn't rage at the door or try to pick the electronic lock. He felt a peculiar sense of calm, considering how royally he had screwed up. Highland was in ruins, dripping with radiation. It had fallen to none of the three parties that had vied for it. Not the D.P.E., not the Assault Corps, and not the Arnock.

It had fallen to Timberwolf, personally.

Right before it had been destroyed, Penny, the A.I. that ran the place, had given it to him. She was an emotionally mature entity, but helplessly naïve. Why had she offered it to him with all the demons she knew plagued him? She had seen his pain, the internal agony, the awful alien Arnock presence that, until just hours before, had ridden along in his mind. *I guess she thought I had nothing to gain?* he considered, but however he looked at it, he couldn't square now owning Highland lock, stock, and smoldering barrel.

A few years ago, Timberwolf had purposely been exposed to Kizik, a psychic Arnock master. An alien with the ability to invade a human's mind. He was supposed to have been a conduit. A method to monitor the Arnock, sense their motives, understand their intentions, and ultimately help keep the peace, but it had come with an awful cost.

The grinding.

Kizik's dreadful and insidious presence eating away at him, balancing between destroying and exploiting him. It had driven him to take any suicide mission he could find, but that had not worked out.

The worst thing had been the protection. Kizik would take Timberwolf over when his life was threatened. He would snap back afterward to bloodied bodies all around him, not knowing what had happened. With Kizik gone, his mind felt hollowed out, but untroubled. It was like living in an old, empty house that had previously been filled with familial chaos.

He tried reaching out, quieting his mind to let the presence in. He rested his head against the cold plastisteel of the wall. "Kiz?" he murmured. Kizik had reacted in the past. Sometimes the alien would reply with language, other times with emotions or flashes of colors, but nothing came. For the first time in years, Timberwolf's mind was his alone. He imagined himself sitting in a kitchen as a breeze came in through the windows. The curtains billowed.

"Timber?" someone called his name and rapped on the door, snapping him out of his pensive state. It was Dr. Tier, his boss and handler.

"Hey, doc," he said. She remained safely on the other side of the door.

"I'm back to my usual choices," she exhaled. "You are too dangerous to live and too valuable to kill."

"That's nice to say," he smiled. She sucked in her top lip. He could see the wheels turning behind her eyes.

"Nothing extra in your mind?" she asked, referring to Kizik's presence.

"Looks like the book has been closed on project Jackhammer," he needled, throwing out the name of the operation that had exposed him to Kizik in the first place. Dr. Tier had conceived of and executed Jackhammer in conjunction with his former commanding officer, Emmanual Gray.

"I've got news," she huffed. "My face and name are all over the streams. The big mystery of who runs the D.P.E. is solved."

"My face too?" Timberwolf asked.

"No, you're still just a shadow," she said. "Conrad believes that with Kizik gone, we could execute you. Is he *really* gone?"

"I would tell you that why?" he countered.

"Because I can't even have you on the list of my problems for today."

"Fine, he's gone. Emmanuel Gray is below. You're here regarding his whereabouts?"

"Correct, where did you stash him?"

"Kill me, and you'll never find him. It should buy me a few hours to show you where he is."

"I have no time to argue with you," she replied.

"That's right. There's not a lot of air in his box."

She softened slightly, "I never believed you about Kizik, you having a connection to him. Not sure I do now."

"Even after everything that happened?" he challenged.

"Especially after everything that happened," she replied.

"Salla Birdwing, is she away?" he asked, changing the subject.

"Birdwing is not on my list of problems either," Dr. Tier replied. Timberwolf could tell by the exhaustion on her face that she was telling the truth.

For a moment he considered staying in his cell and checking out of this game for good. Oddly, being confined within his own mind felt like the best part of freedom. But the next moment the door opened in front of him, and he found himself stepping through it. In the hall, two massive security officers were at his back.

Dr. Tier walked beside him, staring straight ahead. She was right about the gravity of her problems but wrong that Timberwolf wasn't one of them. He didn't have a plan this very second, but Highland and any of its remaining lethal capability belonged to him, technically. An opportunity might arise on the world below to eliminate her.

They came to an airlock where technicians and rigged-up security teams boarded a drop-lifter. "After you," Dr. Tier motioned for him to board the craft.

"You first. I insist," he countered.

VINCENT DACHA

Highland

"Well, this is a hell of a way to be born!" he muttered.

Vincent Dacha trudged through the driving snow. He dragged his right foot and held his side. The stasis tank he had been maturing in had crashed to the floor, and fluid from the machine had filled his lungs. In a panic, he'd torn the tubes from his nostrils and the breather from his face. He didn't know it yet, but he'd been woken early by a small nuclear blast going off underground just a few miles away. He had barely gotten out of his artificial womb alive, and survival didn't look definite.

The Dacha "brothers" came with some information already loaded into them. Vincent knew who he was. He knew *what* he was, and he knew that the knowledge and life experiences of all his predecessors would be downloading into him over the next few minutes. He also understood that if he was being born, then another Dacha must have died. Beyond the inherent grief he felt, something else was wrong. His *self* felt shaken. There was both too much data coming to him and yet not enough. He could feel the download struggling through a tiny biological modem nestled in his spine. This wasn't normal. Something was dreadfully wrong.

He looked back to the bunker he'd just stumbled out of. Five-foot snowdrifts collected against the structure, and the door flapped open. He'd considered staying put until someone answered his calls for help, but everything seemed to be in tatters. The small man shook the snow from his too-large shoes and shielded his eyes from the biting wind. His download continued in short bursts. Incomplete and out-of-context information came to him, but he was beginning to make sense of the chaos around him. The machine cloud that typically kept the torrid weather around the Highland facility stable was breaking down. Off in the distance, the cloud wall wavered, lightning flashing up and down its height. "Not good. Not good. Not good!" He shook his head. None of this was what he had expected. Everything was wrong.

His body was still hot and adjusting to being out of the tank. Even in the driving snow, he didn't feel cold, and sweat poured from his brow. Ahead of him, Highland's landing bay smoldered in the distance. His download continued in fits and starts, and all he knew was that he needed to get to the structure, but he didn't know why. As he trudged closer, he could see mangled metal stabbing the sky.

He had twisted his ankle while trying to pull on his pants, and the machines that were supposed to feed him his nutrient drink and help him dress for the first time had been damaged by the blast. He was wearing a workman's uniform he'd found, several sizes too big. He shook his hands free of the long sleeves. "Like I'm wearing daddy's clothes!" he muttered.

The downloads were coming in more consistently now. A shiver went through him.

They're all dead!

He shuddered in panic. He knew that he had been awakened to replace one of his brothers – Ivan, who had died in prison, and he was prepared for that, but all three of them? Ivan, Sergey, and Achilles, all dead? And Highland was falling apart around him, and the machine cloud was deteriorating. A name suddenly came to him, one that came with warm feelings, protection, and an embrace like a motherly vice.

"Penny?" he asked aloud, his lips feeling the cold now. "Penny?" he pleaded to the chaos around him.

Then he suddenly knew, even Penny was gone. The A.I. that kept this whole place going, that had kept all his selves going, she was gone.

"This is a hell of a way to be born!" he said again, this time in anger. This time with the sting of being cheated.

Wreckage and rubble stuck out of the snow outside the landing bay. He found a thin silver sheet of insulation and wrapped it around his shoulders like a shawl, and he made his way through the jagged ruin of the complex. He knew something important was here, but he did not know what. He was being drawn to a specific point, just a few hundred yards away. As he got closer, his sense of mission swelled, guiding him along.

Then he saw it, a white stasis pod for a… *Sabatin*? That word came to him, and a cold tingle went down his spine. Nothing good at all downloaded to him about that word – violence, war, greed, conquest. Images displayed in his mind. He saw specs for a fierce bioweapon. It looked like a combination tiger/salamander, covered in silver biological armor. Sensors and implants stuck from its flesh. A mouthful of dagger teeth filled an evil smile.

With the Sabatin came images he knew were just a few hours old. A horrific battle deep in the control center of Highland – humans and Phaelon mercenaries holding off an attack by waves and waves of giant spiders – an Arnock landing party. His brothers Sergey and Achilles lying dead by their own hand. The flash of an atomic blast. The destruction of the control center. Penny, he *felt* her fear as the nuclear fire swept around her. He sensed the destruction dispersing her. It was too much for him.

"Stop!" he yelped. He held his head and screamed, desperate for the download to cease. He stomped his feet, and to his surprise, the awful deluge of incoming data did, in fact, stop. He looked to the stasis pod again, to the thing that had triggered so much distress. The pod was propped cockeyed against a twisted I-beam. Atop it, a small light blinked green, indicating it was keeping something alive inside. He somehow knew there wasn't a Sabatin inside.

He broke into a limping trot, his shoes flapping. He quickly righted the pod, his hands flashing over the controls. On a small screen, it showed there was a person inside, approximately one-hundred-seventy pounds, estimated sixty-one years old. There was no name indicated.

But Vincent Dacha didn't need a name.

His gut filled with more dread, more so than when he had realized he was alone and his brothers were dead. More so than when he realized that Penny was gone. He turned the handle and the pod cracked open with a hiss. He knew that it was supposed to have a rancid smell, and he shielded his nose.

The first thing he saw was the man's eye, darting from side to side. A pink membrane was wrapped around him, holding his arms up close to his body. The man's weight shifted, and the contents of the pod slopped with him onto the ground. Vincent tore the membrane from him as the man took his first breaths and coughed up fluid.

"Who are you?" the man asked, and then his gaze wandered. "Who am I?" he asked with fraught urgency. "Who am I?" he repeated quietly.

A small amount of relief filled Vincent. He knew who this was. He was an opportunity and maybe a gift. Someone was responsible for the disaster here. Vincent was beginning to think that it was a collective someone. Maybe everyone. He pulled the last of the membrane from the man, using his sleeve to dry his face. This person could be a tool now, someone who could help even the score for all of this, but there was no way in hell Vincent was telling him who he was.

This man couldn't know that he was Emmanuel Gray.

CRASHING DOWN

D.P.E. Archangel, Over Highland

Dr. Tier glared at Timberwolf. He looked back, a smile on the edge of his mouth. They sat opposite each other in the drop-lifter as technicians and security personnel secured themselves around them. *He better be there,* her eyes said. Timberwolf had told her Gray was trapped below within a stasis pod. He had locked him in there and used his location to bargain for Salla Birdwing's life. She had been sent away on a shuttle, and hopefully she'd scrambled her transponder.

Dr. Tier's whole staff was aboard the lifter, even Conrad Stonefield. Timberwolf had heard whiffs about the young analyst stepping in to deal with Cardinal Jacob for some reason. He was dying to know the story behind that.

"Release in 5, 4, 3…" The pilot left the last part unspoken, and the drop-lifter detached from the belly of *Archangel* with a nudge. The weightlessness came a moment later once they were outside of the cruiser's gravity field. Dr. Tier's hair lifted off her shoulders, and Timberwolf couldn't help but smile.

"What?" she demanded.

"Nothing. Did I tell you that Kizik is gone? Not in my head anymore."

"Yes, you keep saying that."

"Mission accomplished," he grinned, showing his hands like a card dealer.

"You've been given 'ownership' of the Highland facility below, apparently, by the A.I. that ran it. You want to stay there? Fix up the property?"

He nodded. He'd failed Dr. Tier in so many ways. He'd failed to secure Highland, failed to keep the Dacha brothers alive, and the facility below smoldered from a nuclear blast. His only saving grace was that Gray, the man who was the architect behind all this chaos, was trapped below. He had no doubt whatsoever that if he wasn't, then Tier wouldn't let him live one hour. She'd put a blast in him and let the swirling dust and snow of Highland cover his body.

Funny, he considered– just when he wanted to live, forces might finally converge to kill him. Kizik, the Arnock alien spider, was no longer a passenger in his head. He couldn't hear the grinding any longer, wasn't enduring the mental torture. Even as he descended into utter uncertainty, he was almost giddy. Part of it was Salla, helping her escape and earning her freedom for her. It was the first unselfish thing he'd done in a very long time. He thought of her face, kind and naturally striking. He imagined her pressed up against the window of the shuttle looking back at him. For the moment, he knew she was safe, and that gave him some comfort.

"We can't safely descend," the pilot said over her shoulder to Dr. Tier.

"It's not getting any safer. Just descend." They locked eyes for a moment, and then the pilot sheepishly looked away.

"Helmets on. This will be rough!" the pilot advised.

The drop-lifter took a dip towards the world below, and the swirl of the high-cloud layer filled the windscreen. The atmosphere had changed drastically from just a few hours before. Giant weather systems kicked up across the entire planet. The world of Highland looked like an ill Jupiter, its smooth whiteness now replaced by pinwheels of gray and pale orange.

The cabin jerked to the side as they hit the first part of the atmosphere. The pilot corrected manually, taking control of the ship from the A.I. Dr. Tier crunched up her face in aggravation as the pilot hunted for safe entry through the weather. Suddenly, she found a channel and dove almost straight downward.

A deep warbling filled the cabin, and the windscreen shook in its molding. Lightning flashed nearby, and a bolt hung for long seconds just beyond the starboard wing. They broke through layer after layer of clouds, each time like smashing through a pane of glass. In the cabin, heads hung in fetal crash positions, all except Timberwolf and Tier. They were ramrod straight and taking it all in.

"Something's coming at us!" the pilot yelled.

A million shards of the machine cloud, the semi-sentient entity that wrapped the planet, impacted the side of the drop-lifter like sand falling on a tin roof. The swarm moved away and then impacted the other side. The drop-lifter spun, and alarms rang out. The pilot was frantic in her movements, hands flashing to the interfaces. The craft fell in a flat spin now, the G-forces making a tight knot at the top of everyone's neck.

Suddenly, the scream of the engines was gone, and the pilot silenced the alarm. Timberwolf eyed her going for the emergency retro booster button that would throw them back into the atmosphere. Tier saw it too. "Do not abort this descent!" she commanded.

But the pilot had other plans, the drop-lifter was falling without power, the beveled ground rushing up at them. They were just a few thousand feet above the world now. She hit the button, but just for an instant, and everyone's heads jerked against the restraints. The ship stopped its descent, but then began falling a few seconds later. She hit the retro again, once more jerking them to a near stop just above the ground. The ship then dropped the last dozen feet and settled on its gimbaled landing gear with an undignified thud.

Dr. Tier's mouth was open, and she was unusually impressed. "Nicely fucking done," she complimented the pilot.

The gangplank of the drop-lifter wheezed open, exposing the party to the frigid elements. Snow and dust whipped into frenzied pellets, striking their faces. The others rushed out, wrapped in environment suits, but Dr. Tier grabbed Conrad by the elbow. "Stop!" She tightened his breather, making an airtight seal over his mouth.

Two hundred yards away, the smoldering landing bay threw oily smoke into the sky, its superstructure in jagged collapse. Timberwolf pulled his breather away so he could shout to Tier, "That machine cloud is not friendly. It will come back."

"We get Gray. We get out. That's the plan," Dr. Tier responded.

Conrad appeared at Dr. Tier's elbow, "what about some of the inventory here? Maybe we can salvage some… items?"

Dr. Tier nodded; they needed all the help they could get. Assault Corps cruisers *Defender* and *Tranquility,* and possibly *Challenger,* were incoming. If there were any exotic weapons still intact down here, they might come in handy. "And possibly destroy the rest so it can't be used against us," Conrad added.

"That's a good idea. Manage it," she ordered.

"When did you get smart?" Timberwolf punched the young desk jockey in the shoulder.

One of the security team piped up, "I've got tracks through the snow in infrared. Towards that burning structure." In unison, the team switched their smart contacts above the visible spectrum and saw the footprints. "Whoever it was is injured, dragging their right foot."

"OK – who's up for a jog?" Dr. Tier said, making a beeline for the landing bay. "We need to move fast so we don't get killed down here."

They ran towards a triangle-shaped gap in the wreckage where the footprints led. They were close when a call came from the drop-lifter. "Doc! I'm in trouble," came the pilot's muffled voice.

They felt something in the ground – a seismic gallop. They turned back to see a monstrous form bearing down on the drop-lifter. It was a massive creature the size of a rhinoceros, with three angry horns protruding through an armored faceplate. "It's a Trike!" Timberwolf warned – a giant Sabatin used for demolition. They'd attacked the Arnock command ship in orbit, tearing it to shreds.

A security man dropped to his knees and spun up his plasma rifle to fire, but Timberwolf grabbed the barrel. "That thing fell from space! You can't hurt it. Don't get its attention." A second later, the Trike T-boned the drop-lifter, caving it in and smashing it sideways. From the other side, a second Trike joined the game, tearing the back half off the vessel. They tugged at what remained, doing as they were designed and shredding the remnants.

Now the security team let loose, and the staccato pounding of plasma blasts tore through the air. Timberwolf found himself on his belly next to Dr. Tier. He was technically in her custody after everything that had happened, but her eyes begged him to spring into action. This was his kind of moment. Timberwolf thrived in the chaos and bent it to his will.

The Trikes charged at them, moving in fast, straight lines. A security man was flying through the air now, gored by a beast. He landed beside Timberwolf and bounced before laying limp. Timberwolf was up, grabbing the downed man's plasma rifle. The group edged towards the landing bay, but the Trikes circled them, raging inward to pick them off.

One of the Trikes had half the armor over its face missing, and deep, white burns stained its mouth and eye. Timberwolf took careful aim and fired, hitting right above its cheek. It stopped immediately, turning its massive face towards him, the plasma bursts from others bouncing off its thick hide. The beast took a bead on him and charged, its rippled shoulder muscles a manifestation of pure power. Timberwolf fired again and again, on auto-blast now. Each burst hit the exact same spot right under its exposed eye, but it wasn't enough. Just feet away now, the Trike was still coming.

Then suddenly it wasn't.

No goddam way! Timberwolf thought as the beast veered away at the last second, shaking its head like it had just tried to break through a security field. *Nothing made by Highland can hurt me.* He had thought it might be the case but wasn't sure how he would find out until just this moment. As the new "owner" of the facility, the executive safety protocols had cascaded down to him.

The other Trike was charging at Dr. Tier and several analysts now. Timberwolf knew what he had to do and just had an instant to do it. He ran to them, footfall after footfall landing in the snow as if in slow motion. The other Trike had reentry burns from head to toe; its armor sullied and chalky white.

Now's the time to let her die, Timberwolf thought as he moved, now just steps away from Dr. Tier, who huddled for cover behind a snow drift. *I just slow a little...* but then he thought about what he hadn't told her yet. What she needed to hear from him about what happened on Highland. In his momentary indecision, a few more steps fell one after the other, and then there was no stopping.

Shit. Decision made.

The Trike's eyes glowed red in its white-raw face, and mist condensed out of its nostrils with the rhythm of a chugging train.

He was in front of them now, Dr. Tier, Conrad, and a few others. He dropped his shoulder to the Trike, and in that instant, it missed a step. Unable to stop, the beast crashed onto its chin, its giant neck cracking. It cartwheeled over them, the heavy mist from its breath washing down just inches above. It bounced when it landed and then rolled over dead.

The survivors dashed for the landing bay, slipping into the protection of the crumbling structure. They scrambled up the rubble on the inside, and the other Trike pounded against the exterior. "We can't have it following us," Timberwolf said, sliding back down to the wall. The pounding came again and again, and the beast tore at the metal, widening the gap they had just come through.

Timberwolf met the gaze of its giant eye and stared. "Get!" he ordered. "Get going!" he scolded. The beast pushed against the structure again and then paused, slowly backing up. Then it was waddling away, its claws crunching in the snow and grunting like a dog kicked off the couch. Timberwolf fell back on his haunches, taking a moment's rest. He opened his mouth and a sour snowflake melted on his tongue, "Place needs some work."

INTO THE MYSTIC

Highland

"So, you won't say who I am?" Emmanuel Gray asked.

"No," Vincent Dacha replied. The man opposite him shook his head and pushed back from the table. They sat in an empty maintenance shed. It was just the two of them, two folding chairs at a table, and a bare light bulb hanging from the ceiling. Two Trikes sentried outside the structure. One peered into the tiny window, half its armor torn away from its face.

"Am I a bad man?" Gray questioned.

Vincent Dacha laughed aloud, a reaction he suspected should have been internal to hide his intentions. But he was just learning to be alive, and mastering that type of nuance took time.

"I laugh because you've done some bad things. You've killed a lot of people. Three of my brothers. You killed a…" Vincent referred to a small tablet computer "…a whole colony. You're obsessed with war. And just fighting. I don't think you care why. You want your *good* war."

The man didn't speak, the gullies under his eyes looked deep and craggy. He flexed his fingers. "I feel so much energy."

"Yeah, that. Your good friend locked you in a Sabatin pod. You're not a hundred percent a man anymore. You're more like one of them." Vincent motioned to the creatures out the window, the giant Trike Sabatin, the vicious programmable beasts.

"There's a lot here to take in. Who did this to me?"

Vincent smiled, keeping his reaction subtle. "Timberwolf Velez," he said as if he was answering the most obvious question in the world.

Who? Gray mouthed.

"Timberwolf is a man with no loyalties. You did everything for him, but he just turned on you. He'd been hunting you. He'd caught you. Locked you in a Sabatin pod, God knows why. Was coming back for sure. Don't think he cares for you much. If it wasn't for me, he'd have you!"

Gray ruminated on all he'd been told. "What did I do to Timberwolf?"

"Nothing. You never did anything to him that wasn't kind." Vincent leaned back. He enjoyed watching the man's face as Gray worked to make sense of the fantastic lies that he had just been told. Emmanuel Gray had, in fact, done something terrible to Timberwolf, not the other way around. He had sent him on the mission where Kizik had latched on to his mind. He had done it on purpose.

Out the window, the Trikes darted away, something drawing their attention. Vincent knew he had to move fast. "You can make this right, and I have a gift for you."

Vincent stood, taking out a tube that had recently held a cigar. It was supposed to be smoked with his brothers once his lungs were clear, but there would be none of that. He'd tossed the cigar away because he needed the container. He popped the red cap off the end, and a fine mist puffed out. A tiny machine cloud, just a few hundred thousand nano-devices, swirled in the air. "Hold onto yourself, this is going to hurt like hell."

The cloud rushed into Gray's face, entering through his pores and tear ducts. Instantly, it began to burn him, changing his flesh. He grabbed at his brow, shocked by the sudden pain. His angular features suddenly puffed out, his forehead growing an unsightly bump. His handsome and classic looks were muted. His cheeks took on pockmarks and his lips plumped. He fell to his knees and the sizzling subsided. "Why?" he demanded.

"To do your part, you can't be you. Not just yet."

He let him recover for a few minutes, and then Vincent led Gray outside. Row after row of wrecked spaceships were stacked in neat piles, sometimes dozens high. He took his charge to where an intact, sleek model sat alone in a clearing. It was an eggshell color with a racing frame and dual sub-light drives hung under swept-back wings. A long canopy covered its living compartment. "It's built for three, but it'll fit you nicely. My brother Achilles was fixing it up until he died."

A gust of cold air from far away swept around them, and Vincent held himself tightly. Even here, in the cover of the boneyard, the weather was getting in.

Vincent wiped away dust on the ship's hull, uncovering a stenciled name – *Into the Mystic*. "All these ships here are from people we caught trying to find this place. Do you know who the only person was to ever get through?"

"Me?" Gray guessed instinctively. He was learning fast. His answer made Vincent uneasy. Maybe this was a mistake. Mixing him with Sabatin imprinting might have been a recipe for a new disaster. Maybe he should just kill this thing now and make himself more appealing to the landing party that would surely find him soon.

"Yes. You got through."

"This is a nice ship. I don't know much, but I know that."

Vincent pulled a pair of golden cufflinks from his pocket. One shaped like a *D* and the other like a *V*. "You'll need these. My brother Ivan left his pair with another old friend of yours, Salla Birdwing. You'll find her, and then I need you to wake some people up."

"Wake some people up?"

"Some very, very old people. Old people are cranky," Vincent responded. Gray looked back, understandably confused, "And they're bad people, much worse than you!"

Content not to ponder it for the moment, Gray placed his hand on the side of the ship, and its seal opened. He felt dull and tired, but he was also burning. Some sort of strange equilibrium brewed in him, something parallel stirring inside. A small staircase descended, and he climbed aboard, looking back one more time to Vincent. *Do I have to do this?* he asked with his eyes.

"The ship knows where to go. It knows where Salla is. There's a printer on board. I'll send you the rest of what you need."

Having his answer, Gray nodded, climbing aboard. He sat down in the pilot's chair, resigned to his fate – whatever that was. He caught a glimpse of his new face in the reflection of a panel. Everything was muddled and misshapen, except his eyes. They were still him.

Into the Mystic rose on a hiss from its hover jets and headed towards an opening in the ceiling high above. In just seconds, the ship was streaking towards the cloud layer. Out the window, Gray thought he saw a diamond-shaped craft descending far away, well, not descending but falling unpowered. It disappeared from his view before he could be sure, but his stomach sank, and it certainly felt like a bad omen.

Not fully a man anymore, more like those… things. He thought about what Vincent had said, and he had no idea why this "Timberwolf Velez" was hunting him. The only thing that seemed clear was that he was driving towards extreme danger. He feared it was not personal danger either, but a grander and more universal peril – a peril that would go way beyond him.

EXODUS

Highland

The footprints led through the crumbling structure to an I-beam twisted like an old, gnarled tree. They didn't need to get close to realize Gray was not within the Sabatin pod nestled beside it. The door of the pod hung open and creaked in the wind. Someone had carved something on the inside of the door. It was a symmetrical design, maybe a cat. Dr. Tier held the pod open and nodded for a tech to get an image of the interior. The inside was dark, and her flashlight revealed the remnants of the pink, sinewy artificial Sabatin yolk, which was already fading to grey.

"Two people headed off that way." The tech pointed further into the structure, but a tiny man stood right where he indicated.

"Thank you for coming!" Vincent Dacha exclaimed, coming towards them. He took each of their hands, shaking them vigorously. "I'm Vincent Dacha, the proprietor of this place."

"What happened to the man that was in this stasis pod?" Dr. Tier demanded.

"Oh, who? I have no idea. I heard a ruckus and somebody making a lot of awful yelling, and then I hid until he was gone."

"That's B.S. Doc," a tech countered. "I'm reading his DNA on the container. I can tell from here. And two of them went off together."

Timberwolf piped up, "And you don't run this place. This well-oiled machine is mine. Penny gave it to me. You just work here."

"Velez," Vincent sneered, "I thought you were dead."

"No, and I'm your boss."

"Well, I'm three hours old. It's been a shit day. I've just discovered my whole family's been killed, and now… you know, just take me in."

"No," Dr. Tier denied him. "No, Mr. Dacha. You have no value. You just popped out of a grow tank," she shook her head, done with this.

"Please, please! Get me out of here!" he begged.

"Timberwolf, terminate your employee, please."

Timberwolf unslung his rifle and raised it, firing a blast right past Vincent's ear and then another past his opposite cheek. The man shuffled, hiding behind his shaking hands. When Timberwolf drew a bead on his forehead, though, the gun wouldn't fire. "Like I thought. Highland weapons won't work on him. Going to have to use my hands, doc."

"Proceed," she replied, not looking up from her device.

"No, no! Wait! I haven't been straight with you. I let Gray out, and when I did, he threatened to kill me. Said he'd kill me if I told you, so I'm risking a lot now! He stole a ship! My... dead... brother's... ship! One he worked on until the day before he died!" Vincent's cheeks ran wet with tears, and Dr. Tier rolled her eyes.

"Fine – pack him up." She decided.

"Wait," Conrad interjected. "We need you to load up all the weapons that are still viable onto a hauler. And call off the machine cloud. Or else I shoot." The young man held up an old Smith and Wesson pistol, something way below the technology level of anything made by Highland.

Vincent huffed. "This OK, boss?" he asked Timberwolf.

"Sure is," he replied.

CHALLENGERS

A.C. Challenger, approaching Highland

Captain Jephtah found anger to be distracting and unproductive, but she smoldered. Twelve hours ago, *Archangel* had snuck up behind *Challenger* and nudged them out of the sub-light stream by brushing plasma shields. It was one of the most dangerous maneuvers to execute. If successful, it was a non-lethal way to knock another ship out of sub-light and take out their engines. If unsuccessful – everybody dies.

Dr. Tier's taxi driver didn't have the balls for that.

Captain Tirani was reliable and capable but about as daring as tapioca pudding. Dr. Tier had no doubt ordered the bump. It was a classic D.P.E. maneuver, like shooting you under the table. The Assault Corps, for all its blunt instrumentation, preferred a straight fight and eschewed dirty tricks. No, Jephtah wasn't angry but focused. Dr. Tier was playing a reckless game. There were good people on *Archangel,* and the doctor was playing with their lives.

She had gotten *Challenger* back online in just six hours and was running double-hot at Highland. She risked frying the ship's engines for good, but reaching Highland ASAP was critical. The key was stopping Dr. Tier here and now. If Jephtah could take out *Archangel*, then all this nonsense, this wannabe civil war, might fizzle out today.

Jephtah had a big advantage – her reputation. Everybody was afraid of her. Not in person, she prided herself on being approachable and friendly. But in space, in command of a cruiser, she was deadly. *Challenger* and its crew were an extension of her will. *I am bringing a wall of pain, Thea.*

She tapped out a message on all sub-light channels. *Challenger is Coming – Yours, Captain Maria Jephtah.*

Her bridge was abuzz, and when she took her chair, her second, Commander Gage, nodded to her. "We just read your outgoing, Captain."

"Thought I'd RSVP. It's only polite."

"Agreed, Captain. Compliments coming in from *Tranquility* and *Defender.* They're in parallel streams, but we're leading by a nose."

They were coming in from three different angles, blocking all incoming sub-light streams. They would arrive at Highland almost simultaneously. Jephtah considered the myriad of unknowns in play. There could still be active security systems around Highland, the Arnock may still be on site, and reinforcements from Dr. Tier's Department of Peace Enforcement might be right behind them. Risks aside, Jephtah knew she had to get to Highland before Dr. Tier could escape.

"Tell captains Trejlo and Khanya a bottle of Kentucky Bourbon to whoever reaches Highland first."

"Done, Captain."

"Let's make this a race."

AMPLIFY

D.P.E. Archangel, Over Highland

The hauler from Highland connected awkwardly to the bottom of *Archangel*. They'd left in a sleek, state-of-the-art drop-lifter and come back in a flying box container, piloted by a clone at gunpoint. Conrad held his old-fashioned pistol inches from Vincent's ribs. As soon as they were securely connected, Timberwolf lifted the tiny man out of his harness and dragged him from the ship.

"I want this thing unloaded and discarded in fifteen minutes. Ten if you want to be on my good side," Dr. Tier commanded the technicians. "Watch those five crates in the back!"

On the way up from Highland, she'd been appraised of the situation. *We've got 3 incoming A.C. cruisers. Challenger is leading. Thirty-six minutes* was Captain Tirani's message.

Challenger was leading!

Jephtah had somehow managed to get her ship back online in just a few hours, and she most certainly meant business. She was willing to burn her engines to cinders to block *Archangel's* escape, but Dr. Tier had a very bad plan. It was a top-shelf dirty trick – not as low as the sub-light bump, but nothing Jephtah would ever see coming. She needed to let Vincent Dacha hack *Archangel*.

"I hate this idea," Timberwolf said. He hauled Vincent by the collar, going against the tide of personnel swarming aboard the hauler to remove the cargo. "Does Tirani even know?"

"He won't know the plan until it's too late for him to object," Dr. Tier replied. The party weaved through the ship, descending cramped stairwells. Conrad stayed close to Vincent, his palm growing sweaty from tightly gripping his Smith and Wesson. Two assault corps troopers stepped aside as they passed into an area marked "top secret."

In *Archangel's* secure storage area, Dr. Tier scanned her retina to open a locker. Timberwolf's special rig of pressurized fighting armor was inside. It was made from the skin of a Sabatin, and its nearly indestructible, metallic-leather hide covered an unmatchable weapons package. A nearly inexhaustible plasma blaster, Phaelon-grade chemical laser, micro-drone swarm, and more. What Dr. Tier was interested in, though, was the rig's cyberwar unit, accessible manually through the right gauntlet. Vincent reached in and grabbed the prize and handed it over to her with a minor fuss.

Dr. Tier hesitated for a moment outside of the command deck. Just two days ago, she'd been exiled off Tirani's bridge after the spectacle of bumping *Challenger*. Then Tirani had taken her into custody for being high as a kite on Terecine when she'd ordered that maneuver. Now she was walking around free only after blackmailing the man. Even for her, this was a thoroughly burned bridge. "Timberwolf, when they open this door, I need to know how many moves it will take to kill everyone on the bridge," she asked.

"Wait, what? What did I miss?" Timberwolf relaxed his hold on Vincent's collar.

"A lot," Conrad answered. "But please don't kill everyone past this door."

"I'm just going to count how I'd do it. Totally different thing," he replied.

The door slid open to command officers analyzing a rotating hologram of Highland. Three dotted incoming lines marked the approach of *Tranquility, Defender,* and *Challenger.* As Captain Jephtah had no doubt planned, the incoming Assault Corps cruisers were blocking all the sub-light streams connecting to Highland. If Tirani dropped *Archangel* into a stream now, they'd ram head-on to one of the approaching cruisers as they escaped.

Tirani had moved under Highland's South Pole, where the atmospheric storms raged the hardest. That would conceal them from Jephtah's forces, but not for long. In just minutes, the world would be swarming with probes, and they'd quickly be made. Dr. Tier had told Tirani she had a plan, but she hadn't provided details. She gave him the quick summary and got approximately the response she expected.

"They are chugging like bats out of hell, and this is what you bring me? Are you goddamned kidding? Unleash a cyber virus into my nav com?" Tirani questioned, his hands running through his thinning, mouse-brown hair.

Dr. Tier slammed the gauntlet from Timberwolf's rig onto the holographic emitter. "I'm not goddamned kidding," she said, adding nothing more.

"Your stock is low, Thea. After what you pulled, I am considering throwing out peace signals."

"That's called surrender, Les, and you're not thinking this through. It may have been my call, but a sub-light bump was executed against *Challenger* on *your* watch. You think Jephtah is going to go easy on you?"

"Are you high, Thea? This is not a facetious question, considering your past."

"No," she answered.

"Well, I wish you were because this is nuts." Tirani noticed Vincent then, trying to hide behind Timberwolf. "That what I think it is?" Tirani smirked at the tiny man.

"Vincent Dacha has a painful desire to live and brought us some toys," Dr. Tier answered.

"Hello," Vincent said meekly.

"Let's see the Amp," Dr. Tier said to Vincent. He fished in his pocket and retrieved a small black cube.

"That's it?" Tirani reacted to the tiny device. It was just an inch on each side and affixed with a few buttons and levers.

"It'll do the job," Vincent assured. "The Arnock ordered these, and we nicked one. This amplifies!"

"It amplifies a hostile cyberwar package that will now take over my ship!" Tirani snapped.

Dr. Tier locked eyes with Tirani. She needed him to trust her, and she felt about as remorseful as she could for what she had done. He was usually a step behind, but Tirani was a good man and ran a tight ship. If they escaped now, their fortunes would be inexorably linked for the foreseeable future. She could order him, but she would rather he agreed to this on his own. "Please," she asked.

"Well, this looks like all we've got. If you're going to do it, do it!" he relented.

Vincent fiddled with the Amp and wirelessly networked to the gauntlet. "This is great, it'll just hurdle your antivirus!" he bragged. The Amp and the gauntlet blinked in unison, and then all the lights on the bridge began to blink as Vincent's code took over the ship's communications relays. Just as Tirani was about to protest, the lightshow subsided.

Timberwolf reached into the gauntlet, and its innards wrapped around his forearm, dropping sensor threads into his skin. He interfaced with the smart-contact lens floating over his eye, and he saw three exterior views of what appeared to show *Archangel*, but which were actually virtual copies projected right in the path of the incoming ships.

"Am I seeing what I think I am seeing?" Timberwolf asked.

Vincent slapped his knee, legitimately surprised himself. "Really? This is working!" In the holographic projection of Highland, the three incoming cruisers were now streaming towards three faux *Archangels*. "I hacked your ship, now your ship is hacking them!" Vincent said. Tirani and his staff stood, jaws agape and grinning at the scene. A few minutes ago, their situation had been hopeless, but now they might just have a chance.

"Looks like you killed the room," Timberwolf whispered to Vincent.

ARRIVAL

A.C. Challenger, Approaching Highland

"*Tranq'* is losing coolant from its sub-light drivers. That could be a real mess if they blow. They're asking for instructions." Commander Gage kept the urgency out of his voice, but he and Jephtah both knew *Tranquility* was close to exploding, and Captain Trejlo was asking if he could drop out of sub-light.

"We're six minutes out, have them proceed, please," she calmly replied.

Gage sent the message and got the reply just seconds later, "Captain Trejlo has confirmed."

Captain Jephtah didn't betray it to her crew, but she was sweating. *Challenger* was running at one-hundred-thirty-two percent, and all her levels were deep into the red. The view to their front was the typical black void of the sub-light stream. Some Believers said this was a glimpse of heaven you could never reach, but she didn't subscribe to that type of nonsense.

They were coming in right on top of Highland, riding the streams to the very end. Probes were poised to launch. Weapons teams had fingers on triggers, and breacher squads were loaded and ready to drill into *Archangel*. Of course, she was prepared. She was always prepared, but still. "What the hell have you got up your sleeve, Thea?" Dr. Thea Tier was notorious for playing dirty tricks, and she may have just played another. Defense Secretary Bozeman had messaged Jephtah just minutes before.

Under no circumstances can Thea Tier be killed.

She hadn't questioned it. Then Secretary Bozeman had added something.

As per the Chancellor, personally.

The order to bring in Dr. Tier alive didn't seem unusual – but why had Secretary Bozeman added that part about the head of the government making this request directly? Her mind went to various conspiracies. Dr. Tier's Department of Peace Enforcement lived and breathed conspiracies and even gave life to those who served their purposes. Was this part of a bargain she'd made? Jephtah wouldn't put it past Dr. Tier to blackmail even the highest officials, but she needed to put all this out of her mind for the moment.

"We're here! Dropping now," Gage said as the front view screen snapped to the swirling white and orange disc of Highland. "Probes away, breachers standing by, plasma batteries…" but he stopped mid-sentence. Directly in their path, *Archangel* was turning on them. The front visual zoomed in on the massive, jagged whale of a form, its overlapping and thorny composite armor deployed. "It's coming right at us!" Gage announced.

Proximity alarms rang out over the bridge as *Archangel* got within sixteen miles. That frontal armor was like a battering ram, and Jephtah wouldn't put it past Dr. Tier to smash her way out. Though that seemed more like a blunt tactic her attack dog, Timberwolf Velez, might try. "Lateral thrusters. Give her some room!" she ordered. Its thrusters engaged, and the ship lurched to the side, but it didn't help.

"*Arch'* is tracking us!" Gage advised. "Coming right in. Forty seconds."

Jephtah looked over her crew, professionals focused on their deadly serious work. She took a moment to be proud of them and of herself. Gage looked back at her, looking for permission to fire. She was about to give the order when she heard it. Chatter coming in from *Defender* and *Tranquility*. "Turn up the comm!" she ordered.

"… we've got Archangel turning on us… going for the exit… she's rolling a strike right for our comm deck… that armor is deployed to tear…"

That's when she knew. *They hacked us! Somehow, they're showing us false images.* "Mr. Gage – turn off the viewing sensors! Project a view from the bow telescopes." Gage turned off the viewing sensors – which took in data and telemetry from all over the ship and converted it into a composite visual. He switched to a view from the physical lenses, which was as unadulterated as looking out a window.

"I knew it!" What had been the gnarled bow of *Archangel* was replaced by the sickly swirl of the planet Highland. In stark contrast, the proximity alarm screamed. "Turn that off!" Jephtah ordered, and the clamor ceased.

Gage was already on the comm. "*Tranq'* and *Def'*, switch to opticals!"

"Where the hell is she?!" Jephtah demanded to her command crew. The probes were still sending back bad info and would be useless, locked onto versions of *Archangel* that didn't exist. This was going to be a battle of eyeballs, their systems flooded with fake data, unable to tell ghosts from real threats. Jephtah had planned to converge her three cruisers on *Archangel*, but now the script was flipped, negating their numerical superiority. Dr. Tier could charge at one of them, and there would be no way to see her coming.

It was clear which ship *Archangel* would test. "Captain Trejlo, she's coming your way!" *Tranquility's* sub-light coolant leak would be as bright as a Christmas tree on *Archangel's* sensors. Trejlo's ship was the wounded one, the weakest of the herd.

"Roger that! *Tranq'* standing by," Trejlo responded. His command crew scanned the view in front of them. They disregarded their instruments and looked for the telltale dot that would grow into a massive incoming cruiser within seconds. The crew was silent, two dozen eyes searching. Trejlo heard the pilot's breathing from ten feet away.

"Got it!" the pilot announced, and then an instant later, everyone saw. *Archangel* was right on them, going underneath where the sub-light drivers were – and it was too late to do anything about it. *Archangel* unloaded a wall of plasma on *Tranquility's* belly at almost point-blank range. The ship rocked upwards, knocking the crew from their stations and into the ceiling. The view in front spun away from Highland as the ship turned, and a sickening groan came through the superstructure. Gage knew what they'd hit without needing to see the damage report. "Lose them! Eject the sub-light drivers!" he ordered from where he'd been thrown to the floor.

The cylinders holding the ship's drivers burst away, trailing white-hot vapor. *Tranquility* was spinning now, and Trejlo felt the awful lapse of the artificial gravity. Losing that meant that life support was not far behind. His crew had just seconds to react. The pilot was back at her station, working the operational maneuvering thrusters to stabilize them. "I've got a power surge from *Archangel!*" the pilot announced. That could mean only two things, either a deathblow on the crippled ship or *Archangel* was preparing to slip into sub-light. Trejlo felt like a beaten gladiator, waiting to see which way the emperor's thumb would turn.

"Aft viewer on!" Trejlo ordered. The rear-facing opticals showed the quickly receding *Archangel,* its plasma batteries facing right at them. "The Angel, no!" he breathed. But instead of one fate, he got two. Simultaneously, *Archangel* disappeared into sub-light and fired a plasma volley at *Tranquility.* Out of instinct, his crew stood up, ready to take this final blow on the chin. The glare from the glowing balls of gas, as hot as the sun, filled their view, blotting out the dark of space. But the blasts whooshed by, stirring *Tranquility* in their wake and falling harmlessly into the gravity well of Highland.

"Report! Trejlo – James, are you there? *Tranq'* are you green?" Jephtah's voice crackled over the comm. "*Tranq'* are you green?" she repeated.

"We're here. We're a brick. No drivers. Not green, but life support systems stable. Grav stable." Trejlo responded, his heart pounding in his chest.

"OK – good to hear. Commander Gage will be leading a rescue."

Jephtah took a moment to breathe as her crew sprang into action. *Beaten twice in as many days by the good doctor. She'd give Dr. Tier credit for the win but couldn't say she respected her tactics. Dr. Tier needs to be put back in her box.*

She considered the next phase. This event would embolden the D.P.E. to keep fighting and harden the Assault Corps' resolve to snuff them out. A lot of good people would begin dying soon. There were reports of an evacuation of the A.C. fuel depot on Luna due to a D.P.E. attack. The Earth's moon! That was too close to home, but she surmised that that was exactly the point. They were still in the sparring phase of this war, each side showing they meant business and hoping that would be enough.

A message came in from sub-light.

> *TheaTier965: Captain Jephtah, don't mistake my mercy for weakness.*

> *Jephtah101: I wouldn't dare, but we will catch you. Give up so we can end this.*

> *TheaTier965: There is no prize. Highland is a complete loss.*

> *Jephtah101: That goes above my pay grade. I've been sent for you.*

> *TheaTier965: This has nothing to do with me. This is the result of the A.C.'s support of*

Emmanuel Gray. I know you don't care for him.

Jephtah101: My opinion isn't relevant.

TheaTier965: We've met and shaken hands, Maria! You're an excellent captain. They're planning to wipe out the D.P.E. That's a high crime. You don't want to be a part of this.

Jephtah101: Do you have Gray?

Dr. Tier dared not show her hand. She had no idea where Gray was, but leaving doubt about his whereabouts certainly held an advantage. She closed with a warning.

TheaTier965: This is a time of picking sides. Do not follow. Do not track. We are running with all sorts of exotic hardware retrieved from Highland. I'll negotiate with Defense Secretary Jason Bozeman or above from here on out.

And with that, no further messages were exchanged. *Archangel* was gone for now, surely branching off into unmonitored D.P.E. sub-light streams. For Jephtah, it had been a very bad day, but she knew she'd get another shot at Dr. Tier.

Jephtah rubbed her temples. A news feed on her smart device showed a column of black smoke rising from D.P.E. headquarters near Boston. *This is a time of picking sides.* She wasn't a political person, but she had read enough history to know how these things worked. Right now, she was following orders, but soon, decisions would need to be made about loyalty and what one personally believed.

She snapped away from her navel gazing back to the wildcard that was Dr. Tier. She had a job to do. "I may not be allowed to kill you, Thea, but I can sure make it hurt."

HEART AND HOME

Nova Turin

Salla Birdwing bounded across the rolling prairie. Her ankles were clipped into flexing "jumpstilts" that amplified her stride in the three-quarter gravity of her home world. She vaulted left and right, rushing up a small hill crested with a grove of trees. At the top, she leaped halfway to the top of an oak tree and hung onto a branch.

For the moment she was up there, she felt like a kid again. This was a pastime of youth, strapping on springy stilts and leaping about through the brush and tall grass outside the settlement. Child's play or not, it was a great workout and a lot more fun than running. Hanging there, she looked off to the settlement just a mile away, a small town adjacent to a quaint spaceport. It was nestled by a massive lake that held most of Nova Turin's fresh water.

Here on the edge of the settlement, the planet's native ecology mixed with the flora and fauna brought by the settlers. The spongy soil was covered with soft purple moss and fine, brittle shafts that snapped easily as you moved through them. Trails crisscrossed the hills and gullies dotted by more oak and bushes.

A handmade stone wall ringed the outer reaches of the settlement, built by settlers who missed the demarcated fields of home. Up to the wall, the terra-stimulators kept the aggressive native ecology at bay. Beyond it, the landscape was a mass of swirling purple vines and thick black trees only clearable with chemical lasers. Yellow conical spires rose into the air. At night, the spires "spoke" to each other, exchanging arcs of electricity that filled the air with a scent like a campfire spike with ozone.

She dropped down, bouncing on the springy stilts. Down a hill, a young brother and sister ran and leaped. Clearly born here, the children seemed to be made of nothing but long arms and legs. Their laughter reached her, and she took off. She raced them a bit, the low gravity letting her leap far and high with each stride. Nova Turin used to be a place of being able to leap far and jump high. Life growing up here had been idyllic. Pulling sub-light fuel from the mines was hard work but satisfying and lucrative.

No one who worked the mines ever swung a shovel or an axe. It had been a place of engineers guiding machines and fixing breakdowns, of hard-hat roughnecks with PHDs. Her dad ran Birdwing Haulers LLC and took loads of standard-grade fuel to orbit for transfer. Nova Turin was a fair place, a vibrant place, and a place that only had one season. There was always a pleasant chill in the air, but it was never really cold. Earthers described the climate as "permanent October." Nova Turin natives had a saying, *"You don't need a coat, but you should always bring a sweater."*

That was all before Gray took over as Governor. It had happened so fast. This easy place became a nightmare. He'd forced the refineries to produce military-grade fuel that the haulers couldn't sell. He'd broken a strike by having his security men fire on the miners, and then the fighting went on for days. Finally, D.P.E. agents arrived to intervene, but it had been a massacre – over three hundred dead, almost half the colony, including Salla's dad and her two sisters.

She was torn about coming back here. This place held too many hard memories, but there was nowhere else that felt like home. She also knew her neighbors would keep an eye out for her and protect her if it came to that. The day she left to join the Station Corps, she swore she'd never come back, but longing to be up in these hills again came quickly. The desire to forgive this *place* was strong, and not to let Gray take her home from her.

After the massacre, almost no one had left, even as the mines had closed down. Life here was still tranquil, but a gloom filled those that remained. Some chalked it up to the identity of the settlers, most from the *New World Mining Corp*, a company based in Glasgow on Earth. Irish, Scottish, and South Asian accents had merged over the generations into a distinct Nova' brogue. Here were people that had always known melancholy, its brief absence simply a lesson that one should not grow too attached to a kind existence.

But today, her lungs and legs strained, and the thrill of leaping twenty feet at a time made her heart race and adrenalin pump. She'd seen things that she shouldn't have, and she held a benefits card with her picture on it that was stamped *deceased*. She had been present on Highland and had witnessed the whole debacle. She was sure that Dr. Tier was not pleased she was walking around alive, but here on Nova Turin, she knew no one would betray her, and it was as safe as any place could be. Still, she found herself looking over her shoulder for D.P.E. agents, bounty hunters hired by the Clergy, Station Corps security, or worse.

She wondered about Timberwolf and hoped deep in her heart that he was alive. He'd given up his freedom so she could walk out of Dr. Tier's custody on *Archangel*. Without him, she'd, at best, have spent the rest of her life behind bars and, at worst, taken a short walk out an airlock without a pressure suit. She stopped running, catching her breath at the top of a hill that looked out over the lake. Just offshore, plumes of pink algae spread out like pinwheels and lapped against the rocks. "Why, Timber?" she asked.

He could have easily left her to her fate, but he'd given himself to save her. She could tell he wasn't the type to be moved by sentiment. He was a D.P.E. operative, a throat slitter and assassin. They'd built a comradery on Highland, but why had he given his freedom for her? She shook it from her head. Maybe sometimes, even when there's war everywhere and life is cheap, people can still be kind.

She checked the sub-light communications feed on her smart-device with the hope that he might have sent her a message. It seemed foolish to do it, but she checked a few times a day. "Don't keep a girl waiting," she murmured.

She took a path straight down the hill, bounding over the soft moss, getting a rhythm going with the cha-chunk of her jumpstilts and her pumping arms. She found herself outside the spaceport. She clicked out of the bindings and slung her jumpstilts over her shoulder. The doors spread open for her, and she sidled up to a nearly deserted open-air café. "Iced coffee, black, please, Jerry," she ordered from the attendant.

Even though flights were few and far between, the spaceport was still where most people on Nova converged and shopped. A few locals sat at small tables drinking tea, and a whiff of curry came from a stand across the way. She nodded to her neighbors, the tall and angular Mrs. Emery and her round-faced husband, David. She'd only been back two months, and she already knew everyone's name again. It felt nice to be home. She'd even noticed her Nova' accent was returning after flattening her speech patterns during her time in the Station Corps.

She took her bitter synthetic coffee and walked a bit, her sweat drying quickly. At the other end of the space, distorted by an echo, she heard the unmistakable sound of a man preaching. His voice was shrill and high-pitched, a young zealot. As per tradition, spaceports had to provide some public space for those who wished to spread the word of God – any god would do, but mostly Believer adherents would stand and deliver here in the outer colonies.

"Hey there!" she heard over her shoulder. It was Sean Jackson, the remaining lawman for the colony. He had multiple duties, which included keeping the peace and handling customs. He also made extra money doing odd repair jobs too intricate for the automated machines to handle. Last week, in a pique of excitement, he had mediated between two neighbors over the issue of a fence that happened to be six feet over the property line. As a kid, Salla had had a crush on the young officer in his snappy, creased uniform and cowboy-style hat. Now, as Sean approached forty, his midsection bulged a little, and his uniform seemed a bit hokey, even for the boondocks.

"Good afternoon, Officer Sean," she teased.

"Having a nice run up the countryside, are you now?" he asked.

"Sure did. It was lovely." They took a few steps without speaking, and then she asked him. "The ship that came in three days ago, anyone stay?"

"Just that preacher down there embarrassing himself," he answered. "I've got my eye on him, and he's staying in a room above Pan's pub. He's spewing the typical Believer rubbish. Younger than most. Nice full head of hair, but mid-range quality zealotry. No points for originality."

The preacher started in about Highland, like many had been doing lately.

"...and God in the flesh appeared before them, pulling down his sword from the heavens, and swinging it through the hordes and multitudes of sinful beasts. With a bellow in his voice, Emmanuel Gray, The Bishop of the Believers, brought his voice of command and ordered God himself into the breach with him, and the lord of the universe followed!"

Lies, Salla smirked. Not even good ones, just laughable falsehoods. A few locals milled about, one or two nodding in righteous agreement, but most stood crossed-armed and skeptical, taking in the performance as entertainment.

Salla was amazed that in such a short time, the truth of Highland was already being bent. It sickened her, and she hoped it would pass. A lot happened on Highland, but God had nothing to do with it. Hubris, greed, and folly had ruled the day.

"I'll give him two stars, three if he learned to dance," Salla said to Sean, referring to the amateur preacher.

"He's leaving on a hauler tomorrow. I don't know where these fellas get money to travel out here, maybe Believer charities? Cardinal Jacob ought to really have higher standards, don't you think?"

"This latest lot is surely a waste," she smiled. Salla had been as honest with Sean as she could be. She told him that anyone asking about her from off-world was certainly bad news. Groups of strangers asking about her would mean there might be violence brewing. He'd nodded without questioning further, a Nova Turin man through and through.

"Are you having dinner later tonight?" Sean asked, trying to seem innocent.

She bit her lip; Sean was a decent man and wasn't unattractive to her. Above all, she felt she could trust him, but there was too much hanging over her now. She wondered about who might be waiting around the next corner. She hated to put thought to it, but she'd rather be nimble than tied down. Above all, she felt her heart elsewhere right now, not knowing where Timberwolf was or what happened to him felt like a sentence unfinished. She checked her smart-device again, still nothing.

"I'm feeling like just reheating leftovers," she apologized with her eyes in that way that wasn't supposed to disappoint him, but certainly did.

"Roger that," he said. "I've got a hot crossword to get back to."

She rolled her eyes gamely. The preacher prattled on, something about the glory of Cardinal Jacob and his role on Highland, too. Apparently, his excellency had taken the sword right from the hand of God and crushed the hordes underfoot himself. "He was even on Highland?" she accidentally said aloud.

"What's that?" Sean asked.

"Nothing. Absolutely nothing," she replied.

Someone threw a pittance into a pail at the preacher's feet, nodding enthusiastically at the mention of the Cardinal's name. Salla shook her head, truth was certainly being built on lies.

THE RIDGE WAR

Arnock Prime – 6 years ago

The elevator ascended from the warm darkness of the world. Inside, Kizik – an Arnock Master – huddled with two brutes from the warrior class assigned to protect him. They were wrapped in what would pass for Arnock parkas, leather coverings with six sleeves.

The dim light of the surface began to appear above them in the shaft. They looked through the clear top of the moving box and saw the shaded sky, the twilight facing sunward, fading to an eternal black flecked with stars. *Stars* – the very idea delighted the young but filled grown Arnock with dread. Seeing stars meant you were up above. Under the stars, the Farhallen – the Beasts of the Wind – dwelt. They were going to see the Farhallen now.

Murderers, the depraved, the dangerously insane. The Farhallen were the outcasts from Arnock society, cut off from the embrace of the collective mind. They had chosen their fate, though. There were prisons and hospitals below. The Farhallen chose to separate themselves forever and live in this horrible place.

The doors slid open. They were at the top of the twilight ridge. The Farhallen settlement was nestled within the rocks on the dark side. Kizik and his guards ambled down the hill, slipping and recovering in the gloom. Part of this excursion was a desperate maneuver in the war with the humans, part of it was a warning. The Farhallen were in grave danger.

On a flattened ridge. Kizik had the guards float lights. Long shadows fell towards the meager hovels among the rocks.

Farhallen! Kizik buzzed and shook, reaching out with his mind.

He was met with curses, screams, and mindless ranting. A rock came close to his head. One of his guards grunted with anger and raised his weapon, its tip glowing yellow.

Kizik calmed him with a raised claw, and laughter came from the darkness. Depraved, cackling laughter from dozens of minds.

A jovial and meaty chortle overtook them all, and a lone figure lumbered towards them, shielding his eyes.

You're trying to blind us? he asked.

Light breathes life, Kizik replied.

More cacophonous laughter reached him again, and Kizik ordered the lights turned off. The ancient show of respect unappreciated.

Here to talk us into prison? the figure asked.

It's your right to be here, Kizik responded.

It's unpleasant here, but it suits us. The voice had a strange cadence to it. Individual, disconcerting, almost human in its tenor.

Kizik was growing impatient. He had urgent business. *What is your name?* he demanded.

You've come a long way. Call me Far.

Just then, a mad individual ambled out of the shadows, shaking a stick and screaming audibly in three separate octaves. Far grabbed them with his front claw and picked up a nearby rock, slamming it into the side of the Arnock's skull. He swung again, catching him on the other side and dropping him to the ground with a flourish that Kizik could only interpret as gleeful.

Far! Kizik bellowed. *There is danger beyond what you know. There is deep sacrifice occurring. We are at war. Horrific war. With a species that will land here soon. Right here, right on you.*

Far gave the uneasy chortle of someone who was unafraid. *Deep sacrifice,* he mocked. *So, we die, and a problem is solved for you, no?*

I've considered that benefit, Kizik acknowledged. *But about the sacrifice...*

And Kizik told Far about the human's destructive march through their outpost worlds. He told him about how he'd delivered live Arnock Masters to Highland so they could explore their minds in exchange for defensive weapons. He told him the awful truth that Achilles Dacha had relayed to him. About how they might turn their voices on the humans and bend their minds to madness.

Our species is on the verge of nothingness, Kizik concluded.

Far ambled closer. His face was creased and dry from the cold. He wore a filthy shawl around him. Kizik doubted it kept him warm. *Well, it seems this world is in a very sad state, but we are already lost ones. What's this to do with us?* he asked coldly but with aching curiosity.

A human replica from Highland. Achilles Dacha. He told me minds like yours already know!

We do. I could kill you by screaming your name. Kizik, such a balanced name, Far said absently, taking in the stars above.

Kizik recalled the names of those Far had killed below when he'd lived among them. He had liked to stab females and the elderly, dragging them from transit areas and into dark corners. Kizik drew closer to him. *Human minds are separate. They cannot band together. When they land here, you can wipe them out. In exchange, we'll send supplies. We'll sustain...* Kizik could sense Far wasn't listening.

Far drew in the dust with his claw, a human eyeball that he then scratched away. *No. We won't fight for you,* Far murmured.

You will die here. You'll be practice for them!

You misunderstand, Far replied, *you'll fight for us.* Far turned his mandibles to the side in a grin, *I will teach you!*

Kizik recoiled, his shoulders hunching in disgust. One of the guards moved on Far, bringing his weapon towards the bastard's head.

Far leaned in, *you'd let me fight for you? So, your soul stays clean in the pathways of Radem?* Far spat out the name of the Arnock deity with disgust.

With graceful fury, Kizik snatched the weapon from the guard and brought it to Far's head himself. A cold wind came in, blowing hard and making them shudder. This was a desperate time. A Master Arnock like Kizik should never touch a weapon. Violence was not a currency his kind traded in.

Good! Far intoned with delight, *holding a weapon is the first step. You will be a weapon. You'll bring your council here. I'll teach the Masters.*

Any further demands? Kizik sneered.

Liquor never hurts, and it warms the bones.

Kizik took the elevator back down alone. His guards advised they would take the next one and make sure they weren't followed by the Farhallen, but he knew that was a lie. The Masters were supposed to be enlightened stewards of Arnock society. They couldn't stomach being near him after the display beyond the ridge. He had *threatened* violence. He had *pledged* to do violence. The warrior class was not designed to hide their feelings, and Kizik sensed their pure disgust.

They were right to be disgusted by him, but they didn't understand. The Arnock had thrived here for millennia, buried in the shale. The subterranean Ring City wrapped around their entire world. The humans would simply burrow in and destroy them like they had destroyed so many others – the Phaelon, the Tiaski, and the Szykul, just to name a few.

Far was a fallen Master, born from the noblest of egg-mothers. Kizik recalled the satisfaction which flowed out from him as they'd left. Far didn't enjoy murder simply for the act. He relished the fear it caused, the erosion of trust that it created. Turning the Masters into killers was almost too lovely to resist, and that's exactly what he did.

The human attack came 48 rotations later, and the Arnock were ready.

Imagine their small minds. Alone, Far sent his thoughts to the Masters hiding on the dark ridge.

Imagine what they are here for. Imagine our young on the ends of pikes. Remember what I have taught you!

In orbit above, they watched as the snail-shell-shaped Arnock command ships shimmered into view, right in the path of the human cruisers. A cheer went up as human vessels cracked in half from Arnock fire, and the heavy bombers spiraled downwards to crash on the surface.

Achilles Dacha from Highland had told Kizik that the humans would keep coming, even after they lost their air cover. They would send the landers anyway. Their leader was a man named Emmanuel Gray. He was comfortable with the calculus of sacrifice.

The sky flashed with light, and the clouds burst with flame, but along with human vessels, Arnock ships fell from the sky as well. A massive orange plume rose noiselessly far away, and the ground shook long moments later.

Kizik felt the death, the screams of the Arnock in those ships in the instant before they perished. He also felt the screams from below him. The humans had landed on another part of the world as well, breaking through the Masters deployed there. They were streaming into the Ring City via the Great Shaft and filling the Southcaves with flame.

Hold! Far commanded as some of the Masters broke – hoping to rush to the Southcaves.

You will not make it in time, Kizik implored. *Our fight is here!*

Tendrils descended from the sky; countless landing craft trailed by plumes of vapor. Amongst them came a giant object – like a mechanical mountain, blockish and bristling with plasma cannons. It landed on the plain below them, almost on top of their position, so close that they could discern the thoughts of individuals inside the machine.

Confidence oozed from the humans. *They do not know we are here!* Far, expressed joyfully.

It was a command base, massive and self-contained. It could lift off at a moment's notice, but they shut off their engines, and white vapor breathed out of it almost casually. With a disconcerting stillness, it simply sat there.

Kizik could feel the others anxious to attack, to pool their power and repel the humans from their world *right now.* The hours passed, and the carnage from the Southcaves intensified. Region after region fell, large parts of the single planet-wrapping Ring City were cut off from the rest.

They could sense the human infantry and their vehicles collecting themselves beyond the command base now. They knew their intention was to come right through where they hid. Kizik used all his will to hold the others back. *We must wait. We are the wind. We must make this sting to the bone so they never return!*

Then a lament came that filled the assembled with despair. The Southern Nursery, hundreds of generations yet to be born, was cut from its suspension and fell to the caverns below, lost to the world's smoldering mantle.

Unbearable! This sacrifice is unbearable, came the collective cry.

Just when the Masters could wait no longer, the humans approached. Men wrapped in armor came up the ridge, skillfully leaping with the assistance of thrusters.

They are fleas! Far bellowed.

Far's anger swelled within him, his sickness filling the minds of Kizik and the other Masters. He projected his lust onto them, the joy he got from pain and fear. Then, before they were fully ready, a light swung their way.

Twist their minds. They are small. Alone, Far commanded.

A human was just twenty yards away, and they all focused on him. After a moment, he simply brought his own weapon to his glowing faceplate, and with a pop, a red streak painted the rocks behind him.

Kill all of them! Kizik ordered, the joy of murder filling him.

The Masters descended the ridge, stopping and buzzing every few steps to attack. It was like having a new sense, something beyond what they were used to experiencing. They would reach out, take hold of these simple, individual minds, and simply *spin* them. There was no need to imagine the horrors for them, as it was more than enough to simply nudge them towards madness.

Don't look! Far commanded, but for some, it was too late. The Masters glimpsed through human eyes as bleeding tentacles rose from the ground, and a man's head was replaced with black oil sloshing inside his helmet. A human saw the serenity of his youth. A gleaming pond below him. He leaped in carelessly and slipped down into a fissure, breaking his neck on a spire.

Even without looking through their eyes, the Masters saw the results of the horror. Two humans, engulfed in flame, stabbed at each other before tumbling into a crevasse. A trooper removed his helmet and begged for his breath in the thin air. He drove his K-bar knife into his own eye and fell forward. From behind them, a hover tank rolled down the ridge, going airborne and twisting half a dozen times before impaling on an outcropping.

Everywhere, the humans incinerated each other, stabbed each other, lashed chemical lasers into each other's backs. One man seemed to be in command, and the Arnock surrounded him. He lashed out with a flamethrower, keeping them at bay. Far laughed at him, and the man held the sides of his helmet, trying to keep the awful cackling away. With twisted glee, Far approached and sliced off the man's arm with his razor-sharp claw and then plunged another claw into his faceplate.

There's that way too! Far grunted.

Kizik looked over the ridge. The humans looked like a swarm of pests, leaping and running for the cover of their command base.

Go! Kizik willed to them. *Go!*

Almost at his command, the engines of the huge machine began to glow. The command base slowly lifted into the air, troopers still trying to board it. The thrust, hot and vicious, deflected their way. Kizik and the others dove for cover, but three Masters, just a few feet away, were vaporized.

Far appeared next to him. *Don't let them escape!* he insisted.

They pooled their minds, Kizik and Far reaching out to the structure that was now climbing into the sky. They found only panic, coupled with the relief of escape.

Kizik pulled their fear in, enjoyed it. He searched for minds that were on the command deck.

Return to us! Kizik commanded, his voice so strong that even Far could not bear it. Almost instantly, the vehicle's engines ceased. The command base hung there impossibly for a moment and then fell to the ground, a half mile's worth of kinetic energy cracking its innards open like a music box falling to the floor.

Get to them! Kizik ordered, and the Masters scrambled into the jagged wreckage. A human crawled before him, and Kizik stabbed him through the back with his claw, driving his front appendage in up to his second joint. All around, the Masters slashed the humans down, becoming sprayed in slick redness. The Arnock rushed through the wreckage, some dying as it collapsed around them, but they needed to do this, they *had* to do this. They found a dozen humans trapped in a corner. Frantically, Kizik and the others tore into them, tossing hunks over their shoulders until there was nothing left moving.

When it was done, Far fell back, resting for a moment, all of him stained red. *Thank you,* he said to Kizik.

Go see Radem, Kizik moaned, wishing Far dead.

THE BEAR

D.P.E. Archangel

"He drinks a lot of tea," Dr. Tier remarked to Timberwolf. She watched Vincent Dacha sitting across from Conrad in *Archangel's* mess hall. The small man enjoyed occupying space here and would chat with the young analyst for hours. Conrad would stumble away when Vincent was brought back to his secure quarters, exhausted from patiently listening to newly remembered stories and family memories. Conrad prodded and worked him as much as he could, but Vincent never gave up anything on where he had sent Gray.

Dr. Tier had ordered enhanced interrogation, but Vincent had cheerily told them that his physiology would simply shut down if he so desired it. He had discovered that what his brothers Sergey and Achilles had done with poison, he could do with his intentions. Progress!

Conrad rose from the table, his legs shaking. These sessions required him to be "on" for hours at a time, mentally taking notes and needling for information. He shook his head and pushed past Dr. Tier and Timberwolf without saying a word. Vincent waved cheerily as a massive security man, Capote, led him out another exit.

"So," Timberwolf began, "why am I still around?"

Dr. Tier nodded, thinking over the question. It had been over a month, and his fate was still undetermined. "Is this 'the talk'?" she asked. "We're at war, Timber. That's what you're good at."

"And the most I've done is lead a raid on a plasma depot. It was literally robbing a box car." That had been three weeks ago over Djemagon. *Archangel* now hid in the tail of a comet diving towards a white dwarf. In another week, the ice ball would break apart behind the star, and they'd have to find new shelter.

"You got to rig up. Stay nimble. I just have a different job in mind for you. It'll bring you close to Vincent, too, and put you back in your natural element."

"Oh, I get to hear about old times back in Russia before the Dacha brothers became a walking stem cell factory? Did you hear the one about the bear they had on the bus?"

"Dozens of times," she replied.

"Because they had a bear. On the bus!" he declared. She thought he was done, but he had more. "And about how they named a bunch of stuff on Highland to be like the Land of Oz? Like the yellow brick road and the Ruby City. Hilarious."

There was a silence for a few moments, and Timberwolf considered his fate. Dr. Tier was the kind of person to cut losses, remove threats, and eliminate risks. He was all three – a loss, a threat, and a risk. "Again, why haven't I seen the black? Kizik can't help me fight off a security team. If you're going to space me, go with the aft airlock with the high clearance so I don't bump my head."

"I need to show you something," she replied, a glint in her eye.

There were scratch marks covering every inch of the secondary cargo bay. The area was highly restricted, and Dr. Tier had required both a retina and DNA scan to enter. Deep scratches marred the plastisteel floors, walls, and ceilings. She approached five metal cargo crates in the back of the space. Timberwolf noticed that there were purifiers driving air into the containers. "I know what this is," he said.

She snapped her fingers in a rhythmic sequence and then did it again twice as fast. From within, something awoke, and a deep groan came from the crate as the creature within shook off its nap.

"How did you get them in here without anyone knowing?" he asked as the crate lurched to the side.

"I took advantage of the chaos. We brought a lot of stuff up from Highland. Most of it was junk, but Conrad made sure to grab these. He made Vincent instruct the machine cloud to destroy the rest of the hardware down there. They'll eat what they can, like a pack of locusts."

Timberwolf knelt next to the crate and looked in, careful not to get close enough to where he might be sliced by a razor-tipped tongue. "Well, aren't you a full-house?"

"Five Sabatin," she said, proud of her arsenal. Five biomechanical killing machines. Nearly indestructible armored beasts that could be programmed to carry out complicated missions. "When Vincent isn't with Conrad, he's down here with them."

"He's imprinting them? To do what?"

She shook her head. "I've got intelligence coming in about something. I won't say what yet."

"Need to know, huh?" he said. "I assume Tirani doesn't know yet. Will he want to know?"

"He will not," Dr. Tier replied.

"So, I'm still here because you've got something planned for me that involves five Sabatin. What about after that?"

"You never know. Stay in my graces."

"You trust Dacha?" he asked, almost as an afterthought.

"You know I don't. Conrad is reviewing every line of his code."

She seemed buoyant, enthusiastic about the trick she had up her sleeve. That would mean very bad news to whoever was on the receiving end. He didn't trust her, not even a little bit, after everything that happened. But there was something she needed to know, that she had a right to know. He shook his head, trying to find the words. "Thea?" he started.

"If you have questions, I won't answer them," she replied gamely.

"No, nothing. Forget it," he held back, the selfish part of him taking over. He considered that the information he held might be valuable later. "Assume this is double top secret?" he asked instead.

"Triple," she replied.

THE SYMMETRY

Symmetry Lifeship – 2 million years ago

Tanqar Tenock smelled a trap, and he knew his brother did not. He paced within his suite, flexing his fingers within his gloves. There was no escape for their prey. A Srathi Lifeship, holding a billion spawn simply appearing on their screens? *Had they let themselves be seen?* Tanqar worried. His brother Raif Tenock was in command now and would be until day-change, which was just a few minutes from now. Whoever had set this trap might know that Raif was in charge, impulsive Raif, aggressive Raif, impatient Raif.

Warnings sounded, indicating they were drawing closer. Tanqar pulled up a holographic display. The bulbous and delicate Srathi vessel held half their civilization, and here it was, limping before them, five of its dozen drives faltering. It was trying to find refuge between two singularities, where overlapping event horizons would make targeting and combat difficult. A dense asteroid belt and a red giant rounded out this monstrous star system.

"Stop, Raif!" Tanqar muttered to himself, gritting his teeth. The Srathi might be gambling their civilization, but they were gambling theirs, too. They were the Symmetry, and their entire species was aboard this vessel of war.

These were the times of the Obliteration Wars, and worlds had been abandoned by all the species that could flee to the stars. The Symmetry Lifeship was forty-two miles long, a brilliant white tablet engraved with narrow valleys and soaring towers on its exterior. A thousand of its cannons charged to deliver a deathblow to the Srathi race.

"That is not right," Tanqar said when he noticed the distance to the Srathi Lifeship fluctuating wildly as it got closer to the singularities. "That is certainly not right."

Per tradition, Tanqar was not permitted in the *Vejkadam*, or place of command, until his brother's "Semi" was over, the inviolable half-day of authority. He exited his cabin, brushing past the guard whose duty it was to enforce this tradition. "Lord Tanqar, your time is not for twenty-two minutes."

"I am aware. Please slit my throat," he brushed past the guard, daring him to act.

"It is my obligation!" the guard implored, but Tanqar was past him, his command cloak swinging in his wake.

Tanqar's brother Raif stalked the floor of the Vejkadam. "It's like the stars dangling before me. Offering a gift!"

His command officers laughed nervously. Displays covering the walls showed the Srathi Lifeship limping along and its engines faltering. Raif ran his clawed hand through the hologram projected over the room. He was primed to relieve his people of an existential threat they had been fighting for decades.

"It's almost time to sleep, Raif," Tanqar appeared behind him. Never in the history of the Symmetry had one of the ruling Tenock clan interrupted the Semi of another. The command crew stood frozen. Their traditions stated that they were to leap on Tanqar and stab him to death, but when faced with the unthinkable, they faltered.

Raif was just as surprised, and the fur around his throat stood on edge. "Did you bring me my breakfast?" he finally asked after agonizing seconds.

"No, but recall when we were in the womb, and you gave me this?" Tanqar ran his finger down a long scar that traced from his ear to his sternum. "That's always bothered me."

Uneasy laughter filled the command deck, but Raif silenced them with his hand. "What is it? Why are you here?"

"That!" Tanqar moved under the image of the Srathi vessel, its interconnecting bulbs so ripe for destruction, more of its drivers failing now. "Its engines are throwing off sub-light distortion. It's hiding something. It's not in trouble. We're in trouble."

Raif laughed, and his ample frame jostled. Tanqar was the lean one, the one with the keener eyes, but the one less trusted, the one who didn't explain. Raif nodded to his personal guard, the gravity of what was happening settling in. "I have to kill you, Tanqar. Right here as you stand. We all have to kill you."

"You're playing into their hands. I don't know what this is, but if you kill me now, you will join me soon."

From behind, a blade came through Tanqar's shoulder, thick purple blood sprouting. He tried to pull his sidearm, but other blows came down from all present. He felt the blades from all sides, between his shoulders, the back of his knee, even his ankle, but he'd yet been stabbed through the heart. He lurched towards his brother, grabbing the bottom of his tunic. Raif had his own sidearm out now and held it to his brother's neck. He looked down at him, a slash on Tanqar's face cut through the fur to the flesh below.

And then there was a flash of light, and on the screens around them, the Srathi vessel was overtaken in the glare. Flanking it, other vessels appeared from sub-light. There were two dozen from multiple civilizations – the Berun, Verijal, the Sewi, and many more, their only connection being that the Symmetry had driven them from their worlds. Raif turned away from his brother, leaving him reaching up for him.

"They're not attacking," a crewmember said.

"Then why are they here?" Raif demanded.

And as quickly as they had arrived, they leaped back into sub-light, seemingly in random directions. An instant later, it was clear that their actions hadn't been arbitrary at all. Where each ship had been just an instant before, a gravity well remained. Twenty-four artificial singularities encircled the Symmetry. In just a few moments, there was pure density all around them.

"Move us!" Raif bellowed.

"We can't!" the navigator replied.

Their instruments faltered, bringing back impossible readings. There was no time. No matter. No dimension. The light from the massive red giant faded, every photon from the star falling into the singularities before it could reach them.

Tanqar's blood stained his teeth, and he coughed, wiping more of the sticky purple substance onto his arm. His eyes met his brother's gaze as the last of the light faded. The look on Raif's face held all his fear, and Tanqar's dying heart held nothing but anger. They would be locked this way for nearly eternity.

A being appeared before them an instant later. It was male, nearly hairless except for his brow. It had no claws or tail, and a patch covered one of his eyes. "Hello," he said, trying their language. "I have a story to tell you. You've had a long day."

BARRISTER

Tach-Nine Station

Dr. Tier knew that Captain Tirani was avoiding her. She'd been trying to speak with him privately for the last few days, and he had been making himself highly unavailable. She waited by the bridge, and he slipped away when she was momentarily distracted. She came by his ready room, and he had feigned meetings with his senior staff. Now, with *Archangel* docked at Tach-Nine station, he had gone aboard the facility to avoid her. He had no idea how correct his instincts were.

Yes – she definitely had something new up her sleeve. No – Tirani would not want to know what it was.

"He went over?" she grilled Conrad near the airlock. Crew guided floating pallets of supplies aboard.

"He did. I asked him if he would be taking office hours, and instead, he just went aboard Tach-Nine station."

She shook her head, near laughing, and looked out a large viewing window. Just two hundred yards away, over the spine of the station, was the A.C. *Antares*, a rival Assault Corps vessel. It seemed to be poised like a praying mantis, its command deck tilted forward as if it was staring down *Archangel*.

If they weren't docked at a Station Corps facility, they would have been shooting at each other, but the rules of engagement were clear – there were to be no hostilities while in port. The Station Corps had chosen to remain neutral and offer refuge services to both sides and to revoke such privileges if violations occurred. That had held for the most part, but of course there had been scuffles, mostly bar fights. Here at Tach-Nine, Assault Corps crews roamed elbow to elbow with Department of Peace Enforcement personnel. There had been no reports of brawls yet, but it wasn't even lunchtime.

"I hope he took Capote because that place is crawling with jarheads."

"He was with a party."

She bit her lip. She *had* to speak with Tirani as soon as possible. "Let's join the party."

Conrad was following her before he realized what he was doing. "This is profoundly reckless," he complained, taking two steps for her every stride.

They walked along the curve of Tach-Nine's community ring. Assault Corps troopers sneered at them as they passed. "Are you sure about the intel you gave me?" she asked him.

"Very much," he replied.

"Then this is worth it."

Conrad breathed, trying to relax. Two anvil-jawed troopers in black and white space-camo closed on him, forcing him to step between them sideways. Conrad's appearance screamed D.P.E. His soft features and bookish nature left no doubt as to his affiliation. He had no illusions; this place was a combat zone, and he was not meant for combat. Dr. Tier, on the other hand, pushed through the crowd confidently and with purpose. He heard wisps of conversation from the A.C. people as they passed. "Was that Dr. Tier?" someone asked incredulously, not believing she would be bold enough to show herself beyond the protection of *Archangel*.

They found Tirani buying cured soy meat at a stall in the inner ring. She surprised him with a hand on his shoulder. "A cup of real coffee?" she offered. He rolled his eyes, knowing he wasn't getting away.

They sat at a booth in the mostly empty café, untouched cups of non-synthetic Colombian coffee before them. Tirani mulled over what Dr. Tier had just proposed to him. He couldn't say he was surprised at her latest plan, but he could certainly be excused for being incredulous. He had to admit she had done a good job keeping the crew of *Archangel* alive and fighting. Surprisingly, even as the D.P.E. was outnumbered by the Assault Corps four-to-one, Dr. Tier had ordered that all D.P.E. forces go on offense. They worked together when possible but mostly engaged in daring, solo hit-and-run raids out of nowhere. Dealing with an asymmetric threat had kept the Assault Corps from effectively massing their forces. Still, what she proposed was on an entirely new plateau of bold.

Capote, Gordon, and Roberts formed a security wall a few feet away, watching for trouble from A.C. troopers. "Thea, I think that this might qualify as perhaps your best, worst idea yet," Tirani finally responded. Conrad sat at the edge of the table, trying to be both present and invisible at the same time.

"It should result in minimal fatalities and maximum damage," Dr. Tier answered.

"The Station Corps position is clear. They allow refuge for both D.P.E. and A.C. cruisers." Tirani read from the official guidance on his tablet. "'*There shall be no assaults on vessels moored at Station Corps facilities by any party. Doing so will result in the immediate loss of refuge privilege.'"*

"Exactly," she replied.

"But you want to attack eight of Jephtah's cruisers moored at Tach-Four? Tach-Four! You want to go right at the heart of the Station Corps?"

"They won't be moored when we attack."

"Thea, this is lawyer ball, and I don't see how this isn't interpreted as an 'attack.'" Tirani leaned back and crossed his arms.

"Conrad does. He read up on it. Please explain." She ceded the floor to the young analyst.

Conrad began, leaning in to remain discreet. "It's in the definition of 'assault' vs. 'attack.' The Station Corps had used 'assault' in their guidance, which is narrowly defined in the A.C. rules of engagement as 'direct vessel to vessel engagement.' Our plan, narrowly interpreted, does not qualify as an assault. It's definitely an attack, which is defined more broadly and even encompasses threats using strong language. Once the vessels are detached, *then* it becomes an assault, which is perfectly legal."

It took a moment for Tirani to take this in. "The Angel help us. So, this sabotage is perfectly fine?"

"We won't be damaging the A.C. forces until we blow the mooring clamps," Dr. Tier responded.

"You know the Station Corps might still deny us refuge, regardless of what Atticus Finch here digs up for you?" Tirani said.

"This might be the knockout we need."

"And who the hell is leading the incursion to Tach-Four? Who's blowing the clamps?"

"Timberwolf Velez," Dr. Tier responded.

"So, you trust him again. Lovely."

"I don't trust anyone, especially him. He's not going in alone."

"Not alone? I assume that our Wizard of Oz has been training up his merry band of Sabatin?" Tirani asked.

"He has," Dr. Tier responded.

"So, forget Velez, we can trust Vincent Dacha?" Tirani smirked.

"Absolutely not," Conrad broke in. "I am reviewing each and every command he is imprinting on the Sabatin."

"This is your plan? This gets more ludicrous by the minute," Tirani nodded, shaking his head in resignation. Then a clatter came from just outside the café. A chair smashed over their security man Capote's shoulder. He batted it away, almost like it hadn't troubled him, but it was metal with a plastic back and must have hurt like hell.

Dr. Tier saw him going for his sidearm. "Capote! No guns!" she barked.

A lean man with the wiry build of a breacher shoved the mountainous Capote with surprising strength, and the two exchanged curses. The plaza outside the café was filling with more A.C. troopers, and crew from *Archangel* poured in to counter them. The lean Assault Corps breacher laughed mockingly, throwing his arms wide and claiming he meant no harm. His compatriots laughed, still sensing that they had the upper hand.

"We're going to have violence!" Dr. Tier hissed to Conrad, "No guns."

And on cue, the lean man pivoted and threw a haymaker, catching Capote on the cheek. In an instant it was chaos. Chairs flew and the two sides clashed. Tier pushed Conrad away and leaped over a table, kicking someone behind the knee, dropping her.

She turned to a fist hitting her lip, the sharp knuckle splitting her skin. She parried, remembering her Krav Maga, and drove her fist into the solar plexus of her attacker. Then her knee struck his ribs, and she went down with him, smashing her fist into his temple.

Someone grabbed her arm, and she spun to face a wide-cheeked man. She broke his grip and simultaneously punched him in the soft spot behind his chin. He stumbled away, gagging. She kicked him in the chest, knocking him against a wall. He bounced off, and, in that moment, he pulled a pistol from his hip.

At the appearance of the gun, the brawl ceased. Fighters loosened their grip and drifted away from one another, but that lasted just a moment. In an instant, both sides had weapons drawn, and the acetylene scent of plasma weapons charging up filled the air.

"We don't need guns," Dr. Tier said, trying to appear non-threatening. "Can't we just kick the shit out of each other in peace?" she threw out, but no one relaxed.

"Wait, wait!" the man holding the gun on her said. "I know who you are!" He raised his weapon higher, drawing a bead on her chest. A predetermination chilled the air, like everyone was living thirty seconds in the future and had already fired. The two sides exchanged shouts of *'stand down!'* but no one was standing down. Dr. Tier knew that dozens of people would be dead in just seconds if she couldn't diffuse this.

"OK, I am *exactly* who you think I am." She moved closer to the trooper, her chest right in front of the barrel of his pistol, his eyes growing in fear. "And pulling that trigger would make you a hero." The man blinked sweat away from his eyes. She motioned to the dozens around them. "And then he shoots, and she shoots, and everybody shoots, and we all die." She was an inch from his barrel, arms at her side. If he pulled the trigger, she'd be dead in an instant. "Are you ready for the last second of your life?" she asked softly.

"Look, mam…" he tried.

"Call me Doctor!" she demanded.

"Doctor Tier, I just want to…"

"You just want to put that gun the fuck away."

He blinked and his arm shook. In that moment, she snatched the pistol from his grip. Those in the plaza gasped, but instead of weapons being trained more directly, the crowd relaxed, losing its energy. "I've got a souvenir!" she said, putting the weapon inside her jacket.

Knowing it was time to go, she moved to depart, and the crowd parted for her, Tirani, Conrad, and the others followed. She tried to hide her excitement, but she was giddy from the action. She had been behind a desk for way too long. Her heart was still racing when they reached the outer ring. Timberwolf raced towards her out of *Archangel's* docking port. "Go back," she told him, wiping the blood from her lip. "But I've got a new job for you."

PREACH

Nova Turin

The man who had been Emmanuel Gray didn't know who he was or exactly where he was going. *Into the Mystic* took him on a roundabout journey, but it seemed to know where it was headed, landing on various worlds to refuel. Each time, the ship's A.I. had given him one basic instruction. "Go into all the world and preach," and so he would preach.

He talked about the places he had been, of being reborn and seeing through new eyes. He mumbled and shuffled at first, but then an innate talent woke within him. He was filled with energy when he spoke, and he realized that in his past life, people felt compelled by his words. He said he was *here to wake people up.* He met with indifference on most worlds, understanding nods in others. And so on, though things began to come to him, words out of his rote memory.

He found himself talking about marching off to war, of men experiencing horrific things. The spiders tearing at their minds. Entire platoons obliterated in the Red Forrest on Phaelon Prime. He didn't know where he was getting these words, they were simply coming to him, flat and direct and with almost no feeling. Through all of this, he was kept alone. When anyone spoke to him directly, he'd feel a ringing in his ears that quickly became unbearable. He went about his way, connecting with no one. After a day or two, the cufflinks Vincent had given him on Highland would buzz, calling him back to the ship.

In between worlds, he looked through the ship's A.I., searching for some sort of clue as to who he was or where he was going. The memory banks were selective and only showed him the most basic news feeds, mostly about the brewing conflict between the D.P.E. and the A.C., which was now being openly referred to as a civil war. He wondered if his purpose might have something to do with that. It seemed to have started at around the same time Vincent had found him. He knew he had been a very bad person, maybe he was somehow involved? He brushed that off, unsure how to process that sort of thing.

He felt simple, but that wasn't quite the right word. It was more that he was *emerging*. He could feel that there was something infinite within him that he wasn't aware of yet. It was weeks into his journey when he realized he hadn't eaten or drank anything since he'd left Vincent. He didn't feel at all hungry, but he opened up the stores on *Mystic* one morning. Unable to stop himself, he ate almost everything inside, self-cooking rations of synthetic coconut chicken, steaks, pasta primavera, and more. He drank bottles and bottles of red wine, the notes of rich caramel and the earthy tannins dancing on his tongue.

He found himself only momentarily drunk, and momentarily full – his body processing the calories and the alcohol almost instantly. He slept for a few minutes, not because he needed to, but because it gave him some pleasure. When he awoke, he searched through the ship's computer. In a folder he had never looked at before, he saw that he had no restrictions. Inside was a file called *Symmetry,* and it was just a few lines of text.

```
The  Obliteration  Wars  were  waged  by
several species driven from their worlds
by stellar conflict. Entire civilizations
quartered in massive 'life-ships' which
were  free-floating  arks.  They  fled  one
common enemy. The Symmetry hunted them all
one by one. Finally, the Symmetry life-
ship was trapped by dozens of artificial
singularities in a structure called the
Rubicon Cluster. They are still trapped
after two million years.
```

"Two million years?" he considered. That was an unfathomable amount of time. "Two million years sleeping."

Vincent had said he was going to wake up some very old people – bad people, much worse than him.

Much worse than me. He mulled that over in his mind. A lot had come to him in the last few days. Horrific images of war – lifters slicked with blood, thousands of aluminum caskets, mushroom clouds rising. He knew he had been responsible for it all. *Much worse than me?*

He doubted it.

He knew why he was taking his time to get where he was going. He was getting stronger, more focused. He needed to know himself at an animal level. He began to sense his purpose. Whoever Salla Birdwing was, he was starting to understand what he needed to do when he found her.

Somehow, she was going to help him wake the Symmetry.

The ship dropped out of sub-light over Nova Turin, a far-flung colony world. He knew that this was the end of his journey, and he would find Salla below. The cufflinks on his arm buzzed, and the A.I. had one instruction for him. "Wear the jacket. The one you had on back on Highland. The jacket still covered in dust."

OZ

D.P.E. Archangel

Archangel sat nestled within a crevice of a hunk of iron. The asteroid orbited a binary pair of brown dwarves in a wide elliptical orbit. The magnetic field of the object did a fairly good job of masking the cruiser's energy signature, keeping them off long-range scans.

The Five Sabatin knelt before Vincent Dacha in the secondary cargo bay of *Archangel*. Their silver bio-armor gleamed under the bright light. With hand motions, he guided their attention left, then right, up, and down. Then, they rested their massive heads over their front claws. They waited for the next instruction, growls and hisses coming intermittently and long, razor-tipped tongues sliding in and out.

Timberwolf watched the exercise as he always did. Once Dr. Tier had confirmed her intelligence about Tach-Four, Timberwolf had been brought in – now having a need to know. He wore the shoulder harness for his rig and the right gauntlet with the chemical laser. Part of his role was executioner. If Vincent made a move to let the Sabatin loose on *Archangel*, his job was to kill him instantly. Dr. Tier had stationed Conrad in an observation room at the back of the bay. His job was to blow the whole thing into space if Timberwolf misbehaved. Timberwolf was slowly moving back towards the circle of trust but wasn't there yet.

The Sabatin were code-named Dorothy, Tin Man, Toto, Scarecrow, and Lion. Vincent had become fascinated by memories of Highland's heyday, before it was automated, and the place employed thousands of people. The employees had nicknamed parts of the facility after the Wizard of

Oz, and a golden path had wound through the command center loading area. He recalled that some awful woman in procurement, which was in an area called the Crystal City, had been known as the "wicked witch."

Once the Sabatin were warmed up for the day, Vincent donned a holographic viewer that was synced to smart-contacts floating over their massive eyes. He took them through their imprinting, running them through the entire attack plan, accelerated by a factor of ten.

Lion was living up to his name and was proving to be the most aggressive. Tin Man was the nimblest and was focused on the intricate task of breaking the moorings. Scarecrow had the most acute senses and would be focused on in-mission intelligence. Dorothy and Toto – fast and precise, would plant the bombs once the cruisers were floating free. Timberwolf was what Vincent referred to as the "glue" that held the team together, but the tiny man had also gone out of his way to emphasize that he felt he was a useless appendage to the whole operation.

"I know you love this part," Vincent said.

"Come on, we did this yesterday." Timberwolf tensed and waited for the final step of the daily imprinting. During the mission, Timberwolf would be their handler, and they needed to trust him more than they trusted each other.

"Do it!" Vincent commanded, his voice rising above its chirp to an authoritative bark.

"Bo heh-nah!" Timberwolf commanded. An instant later, there were five blurs of silver swarming to all parts of the cargo bay at once. Then they encircled Timberwolf, brushing their musk onto him and swiping at his body with the dull side of their claws. He fell into a pile of them, not able to tell where one ended and the next began. He kept his arms limp at his side to not appear threatening, and their sour breath was everywhere. They knocked him about roughly, tossing him like he was a ragdoll.

Finally, Timberwolf uttered "aht sor," and the session ended, the beasts returning to their exact prior positions in front of Vincent. The small man turned to Timberwolf, feeling satisfied. "You know, it would have been great. You running Highland. Me not needing to be born yet. You and my brothers could have built the place back up. Maybe brought actual people back to work there, nice days."

Timberwolf sensed an opening and decided to needle Vincent. "Yeah, too bad Gray came along. That wasn't a factor you controlled for. He's still alive. I know it."

"He's serving his purpose, so is she," Vincent said, instantly realizing he had slipped. He looked to the Sabatin. They waited with bated breath for their next command.

Timberwolf knew better than to dive right in, but the hair stood up on the back of his neck. *So is she* could only refer to one person – Salla Birdwing. *How was Salla Birdwing part of this!?* "I guess Gray is serving his purpose," Timberwolf answered, pretending he hadn't heard the second part. The two men stared at each other, though, silently acknowledging the misstep. The astute Tin Man could sense the tension.

Vincent knew there was no denying it. "Look, my brother Achilles cared for her a lot. Trusted her a lot, but this is bigger than Salla, believe me." Timberwolf assumed she was on her home world of Nova Turin – a small settlement where her neighbors would protect her and someone from off-world, with bad intentions, would stick out like a sore thumb. Somehow, whatever Vincent was cooking up involved not just Gray, but Salla – and maybe both of them together. He shuddered at the thought of Gray tracking her down. She'd been through enough. Though, the upside was that it was also possible that she might kill Gray on sight.

"If your brother cared for Salla. You care for Salla. I know how this works," Timberwolf twisted the knife a little. "What sort of danger is she in?"

Vincent shuffled, knowing he was out of deceptions. "I'm not going to lie to you. She's in all sorts of danger."

"Huh. Thanks," Timberwolf said, shaking off his rig harness. He made for the door, banging on it until Conrad buzzed him out of the cargo bay. He stalked up to the command deck, Conrad following him.

"I heard all of that. Nicely done, but…"

"Not now, haircut," Timberwolf pushed past him and climbed a service ladder.

"Where do you think you're going?" Conrad asked.

"I need to ruin the doc's day," Timberwolf responded.

He banged on her office door, and after a few moments, Dr. Tier slid it open. "Can I help you, Timber?" she asked. He pushed in, Conrad behind him.

"I had a breakthrough with Dacha."

"That's excellent, so why are you so… acting like your old self?"

"Whatever Vincent is planning for Gray involves Salla Birdwing in some way. That puts the locus of all this on Nova'."

She stopped him. "So, you should get there on your white horse?"

"That's secondary."

"Oh, the hell it is! I suppose you want to leave now?" she asked.

"I would not advise that," Conrad interjected.

"Well, isn't this about choices, Doc?" Timberwolf said.

In a way, he was right, Gray could serve as a linchpin in this struggle, an object to be bartered with. Then again, the strike on Tach-Four was only three days away. That could take the backbone out of Jephtah's forces. She had six of her fleet there now, and two more would be joining soon. Dr. Tier sighed, weary of this. Weary of all of this. "Look, thank you for your service. You have done a lot since Highland. I expected much less, but I can't let you go after Gray. We don't have time for personal asides."

Timberwolf nodded, unsatisfied. He had hoped he wouldn't have to play this next card. "I need to tell you something about Highland. You need to sit down."

Sensing the gravity, she nodded, and Conrad departed. She slid into her chair, waiting for what was to come. "Michael Solandro was on Gray's crew," Timberwolf said. At Michael's name, some shine came to her eyes and then dropped away instantly.

"Michael is dead, isn't he?" She knew the answer before she asked. She shook visibly, wrapping her arms around herself.

"Yes."

Michael Solandro had come up with Timberwolf in the special forces but had washed out and become a mercenary. Dr. Tier had met him almost twenty years ago while in the field. Their relationship had been brief and under duress, but it had resulted in a child. She rose, looking out the window at the stars slowly churning in the blackness. She needed a minute and took almost a full one before answering. "You held this from me?" she murmured, shaking her head. "Why?" she demanded.

"I don't have a good reason."

"So, Camille's father is dead, and you felt like keeping this to yourself? What the hell is wrong with you?"

"I didn't care about you, Thea!" he snarled. "I didn't care about anyone! After all that happened, after all *you* did? You put Kizik up here!" He tapped his temple and lowered the growl in his voice. "You didn't deserve kindness."

"You held this back until you could use it on me." He started to say something, but she cut him off. "Nicely played. Cut to the bone like a professional."

"I am a professional. This is what we do." Timberwolf felt the shame building in him. He hadn't intended for this to happen. He hadn't thought he would end up cooped up on *Archangel* in Dr. Tier's service. He assumed he'd be forgotten in a cell or left to the black within a few days.

But here they were, forced to relate to each other as human beings in the midst of all of this chaos. Through her steely demeanor, he had forgotten that she could be hurt just like everybody else.

"Gray killed him in front of me. I'm sorry," he continued.

"Well, thank you for telling me, eventually." Her head was spinning. She went to her pocket, where she used to keep her unmarked bottle of Terecine, and then remembered she had tossed it. *Gray killed Camille's father.* That realization came over her. She realized she would have to tell her daughter about this very soon, in case something happened to her, and she lost the chance.

"Michael didn't buy into any of that Believer bullshit," Timberwolf assured her. "He was there for the paycheck.

"Huh," she said, a smile fluttering, "that tracks." She hung her head for a moment, making her decision. "You give me Tach-Four. I'll give you Salla Birdwing, and maybe you put a blast into Gray for good measure. Reduce life's complexity."

"And if I just leave for Nova' now?"

"I'll take a detour to tear you apart. Don't tempt me."

He nodded and turned to go. When he was gone, Dr. Tier found herself dropping to her haunches against the wall. Tears came from what felt like an endless well. She mourned for Camille and the loss of the girl's father. She also mourned for the life she was living without ties or close friends. Gray had taken the family from her that she had sometimes imagined. Michael had been an embittered man she had avoided for the most part, but the fact of his existence held something for her. There had been someone out there she had come together with to form a triad, to create something more than herself. Now, even if that had been a threadbare, sorry wisp, it was destroyed.

She was wrong, there was time for personal asides. Gray had to pay for this.

THE BEAST OF THE WIND

Arnock Prime

Kizik was the first and last of his kind – or at least he hoped he was. A Master who had cast aside everything and turned to war and violence. He hadn't asked for this role. It had simply fallen to him when the humans attacked. It had to fall to someone. Still, he was an outcast Arnock. There was a word for Arnock who separated from the collective consciousness, Farhallen – creatures of the badlands, beasts of the wind. It also referred to the self-exiled, the forsaken and hopelessly insane.

He'd done horrible things to protect his people, and it had all been for naught. No one who had set out to claim it had secured the prize of Highland, not the competing human factions nor the Arnock landing force. Kizik had been the only survivor out of thousands of Arnock. He had made a poor wager by taking the last military assets of his civilization to move on Highland, but he had seen no other way. It had all failed, and now he had nothing, nothing but this awful box.

A box of death. He held the small cube in his claw, focusing on its black edges. It had the capability to do many things, but he had commissioned its construction as a weapon. Something that could take the Arnock ability to control human minds and amplify that many times over. He considered where his journey had taken him. He had left his world to secure the future of his people, but instead, he had sealed their fate. Now he sat in a tiny shuttle, his only companion was Droma, a Phaelon warrior he had rescued from Highland, or more accurately, captured. The creature showed him no aggression but provided him no more than minimal regard.

He turned the deadly cube over in his claw. He was sure the humans had at least one of these as well. There were supposed to be two in the delivery container, but when he had opened it, there was only one. He wondered how they might use it, perhaps to amplify their technology. Humans were so small, so simplistic, so dependent on machines to extend their capacity. They had one horrific quality, and that was adaptability. Most species evolved over millennia, but humans hadn't even left their own atmosphere until three hundred years ago. *Can I dare stop them? Am I too late? Would this Amp even matter?*

Before he used the Amp as a weapon, he had to try something else at least once. He'd done some experiments with it before but had been unsure if they had worked, though he felt he knew how to use it better now. He input the commands that would activate the cube and the thing sprung to life, blinking on all six sides. He held it close, and an energy field enveloped him. After a few seconds, he felt expansive, like he was actually present in places where his mind wanted to be.

He found himself looking over Highland and diving between the swirling clouds. He saw the smoldering ruins and felt the caves simmering with radiation all around him. An entity swirled in the dust and snow, something alone and desperate. He pushed himself away from that place.

He saw Timberwolf aboard *Archangel*, planning military maneuvers with the person he knew as Dr. Tier. He lingered on the man whose mind he had once been so intimately connected to. Without trying to reach him, he waited for Timberwolf to turn toward his presence, but it didn't happen. Instead, Dr. Tier turned to him, looking directly at where he was projecting himself. She actually stood and came towards him, but then he pulled away and moved his mind to home.

Arnock Prime, the windswept husk of a world. The remnants of his people lived in a single underground metropolis called the Ring City that wrapped the planet. He felt like he was knocking on the door. *Hello?* he called out softly. He moved through the dim streets and alleys, over the cocoons and public areas. He had spent so much time away from home that the gray monochrome place shocked him with its dullness.

Hello? he asked again, feeling numb from the lack of response. He found himself on the surface, at the place of the exiles, the Farhallen that he swore he would never join. One of the Farhallen knew he was there but he couldn't see who, then suddenly, like in a dream, the Arnock turned to him. It was Far, the one who had taught him how to invade human minds. *Oh no. Not him, anyone but him.*

From below the surface, he heard a response. *Who is it?* a voice asked, it wasn't exactly familiar, but close.

Dremis? Kizik asked, but that was impossible. Dremis was dead. Kizik had killed him.

This is Tallis, ninth daughter of Dremis.

I am glad to hear your thoughts, Kizik replied.

What is happening? Where are you? You seem to be everywhere. I do not like this. It feels like you are screaming.

I am sorry.

You killed Dremis and the others. You led us to war. You brought us nothing.

All of those things are true, Kizik admitted.

There was a long pause with no response. Kizik suffered under the silence of the entire Arnock race. He finally dared ask the question that burned in him. *I want to come home. My bones are in agony.*

I am now leading our kind. If you come near this world, you will be killed. If we find you, you will be killed. If you try to join the Farhallen, you will be killed. You are not even worthy of exile. We do not have a word to describe your betrayal.

With that, he felt a surge pushing against his mind, like a tide crashing on an infinite shore. The entire civilization was making known its disdain for him. *So awful,* were the waves coming at him. He tried to face it, but it was more than he could bear.

He was about to flee, but there was something else here. *Something new?* He didn't understand, but there was a massive presence in a place where there should be nothing at all. He started to look at it, *minds like mine? Hello? Can you hear me?*

Then Tallis and all the others were pushing him away again. Such disdain and hatred coming from them. A hatred that felt ancient and brittle, the hatred of a crumbling race. After a few moments, he removed his mind from his home, taking it back within his tiny shuttle. He wasn't physically near Arnock Prime, but someplace else.

Below him was Nova Turin. It was a beautiful world, and on it were three hundred and thirty-eight humans. Kizik only cared about two of the lives down there, but he would never have even considered taking this next action if they hadn't found themselves just steps from one another. *Not doing this would be a horrific mistake, and he had made enough horrific mistakes already.*

His heart, cold from the rejection of his people, took no pity on those innocents below. They would die to send a message to Salla Birdwing and Emmanuel Gray.

TACH-FOUR

Tach-Four Station

Timberwolf was wrapped in Sabatin, their claws and limbs surrounding him. The five beasts were connected to a booster sled by his feet. "You look like a rock," he heard Dr. Tier say through his rig helmet. He was falling towards Tach-Four station. A few moments ago, he had disconnected from *Archangel* and dropped out of sub-light. The cruiser was now swinging around the system and would come out of the stream in a few minutes from the opposite direction, right on top of the target.

"I've got Tach-Four on short range," he reported, checking the heads-up in his helmet. The rig that surrounded him felt natural, as if it had gotten to know him. Its armor was made from the hide of a Sabatin, and the cluster of the beasts around him had become accustomed to it and pressed into him tightly. It was actually his second Sabatin rig. Penny had given it to him on Highland.

Highland memories of the place came to him. Crashing through the tunnels pushed by the nuclear blast. Finding himself face-to-face with Kizik. The mind-bending spider speaking to him with three audible voices at once instead of talking directly to his mind. The events replayed for him, the sudden relief as Kizik had released his awful hold. The *grinding* in his mind finally going silent.

He was free now, but Timberwolf admitted that Kizik had kept him alive – more forced him to prevail. The Arnock had taken control of him when he'd tried to end the torture and prevented him from taking his own life. He'd heightened his senses and made Timberwolf unbeatable, but now…

Hello? He searched for the grinding in the back of his mind – nothing.

He was free and totally on his own. Kizik was no longer taking from him, and Timberwolf had gotten everything back except one thing. He breathed in through his nose. Usually, one's rig helmet had a *unique* musk that built up over time, but there was nothing, no sense of smell. He couldn't detect one offending molecule. "I'll let you keep that Kizik," he said to himself.

He switched to visual. Tach-Four orbited a dwarf planet composed of silicon called Nero. He could make out Jephtah's fleet, sticking out from the station's wagon-wheel superstructure like eight spurs. He checked the vitals of his team. Dorothy, Tin Man, Lion, Toto, and Scarecrow were all green. They were clumped together so that they were head-to-head and facing inwards towards him. Protective linings covered their front claws, and thruster pods wrapped their back appendages.

He took in their angular faces, somewhere between a salamander and a panther, protected from the vacuum by goggles and breathers. They were placid, waiting for his orders. The aggressive and restless Lion shook his head from side to side; he always did that when Timberwolf looked right at him.

He checked for chatter on Assault Corps channels and saw nothing. Within a few minutes, though, he knew Tach-Four would light up when its proximity sensors detected a bogey. His stealth package would deflect scans, but ever since the trick they pulled on Captain Jephtah over Highland, the A.C. had prudently switched to opticals. Closer now, he could make out the profiles of the docked cruisers. "I've got a full boat, Doc. *Tranquility, Defender, Antares, Intrepid, Falcon, Orion, Eagle*, and the big dog – *Challenger*."

They were *all* there. Conrad had been right – every ship under Jephtah's command was moored here at Tach-Four. "We are go for Bulldozer," Dr. Tier told Timberwolf, setting the attack in motion by using its code word.

"Confirmed, Doc. Cheers to bad decisions."

"Get 'em all, Timber," she responded.

At that moment, alarms lit up in his heads-up, they'd been seen by Tach-Four. A sensor-laser had swept by but hadn't locked. They might perceive them as an errant rock from the system's asteroid belt, but they'd be moving to destroy them either way. "Starting the burn. A hundred and thirty-eight miles out."

Timberwolf activated the booster sled's thrusters and began evasive maneuvers. The Sabatin tightened their grip to stay together as the g-forces pushed and pulled. With an arterial pulse, kinetic slugs the size of fire extinguishers started to come at them from turrets at the top and bottom of the station.

Without a target lock, hitting them should have been a near impossibility. But suddenly there was an empty space above him, and he saw Scarecrow flailing as she fell away, an arc of the beast's thick blood trailing her. Timberwolf took manual control of the thrusters, diving the booster sled right at the station instead of risking another hit making an evasive approach.

"Ten miles, nine, eight, seven, four, breaking!" Timberwolf slammed on the retro thrusters just a half-mile from the superstructure of Tach-Four. His head filled with blood from the sudden reversal of g-forces, and he wavered on the edge of consciousness.

Timberwolf and the Sabatin separated from the sled, scattering in different directions per the plan. He launched his grappling hook from his left gauntlet, and it caught on with its magnetic grip. Firing the thrusters in his boots, he made a hard but controlled standing-contact. The four remaining Sabatin landed by him on the outer ring of the station. Lion announced himself by hissing into his breather.

"We're here. We're down our eyes and ears. Scarecrow was hit." She had specialized in reconnaissance, and now they might not see threats coming until they were right on top of them.

"Understood, proceed," Dr. Tier responded.

A hundred yards above him, the turret swiveled on his position. He knew it wasn't going to be a kinetic slug coming at him, that would tear through the station's superstructure. Instead, the turret fired an object that burst almost as soon as it was out of the barrel. A webbing of silica fell towards him, and he dove under an overhanging exhaust port. An adhesive silica webbing fell around him, a bit of it catching his left shin and sticking him in place. It took him a long ten seconds to burn through it with his chemical laser. He leaned from his cover to get a look at the tower above.

He could see the turret switching to another chamber, like a giant revolver. But before it could fire again, *Archangel* dropped out of sub-light just two thousand yards away, its retros blasting and front armor deployed like a spiny battering ram. Its bow plasma cannons fired, shattering the turret into a disk of debris.

Timberwolf was moving now, careful not to get caught in the webbing stuck to the surface of the station. He pulled himself along handhold to handhold in the microgravity. Tin Man was at his side, and Lion waited for them up ahead, roaring noiselessly into his breather, eager for them to join the fight. Dorothy and Toto struggled under sticky silica webbing; both their back halves captured. Timberwolf quickly freed them, and they shook the rest of the adhesive away. Their first target, *Falcon,* was just ahead. Its mooring lights blinked lazily, not yet indicating any emergency.

Tin Man was on the docking clamps. He recalled his imprinting perfectly and avoided touching the cruiser, only the clamps connecting to it. He spread apart the connectors until they popped, and just as planned, the atmosphere from the connecting airlock pushed *Falcon* free. Toto was at the back of the cruiser now, dropping a payload of implosion grenades into its engine block as the ship slowly arched backwards.

"Zuz!" Timberwolf ordered, and the Sabatin scattered back to the superstructure of Tach-Four. A moment later, the implosion grenades went off with a noiseless flash, and the tiny singularities pulled the engine together into a mangle of metal and plastisteel. Plasma spurted from the seams at the rear-quarter of the vessel, and emergency bolts detonated at the back of *Falcon,* throwing the engine block away.

"We're reading *Falcon*'s engines as null!" Dr. Tier told him. "Move to *Eagle!*"

Timberwolf looked over to see *Archangel* turning just a few hundred yards away. So close that he saw crew running past its portholes. Its cannons were swiveled towards Tach-Four, but not firing. Timberwolf knew that breacher teams were spinning up aboard the docked cruisers, and they had just a few minutes to hit their targets before *Archangel* was fighting off a dozen boarding parties.

Tin Man was on *Eagle's* clamps in just moments, performing exactly as he did against *Falcon*. It seemed like an eternity as Timberwolf watched, but in less than a minute, the cruiser was free of the station, and its engines were mangled. Then he saw something on his scope: three small signatures headed his way. Rambler units were coming across the structure, men rigged up in pressurized fighting armor to repel borders.

"I've got ramblers. That was fast!" Timberwolf reported to Dr. Tier. Without Scarecrow patrolling their perimeter, they were vulnerable to threats like these. The ramblers appeared over the lip of the station ring, taking in the scene of Timberwolf and Tin Man still at the docking clamp and *Falcon* unmoored, critically damaged and corkscrewing away. Timberwolf cycled through his cyber-weapons packet and accessed their communications channels. He felt it best to introduce himself.

"This is Colonel Timberwolf Velez of the D.P.E," he said calmly. "I suggest you fall back while we operate here. Our actions are 'technically' legal," Timberwolf calmly informed them.

"The fuck?!" one of them said, firing his weapon and stitching Tin Man's armor with plasma blasts. Timberwolf ducked behind one of the massive L-shaped docking clamps. He pinged his two brawlers patrolling the perimeter. From both sides Toto and Lion smashed into the unsuspecting ramblers, sending them flailing off the structure.

On the opposite side of Tach-Four, Timberwolf saw *Tranquility* throwing its moorings and backing away. But *Archangel* was there, turning its battering ram of a bow right into its path. *Archangel's* jagged armor smashed the rear of *Tranquility*, spinning it parallel and directly into *Orion*, breaking that vessel clear of the moorings.

"We've got two free ones!" Timberwolf saw the opportunity. "Kof!" he ordered. Dorothy and Toto broke away to drop their grenades into the engine wells of the free-floating vessels.

"Moving to *Antares*," Timberwolf told Dr. Tier. He grabbed ahold of the structure and pulled himself to the next moored target. Tin Man was already working the next set of docking clamps, and he was getting faster each time. Timberwolf saw five more ramblers coming at them on his scope, red dots trundling closer. He pulled himself over the lip of the station ring and let loose with a volley of plasma fire, strafing the attackers from left to right. They fired back, one of them getting off a silicon net, which nearly wrapped Timberwolf's left gauntlet. Behind him, he felt the station shudder as *Antares* lifted away, liberated from its docking clamps.

His attackers momentarily distracted, Timberwolf pivoted, his plasma driver on non-lethal auto-fire. His blasts smashed into the chest armor of one of the attackers, sending him flying. He swiped through the rest with his chemical laser, forcing them to dive for cover.

Lion was in the mix now, maneuvering behind the attackers. He landed almost on top of one of them. Lion's razor-tipped tongue sprang through his breather, and with a flick, it took a rambler's arm clear off. "Jesus!" Timberwolf muttered. The objective was to use non-lethal force as much as possible and to stay focused on crippling the fleet, not killing people – but an arm floated past Timberwolf, crusted with freeze-dried blood.

"Lion, stop! Taf-seek!" he ordered the beast to get out of the fight and fall back. "I've taken Lion out. He just killed a guy," Timberwolf told Dr. Tier. He took cover behind an exhaust port, plasma bursts pinging around him and silica nets wrapping close.

"I see that. Proceed," Dr. Tier responded as a rambler appeared just a few feet away from Timberwolf. He felt the sting of the plasma burst on his shoulder through his armor. He got off a concussion burst in response at near point-blank range, knocking the attacker away.

For a moment, he dialed up his weapons package to lethal. He leaned around the barricade, firing a barrage of white-hot plasma in front of the attackers and buying a few seconds. He pulled back and cycled through his cyberwar package. There were twelve ramblers on him now, not counting the man Lion had killed. In a moment, he had locked onto all of them and accessed their thruster units.

Timberwolf entered the command, and their thruster packs began firing at once. He saw them flailing by him, hurtling off the superstructure. He could move now, and he scrambled along the superstructure, pulling himself towards *Intrepid*, the next target. *Antares* floated free above him, bits of flotsam twinkling. The ship's insectile shadow fell in front of him, but then there was something wrong with it. Blossoms and black tendrils snaked from the shadow's form.

He felt the concussion from above him, the jagged shrapnel tearing into him and slamming him down face-first into the station. He had nothing on his scope for a good twenty seconds, just static and the ping and shatter of debris impacting around him. He held on, pressure and shock waves tearing from all sides.

Finally, his scope came back, and a yellow and black symbol blinked in front of him. He heard Dr. Tier's frantic voice. She'd been trying to reach him while his communications were out. "...nuke detonation! Are you reading? Are you reading?! Look out!"

At her warning, he switched to his rear-view and saw *Antares* crashing right towards him. He pulled himself to the side, barely getting clear. The ship's bow was just a few yards away, scraping crudely across Tach-Four's structure. Timberwolf saw that its slender mid-section was mangled.

The nuke must have been under a tenth of a megaton, just enough to crack *Antare's* spine.

What was happening? Who had hit Antares? He checked his squad and only three were green. Lion was missing. "Lion nuked *Antares?!*" he questioned Dr. Tier as much as himself.

His rig was nuclear survivable, but something was wrong. His system levels were way into the red, even his gyroscope was off. He careened away across the surface of Tach-Four, nausea gripping his stomach. He managed to catch himself by holding onto a maintenance railing. He found himself face to face with Tin Man, the beast shrieking noiselessly right in front of him.

He looked back, and *Antares's* belly was scraping the superstructure now, the mass of its engine block driving forward. "Oh no," he grunted. He knew what was about to happen. The cruiser's damaged midsection buckled, and it almost looked like it was going to spring back, but no. The ship cracked in half, its dense rear-section careening forward, smashing into the back of the command deck.

Timberwolf braced for the shockwave as the racks of plasma cannons and laser batteries shattered. A bright light came first as ordnance burst, and then he felt it. The shockwave came, battering him like he was being kicked by a dozen horses. The next moment, he was tumbling, thrown free of Tach-Four. His heads-up display flickered, and then there was darkness, but his rig wasn't catastrophically damaged. Something had shut him down.

He was able to get out a single message, "I've got a code black!"

"We see you, switching to reco-" Dr. Tier was cut off as Timberwolf lost all power. His arms felt like lead, but he was able to force the servos in his suit. He tapped the button up at his temple and opened the viewer. He was miles off the superstructure, and Tach-Four spun sickeningly before him. The station listed almost perpendicular to its axis, its maneuvering thrusters trying and failing to keep it steady. He saw the puffs of evac pods all around its central disc.

Shit. Tach-Four is a loss.

Coming out from behind the station, *Challenger* was free and closing on *Archangel*. The cruiser's plasma cannons were charged up and glowing. Before he could see what happened next, he struck something and was spinning.

Timberwolf found himself entangled with Tin Man and grappling desperately in the weightlessness. The Sabatin was missing both limbs on his left side, and the beast's thruster pods sputtered. Timberwolf could feel him struggling to inhale, his chest heaving against the breather. Then, Timberwolf's keen ability to sense his orientation in microgravity kicked in.

Nero. Where the hell is Nero?

Where was the small silicon world that held Tach-Four in its orbit? If his instincts were right, it would be in exactly the worst possible place. "Oh shit," he hissed as the pale-yellow disk rose before him, terminally close. The writhing mass that was him and Tin Man broke through Nero's wispy atmosphere, barely feeling any drag.

Having only seconds to orient himself, he grabbed Tin Man around his trunk of a neck. Reaching over, he grasped the thruster on his right front hoof, activating the manual controls. Nero was everything below them now, and Timberwolf arched over, using the thruster to position Tin Man underneath him. "Sorry about this," he said as the beast tried to pull away. He looked up and saw *Archangel* escape into the spectral disc of sub-light.

He closed his eyes for a moment. *Well, I guess I'm not getting out to Nova' this week.* Salla's smile, something he had seen only a few times, flashed in his mind. He'd made a pledge to himself to keep her safe. Safe. Whatever the hell safe was was impossible now. They began to spin, and he closed his eyes to control his nausea. Tin Man futilely writhed away from the approaching surface. Timberwolf, straining in his powerless rig, struggled with him. "Really, really sorry, Tin Man."

Just a few miles up now, Timberwolf reached under Tin Man's jaw and forced his gauntlet under his breather, breaking the seal. Instantly, the Sabatin stopped struggling as the vacuum reached his lungs. Timberwolf leaned into him, putting the beast between himself and the planet. He counted down the fall. "Four-thousand yards, three-thousand, two-thousand, one-thousand —"

Right when he expected, they hit, Tin Man breaking his fall. They parted the world below them, driving them far into the brittle surface. He waited for the pain to come, for something to let him know if he was alive. He felt the burst of the emergency-nano menders entering the artery in his leg, and a tinny taste instantly came to his mouth. He knew what was coming and what it meant. *Coma.* He had about ten seconds of consciousness left before the medically induced hibernation would kick in to try to keep him alive.

Ten awful seconds. The pain came like floodwaters through the front door, mostly on his left side. He sensed the dull heaviness of broken bones and an awful burning which lashed up and down his body from head to toe. *Hey, I guess I won't die paralyzed! Vincent Dacha, you little son of a bitch!* A verse came to his lips, one he swore he would never utter. "When I die, Hallelujah by and by. I'll fly away," and then everything went black.

His throat was dry, and his mouth felt like sandpaper. His eyes fluttered as he awoke, and soft white light was above him.. He was alive somehow, and his body had the numbness of heavy drugs. It seemed to take a full minute to blink and when his eyes fully opened, he had to tell himself he was alive again. A kind-eyed woman leaned over him, looking in at him through the transparent shell of a medical pod. He could see his name in reverse projected on the clear plastisteel.

He knew the woman looking down at him, he didn't know exactly how but she was familiar. His brain was too scattered to put it together, but he knew that his situation was very, very bad.

"Glad you're awake, Mr. Velez. I'm Captain Jephtah, but you can call me Maria. Welcome aboard *Challenger.*"

RUBICON

Rubicon Cluster – 60 years ago

Joseph Dacha hoped he wasn't about to die. Sure, he'd regenerate, and his memories would live on, but who wants to go through all that trouble? Ahead was the cluster of black holes he had become obsessed with. He scanned the screens before him in the cockpit of his Traveler 42. The ship was sturdy and reliable but had the styling and grace of a tugboat. He'd stenciled *Hercules* on the side.

"Four, five, six... at least eleven." He counted the objects aloud, but the extraordinary cosmic structure blurred together making an accurate accounting impossible at this distance. He was two light years away and couldn't prove it yet, but he knew one thing for certain. This formation wasn't natural.

The cluster orbited a waning red giant that was compressing inwardly at an exponentially accelerating rate. He did some quick calculations and the star had about ten thousand years before it died – a blink in galactic time. He couldn't tell exactly why, but the gravity from the cluster was having some kind of effect on the star's core.

He saw a bonanza of pure science, and dollar signs, but before he could claim any of the prizes, he had to do something extremely reckless.

His plan was to fly into the center of the cluster.

That was the only way he would be able to get the readings he needed. Someone had arranged these objects into this configuration, and he had to know why.

He only hoped that the null-field around *Hercules* would hold the incredible gravitational forces and mangled space-time at bay. He pulled a protein bar from his jacket – chocolate and blueberry. He liked the peanut butter ones better but had grabbed a handful of the wrong kind in his hurry to leave Highland. He engaged the sub-light engines and pulled closer to the maelstrom.

He didn't have much choice but to trust the null-field – or at least pray that it protected him from being squeezed into atoms. In a little under an hour, he had reached the cluster. He dropped from sub-light and curved around his target, coming up behind the inky black objects. This close, they appeared as twenty-four distinct singularities spaced in an *exactly* consistent geometry. To the naked eye though, they formed an oval blob of absolute negative space. No light escaped and no features were visible, but he could tell by using a sub-light scan that there was passable space between them. In fact, the whole structure seemed to be designed to *sustain* something. He suddenly got a sense of what he was looking at. "A Prison?" he whispered to himself, as a chill went through him.

He noticed an arc of material before the cluster, the gravity well was lining up mountain-sized asteroids into a reverse assembly line. He watched as they stretched and turned themselves into molten threads. After observing for a few minutes, his computer-sharp mind had figured out the optimal approach vector. He ran the numbers and had the onboard A.I. triple check his findings just to be sure. When he was reasonably satisfied, he wasn't about to die, he steered *Hercules* over what would be the north pole of the cluster. He engaged the engines, and the ship shook just a little as it passed between two of the singularities.

He chuckled a bit. "Nobody but a Dacha!" he remarked, and he was right. If anyone else had found this object, they'd have to spend years just uncovering the science before even thinking about entering it. The collective intelligence of Joseph and his brothers, combined with their mastery of technology, had allowed him to penetrate the cluster in just a few minutes. Still, he was annoyed with his kin. Vlad and Georgy had been incredulous about this adventure. They'd gone as far as dissuading the R&D leads from helping him plan his trip. It was a combination of Vlad's mantra to "focus on core businesses" and Georgy's superstition, "you don't mess with ancient alien tech," had been his head-wagging opinion. "There's some serious voodoo hidden out in the galaxy."

"Operation Voodoo looks good so far," Joseph said to himself and grinned. He'd code named this project to annoy his brothers, but it also helped to ground him. He was stepping into some unknown territory here and he needed to remind himself that this was more than simply a scientific venture. There was a profound intelligence at work here, a very old intelligence – two million years to be exact.

He continued deeper into the cluster, and exotic particles of all sorts streamed past him. He got a pit in his stomach that told him this was a place best visited briefly. Ahead of him, light was stretched to the red band and the singularities distorted space-time to appear solid and physical. It spread apart like he was passing between muscle tissue. He slowed to let the sensors take this all in and to wonder at this with his own eyes. The null-field held, but the ship shuddered slightly, and he corrected course. Soon the red space faded to a misty white and the sensors told him he was approaching a vapor wall. Lighting flashed around him as he passed through, and he could hear the whistle of gas and dust outside.

Behind the barrier, a soft pink hue filled the massive space – half the size of earth's orbit around the sun. He could see what appeared to be a luminous object in the center, from here it looked like a splinter. The sensors told him the object was solid and about forty miles long. Joseph assessed that it was artificial, as it held an atmosphere – also it wasn't compressed by gravity into a sphere but was shaped like an elongated tablet.

He would have been trapped for eternity if he hadn't reached for another protein bar. As he opened the wrapper, he noticed the subtle flashing icon on a small screen at the top of the dash.

"Whoa!" he slammed on the retros, bringing *Hercules* to a sudden halt at about the distance from the Earth to Luna. The icon of a frozen alarm clock blinked lazily. "I have to make that bigger!" he cursed himself. If he'd traveled just a few thousand miles more, he would have been frozen in time. Around the object, the gravity of the surrounding singularities conspired to create a bubble where space and time merged into one and stopped moving altogether. "Temporal constipation," he noted with a grin. "I christen thee – entropy bubble."

He compensated by reflecting the null-field outward and creating a little enclave that took normal space-time with him. A realization came over him and he turned on his 360-degree viewer, switching the filter to infrared. All around the space, the singularities stood like endless, unblinking sentinels, watching over whatever was before him. "Yeah, I'm visiting a prison."

He pushed into the entropy bubble and made a pop sound with his lips when he squeezed through, slightly relieved that he was still experiencing the passage of time. He didn't miss the irony that if time had suddenly stopped for him, he wouldn't have known it – just as whatever was trapped here had no idea they were imprisoned. He was getting readings from the surface of the object now. Under an oxygen/ nitrogen atmosphere, the gleaming white and pink surface was carved with rivers and valleys. Urban areas covered the surface, and he could see that structures rose both above and descended deep underground, indicating that the object had both an external and internal profile.

He descended further, engines adjusting to an artificial gravity field that surrounded the object. Like the atmosphere, gravity was earth normal. He noticed that an energy field also wrapped the artificial world, one designed to keep out radiation, but he surmised could also be charged to repel incoming attacks. He noted that massive plasma cannons arrayed on the surface were charging to fire. A huge amount of charged plasma had been about to be released at something, but it never happened. "Looks like someone drew quicker!" he remarked to himself.

Giant spires stroked the sky, reaching into timeless cloud layers, in which not a molecule stirred. He got a sinking feeling in his stomach. There were millions of structures below. He could only guess at the sheer magnitude of beings that were down there. As if to answer, an alert blinked on the panel in front of him. He swiped it and a message appeared.

Approximately Five Billion Residents – Species Unknown

A hologram of a bipedal creature slowly spun. It was muscular, with a body structure that was similar to a human's, with a few key differences. A tail hung down and striped fur covered its body. Its hands ended in claws, that the A.I. surmised were retractable. The image changed to the creature's face and Joseph lost his breath. "It's beautiful." In most cases, aliens were abominations of familiar forms – giant arachnids or massive pale mollusks – and were rarely appealing.

This species was downright striking. A broad feline face looked back at him, a flattened nose, and wide, yellow eyes. This composite example was definitely male, with high cheekbones and a sharp gaze. Whiskers extruded from the creature's cheeks, making him appear alert and prepared.

The A.I. processed more information and began to show variations of the species. Infinite color combinations and markings, softer-featured females and ample-cheeked young. One thought came to Joseph's mind – *hunter.*

The A.I. suggested a name, the *Symmetry.* Joseph nodded – that was perfect. "What immortal hand or eye, could forge this fearful symmetry?" He swiped the display away and prepared his final descent. He moved low over a dense urban space. The streets were filled with Symmetry – all were frozen in place but appearing to be headed somewhere collectively, maybe to shelter. "Looks like they knew they were in danger," he surmised.

He crossed a narrow river and was over what appeared to be rice paddies interspersed with rolling hills covered in pale green and dark red vegetation. This close, the gleaming white appearance of the Lifeship was overtaken with a pink hue. The buildings and structures reflected light from floating orbs spaced every few hundred yards. He couldn't immediately tell what the orbs were but planned to investigate once he got out on foot.

He landed *Hercules* in a clearing. He took a few minutes and figured out how to make the null-field emit from his jumpsuit. The air outside appeared to be perfectly breathable, and he was sure it was fresh. It hadn't moved a molecule in two million years.

He descended the ship's gangplank cautiously, donning a baseball hat and dropping sunglasses over his eyes. The place practically glowed. Reflected luminescence came from almost every surface. He began to walk along a path that spilled out into a settlement. Everywhere he went, Symmetry stood like statues, all stilled down to their last atom.

In person, the beings were more striking than he had imagined. Adults were all over seven-feet tall, adorned with colorful clothing in countless styles. Though they were unmoving, Joseph's supposition that they were communally headed someplace still seemed right. Most were collected near wide funneling staircases that led underground. He recalled the plasma cannons charging. "Were they attacking or defending?"

He avoided getting too close to any of them, for fear of catching them in his null-shield bubble and possibly unfreezing them. He wasn't exactly sure how their temporal impasse functioned, but amazing data streamed into his smart-device. This trip would certainly be worth it. What he had collected in just an hour would keep Highland's best scientists busy for years. "Voodoo indeed!" he huffed.

Ahead of him, he could make out one of the glowing orbs floating above the ground. He tried to move towards it, but as he weaved his way along the twisting streets and walkways, he'd find it obscured behind buildings and vehicles. He hurried down a curving avenue with blocky buildings on both sides, too distracted to acknowledge a beeping from his smart-device. When the street opened up to a wide circular plaza, what he had been seeking simply hung there – a small, miniature sun. The smart-contact he wore displayed the distance and density of the object, but he discounted it. "That can't be right!"

He pulled out his smart-device to take a more thorough scan and it gave the same readings. The glowing ball of gas ahead of him was almost eighty-million miles away, with a diameter of seven-hundred and fifty thousand miles. He analyzed more carefully and found that the curve of space-time was like a nearly infinite funnel into the object. Even he couldn't make sense of how the science was working. He pulled in billions of data points, but like everything else here, the ball of glowing gas was unmoving down to the molecule. He wished that it could spring to life for just a few moments, not so much that he could capture more data, but that he could experience this impossibility for himself.

Again – his smart-device beeped, but this time he minded the alert. *Proximity Alarm.* He was being followed.

AFTERMATH

Conrad Stonefield placed one foot in front of the other, utterly numb. The hallways pulsed with crew, running frantically past him in both directions. "Go back to bed!" A crewman shoved him into a wall, sneering at his D.P.E. uniform. It was clear that Tach-Four had been a massive disaster, and the crew was already placing blame on their D.P.E. passengers. *Archangel* streaked away from Tach-Four through sub-light.

"We are on violet alert," a pleasant A.I.'s voice repeated through the klaxons.

Violet alert. Conrad actually had to look it up. It meant that pursuit through the sub-light stream was probable. Crew rushed to stations, mostly at the aft of the ship. Violet alert was a nightmare scenario, since usually only friendlies traveled in the same stream, but all of this was a nightmare now, and it kept getting worse.

"Oh God. I've screwed it," he muttered. Just then, a crewman came down a ladder shaft, her foot striking the bridge of his nose. She bounded away without apologizing.

"Conrad!" he heard the pierce of Dr. Tier's voice behind him. He turned and found her just a few feet away. "You said, you were sure!" She shook him by the shoulders, the rage pouring out of her. "You said, you were sure!" she repeated.

"I was sure, but he screwed us. He found a way to drop in malignant commands. He sent Tach-Four telemetry. He shut down Timber's rig and he imprinted Lion to set off a nuke."

Her mouth hung open in disbelief. "What is it we do, Conrad? Of course, he screwed us!" She stalked down the hall, crew parting for her. He knew he was to follow. She pounded the sensor on her door, and it opened. Once inside, she turned on him. "He screwed us and then he showed us he did it." She tossed a tablet computer to him. "Even I could find it. He's rubbing this in your face!"

Conrad scrolled through the imprinting sequence, every bit of it looked familiar. He'd lived and breathed the planning of operation Bulldozer for weeks. He had reviewed and scrutinized each and every line of code Vincent had used, but sticking out like sore thumbs, were the interloping commands. "I had three other analysts checking this! I don't know how he did this."

"What is it we do Conrad?" she demanded again.

"We keep the peace," he stammered.

"We push the knife in! We hit when they're not looking. We do not play nice!" The ship shuddered, dropping into another sub-light stream. They were executing switchbacks to try to shake pursuers – violet protocol in action. "You should have known he was trying to screw us because that's the game *we* play. Vincent Dacha played it better."

He straightened up. He'd never felt true failure before. He'd been around failure and been a neighbor to it, but he'd never owned it. This was his mess. "So, do we have a hand to play?" he asked.

"We run. We've lost Timberwolf. We've screwed the whole D.P.E. out of Station Corps refuge. We've escalated this fight by using A GODDAMNED NUKE. We look like terrorists. I'd brand us terrorists! Tirani is… I don't want to think about the captain right now."

He hung his head, wishing he was like Vincent and could simply wish himself dead. "What about Dacha? Do we kill him?"

Her gaze pierced through him. "That's the kind of question I would ask you, Conrad!" He wished he was anywhere but here and prayed for *something* to get him out of this room.

Capote, the head security man, called to Dr. Tier over her smart-device. "Dr. Tier, you might want to come down to lock three. It's Dacha."

Conrad exhaled as he had his reprieve but, whatever this was couldn't be good.

LOCK THREE

D.P.E. Archangel

The blows had rained down on Vincent's tiny frame. A foot to the ribs, a knee to his face. His mouth spouted blood. He had called for the guard that stood outside his secure quarters; the one he knew had a nephew serving on *Antares*.

"So, just so you know," he had begun.

More blows came down, to his kidneys, his back, his groin.

"I didn't want the grapevine to get outta hand, like it does."

A fist like a brick hit his temple. The guard pulled him up by the hair, and Vincent was still smiling, teeth stained with blood.

He had summoned the guard close, to make it intimate. "But I nuked Antares! I really was behind the whole mess out there! Sorry!" He'd shrugged his shoulders with a careless grin.

Then the guard was dragging him towards Airlock Three, but he would get more blows in before sending him into the black. As the guard had beaten him, the little man had just laughed.

Capote had fired, striking the guard square in the back, and sending him into the bulkhead. Dacha rolled over on the ground. "Gee thanks!" he said, giggling blood.

Vincent awoke to Dr. Tier staring at him. He waved to her from behind the glass. He laid on the hard floor of the airlock and propped himself up on his elbows.

"Mr. Dacha, glad you're awake," she said. Her voice crackled over the intercom.

He pulled himself up to a sitting position. He cracked his neck and rubbed the bruises up and down his side. "Well, thanks for the nap."

"I gave you something to sleep. I needed some time to think."

"About what?" he asked, bringing himself to his feet. Blood caked his hair. A gap where a tooth had been showed when he talked.

"Somebody had the right idea, beating you like that. You had it coming."

"That guy dead? I heard the blast."

"Yes, he's dead. That's another one for your tab. Add that to *Antares.*"

He took in his surroundings. "So, you needed to think about opening that door, sending me for a short walk. Did you put me to sleep so you didn't have to hear me beg for my life?"

"I wouldn't have cared about that. I'm not Conrad."

"How is that boy? I really took advantage of him. Covered my tracks though! I wish I could have seen the look on his face!"

She sighed, already sick of this. "You're not living through this. You die today. You know that. What was this for?"

He searched the air above him. "Oh, where to begin?" He brought his gaze to her. "It's the hubris, really. I've been alive for maybe a month now and I *hate* you. I mean, I really hate all of you. Killing you all will be hilarious."

"Would it help if I said 'sorry' for what happened to your brothers?" she sneered. "So sorry they're all dead, and you'll be the last?" She thumbed the exterior door release, and his eyes went wide. "There will be no more Dacha brothers. You'll die in less than half a minute. You won't be able to even look back because your eyes will freeze over."

He swallowed, even though his throat was dry as a bone. "So, what did Conrad say? I know you lean on him. Where's he at?"

"He went to get his gun. He thinks he's going to shoot you in the head."

"Oh," he said, understanding his fate.

"Any last words?"

"I already said it," he said, huffing with impatience. "Killing you all will be hilarious. The universe will laugh. I will laugh."

"Shut up. Where did you send Gray? What does Salla Birdwing have to do with this?"

"She's a nice girl. She'll probably die too though. Tough huh?"

"Where did you send Gray?!" She shook with anger.

He spread his fingers wide and moved his hands from side-to-side, like he was in some sort of hokey musical. "You'll never know," he sang sourly, with a wide bloody grin. "You'll never know. Wherever you go, you reap what you sow, you'll never know!"

He gasped with faux anticipation and covered his mouth as her hand slipped to the door release.

Vincent continued. "You're all so stupid. You believed I could stop my heart just by wishing it so! You wonder now, 'do I keep him alive and maybe I can wring something out of him, or do I kill him in cold blood?'"

"Decisions, decisions," Dr. Tier mused.

"I'm a lovely problem. Us Dachas were always the keys. To Highland and to what is going on now." He lifted his small arm, letting her see into the sleeve of his shirt. "But what's here? What's up my sleeve?"

She stared into his hazel eyes. Old and yet so young with mischief. *This thing can only lie.* She thought to herself. Had he outlived his usefulness? Where did it balance out?

"Where did you send Gray?" she asked with finality.

He smashed his palm on the glass, leaving a brown bloody smudge. "I got what I wanted! That whole disaster out there. So why tell you anything more?" He shrugged his shoulders. "You'll never know!" he sang like a tenor, holding the last note.

"Fuck off Vince," and she opened the exterior airlock as his voice crescendoed. Instantly klaxons began to wail and yellow warning lights spun as a white trail of atmosphere bled through the crack into space. As he was being pulled away, he mouthed something to her through his sickening smile. He held onto the outer door for just a moment and then Vincent Dacha jerked backwards, disappearing into the void.

She closed the door, silencing the alarms. "Shit," she exhaled, holding onto her knees.

"Thank you," she heard from behind her. Conrad was there, holding the dark handle of his Smith and Wesson pistol. "He said 'thank you' before he slipped out."

"I had a choice there, didn't I?" she asked, and Conrad nodded affirmatively. "I need to refocus," she said, knowing in her gut that she had played her part in the next part of Vincent Dacha's twisted production.

NEWS OF THE DAY

Nova Turin

Salla swiped through her news feed over her morning coffee. Around her, the low-grade bustle of the spaceport went on, her neighbors getting breakfast and exchanging pleasantries. "Oh my God," her breath left her, and she put her tablet down. There had been a major engagement at Tach-Four station. It was being described as a D.P.E. terrorist attack. Four A.C. cruisers had had their engine blocks fused. *Tranquility, Falcon, Orion,* and *Eagle* were essentially floating bricks.

Worse, *Antares* was completely destroyed. A nuke had been used.

There were almost five hundred dead. A.C. crewmen and Station Corps personnel. Tach-Four had to be evacuated and was looking like a total loss. The A.C. was now being denied refuge and resupply at all Tach stations.

She didn't want to know, but she flipped to the next part of the story. "Please don't let it be…" she muttered, but her worst fears bore out. A single ship had attacked – it was *Archangel.* Apparently, four Sabatin were part of the attack and there was one D.P.E. prisoner. He was described as a *high value operator* but was unnamed. She knew it could only be one person. "…Timberwolf." She looked off to the middle distance; a new preacher was at the other side of the spaceport. His mumblings barely carried, and she couldn't make out what he was saying.

She closed her eyes for a moment, exhaling slowly. She'd never known anyone like Timberwolf. He was an effortless force of violence. Someone who had torn through all of Gray's men like a hot knife through butter. He had been more than a force of violence, he had protected her, put her own freedom ahead of his own. A slight smile reached her lips when she remembered that. *If anyone can get out of this mess, it's you Timber,* she thought.

"Jesus!" she heard from behind her. Sean Jackson was at a nearby table, reading the news. "Well, the Department of Peace Enforcement is *not* living up to their name. A bloody nuke? You've got to be joking!" the lawman muttered in disgust.

"A small nuke," she said, absently.

He shook his head. "But that's crossing a line. The D.P.E. are fucked, pardon my French. They've got a month or two at most without supplies. This is serious."

Her mind was still wandering, thinking of what Timberwolf's fate might be. Her stomach sunk as she processed all that had happened, trying to weave it together.

She had been in the Station Corps and stationed to Tach-Four before her transfer to the Outpost. She undoubtedly had friends in body bags. Something must have gone wrong in the attack. Maybe it was an accident? Nuking *Antares* was stupid, and that wasn't Timberwolf's style.

"It seemed like *Archangel* was trying to take out the fleet's engine blocks, not destroy the cruisers entirely," she said to Sean, but more to herself.

"Well intentions don't matter when you're popping nukes. The D.P.E. are traitors. Always have been," Sean responded.

She hung her head in silence for a few moments. Conversations between neighbors were now strained with the overhang of politics. It came down to infinitely complex issues boiled down to for or against, black or white. Now that the two competing points of view had led to killing, nuance was pointless, and the thoughtful kept quiet.

After a few minutes, Sean got up and walked over to listen to the preacher. Without giving it much thought, she followed him. They had come to an easy ritual. They'd listen to the latest zealot and give a running critique. It was usually fun and a bit obnoxious. Salla wasn't really in the mood right now but felt uncomfortable breaking routine.

They got within earshot of the preacher. He was the typical stooped and rumpled traveler, a bloated face, misshapen by age and a life lived roughly. He spewed the classic Believer hits about the cancer of aliens and the duty of God's children to wipe them out. He didn't bring his voice to the rafters, which most preachers knew to do, and his patter came out as barely intelligible mumbling. "He's new to this," Sean nudged her.

The preacher's coat hung heavily on him, still coated with dust from his travels. He shuffled about on the small, raised platform, seeming to lose his place. His mouth hung open, but nothing came forth. Salla pitied him and cringed empathically. She was about to go, when he snapped his gaze to her, locking eyes for just a moment. "And then came Highland…"

Preachers lately had been going on about the events that had happened there, and all had repeated the talking points coming from the Clergy. "Oh, more about Highland, let's hear it," Sean whispered to her.

"God sent his mission there, to open the doors and take what was needed. We all fought the Arnock. The spiders! You, and you, and me!" He stabbed at the air; a speech prepared for many more people than were currently listening. "We all gave too much to them. Like no other enemy. They took our minds. Drove us to madness on contact. There are no veterans from that war." The preacher stared daggers through Salla, and her stomach dropped. "We're the knights of a new crusade. The Arnock are what drives us. Our peace with them is a sin and those that forged it will perish. Highland was our first step towards healing from that peace. We came to make an army and finish our work. God's will be done, on all our worlds as it is in heaven, but ashes to ashes, dust to dust." He beat the dust from his coat, and it puffed into the air.

Salla gripped Sean's arm, nearly pulling the man over. The dust. *Oh God the dust.* It was a smell she could never forget, the chalky, slightly sour smell of the dust that had covered everything on Highland. The preacher continued to rant, but Salla found herself running through the sliding doors to the outside, with Sean trailing.

"Salla, wait! What's the matter?" he asked, catching her by the arm.

Her eyes met his. He'd been so kind since she'd been back and had certainly been a perfect gentleman. She *wished* she could tell him. She wanted to trust somebody, but she knew she couldn't – as much for his safety as for hers.

"That dust on his jacket, where did he come from?" she asked, tears welling in her eyes.

"Jeez, Chimera, Ceres a few ports near Earth. He's new to the outer colonies. Never been this way before."

"Listen," she grabbed him by the shirt. "I want to give you the details, but I can't. It wouldn't be safe for you."

"Wait, what?" he asked.

"Just trust me, OK?" she said, and he nodded in unsure agreement. "There's a hauler leaving tomorrow. Make sure he gets on it."

"Of course, that's my job."

"And put a micro-drone tracker on him."

"Well, that's totally illegal, but of course, that's my job."

She wiped her eye, "I'm sorry. It's been a rough time after I left the Station Corps, but I didn't do anything wrong, OK? I don't want you to think I'd deserve anyone coming after me, or that I'd bring anything here. Especially with all this craziness."

"Sure, sure. I believe you," he smiled. "Look, if you went AWOL, they've got other things to sort out now, you know?"

She laughed, uneasily. "It's not that. Nothing like that." *God, I wish it was just that,* she thought.

"OK, I'm on the case. I'll keep an eye on Dusty Spaceman and get him off this rock tomorrow, OK?"

"Thank you," she nodded. She needed to get home and curl up behind locked doors.

He turned to go back to the spaceport and held up a cylinder containing the micro-drones he would use to put a tail on the preacher. He waggled it in the air to reassure her. "I'm on the case."

It was midnight and Salla checked the locks for the tenth time. She pressed her back against the door. *You're being paranoid. He's just a crazy old man.* "WWTD?" she said aloud, wondering what Timberwolf might do in this situation. "Maybe go throw the guy through a window?" She checked the small plasma pistol she still had from her days on the Outpost. It was charged and ready to fire.

She checked the back door again and the windows too. She had a surveillance system that would tell her if any visitors came near the property, but she was still on pins and needles. Sean had sent a message an hour ago and the preacher was asleep in a room above Pan's Pub. The micro-drones were perched on his windowsill.

"OK, just relax," she said, sitting on the sofa and taking deep breaths. This had been the house she'd grown up in and she knew every inch of it. Somehow, that thought helped her relax. Still, she needed to talk to someone. Sean had offered to come sit up with her, and she regretted not taking him up on that.

She connected to Sean's smart-device. "Hello," the tired man answered.

"Hi, I just wanted to say thanks."

"Yeah, sure. It's honestly the most excitement I've had all year," he said.

"But what about the fence dispute you just mediated? No blood was spilled. You're a big, damned hero."

"I sure am. I just wish…" he huffed.

"What?"

"Look, whatever it is. Just let me know. What the hell's going on?" he pressed.

She paused, exhaling. "OK, look. I don't… I didn't go AWOL, but I was on the Outpost."

"What? The Angel! What happened there? Thank God you're alive."

"It was awful. But that's not it, I wish that was it. I…"

"Shit!" he muttered. "He didn't come in on a hauler."

"What?"

"Yeah, he has his own ship. I just checked his creds. He's got his own ship. He parked out south of town in a clearing through the ridge woods. Oh, this guy is fishy."

"Can you come down? Please," she asked.

"On my way," he responded. "Oh, shit again. I lost him!"

"Lost who?" she asked, already knowing who.

"The preacher. I don't know where he is. Maybe he went to the john, hold on. Don't panic."

"He's here." The smart-device slipped from her hand. There the old preacher was, standing in her kitchen. He was simply present. He hadn't tripped any alarms or made any noise entering.

"Hello," he said, waving simply.

"Who the hell are you?" she asked. He realized that he'd left the back door open when he came in, and he politely turned and closed it.

"Me? Well, I'm new."

"You mean born again? I don't buy that Believer shit." She had her pistol on him and spun the setting up to maximum. "Get on the damned floor before I put you there."

"OK, OK."

"I'll ask you again. Who are you and who sent you here?"

"I don't rightly know. His name was Vincent. He'd just been born too."

She checked her pistol. "This thing does not get any hotter. Please start making sense."

"I'm not the darkness," he said calmly. "I'm the judgment." He slowly went to his knees, his hands behind his head. "By chance, do you have a set of cufflinks? Golden ones. Maybe in the shape of letters?"

That's enough, she thought. This guy was playing games. He knew things he shouldn't have, deep and dangerous things. She didn't realize she was doing it until after she had, but she pulled the trigger, with the intent to kill him.

But the pistol didn't fire. Maybe in the chaos, she'd neglected to take off the safety, but it didn't matter. In that instant, Sean slammed through the back door, his weapon instantly trained on the man on the floor.

"You OK?!" he asked her.

"Yeah," she replied.

"Looks like you've got this under control."

"Barely. There was almost a dead man here. You saved his life."

Sean fumbled for his handcuffs, and quickly got them around the preacher's wrists. The man didn't complain or resist. He peaceably got to his feet and let Sean lead him out the door.

"OK – I'll be back." Sean said.

"No, I'm coming with you," she countered.

Sean led the preacher down the cobbled street and around the curve to the old police station that hadn't held a prisoner for several years. "You can wait out here, but I'd rather you let me at least get him secured," he advised Salla.

"I want to know why he's here!" she retorted.

"We'll find that out, but please give me a minute to get him settled."

"He *knew* things," she said bitterly.

"You can wait at your place. I'll message you." Seeing that she wasn't going anywhere, he handed her his sweater. "OK, fine. Wait here in the square. Try to stay warm."

Sean led the preacher into the station and the lights inside came on. She sat on a bench and exhaled. "Jesus," her mind was spinning. *Who was Vincent? And what did the preacher mean by 'he was just born too?' and how did he know about the cufflinks?!* She could have excused everything as the ranting of a crazy person, except that last part.

She pulled out the chain that hung around her neck. Golden *I* and *D* cufflinks were attached like pendants. Sergey Dacha had given them to her as a gift. They had belonged to his dead brother Ivan; well, he was sort of his brother. All of the Dachas were clones that downloaded their brothers' memories and experiences after they were "born" from grow tanks. All three of the Dachas had died, either killed by Gray or by their own hand.

But what if they weren't all dead? Salla had of course assumed that as clones, they could replace themselves if one of them died. What if "Vincent" was a new Dacha brother?

Newly emerged from a grow tank? The thought chilled her to the bone, and she pulled the sweater tighter. If so, then the preacher was straight from Highland! She stewed for a few long minutes, the pit in her stomach growing larger.

Inside the station, the illumination faltered, and she saw a light hanging from the ceiling sway back and forth. She heard a single plasma blast and the distinct sound of something heavy falling to the floor. She was at the door in an instant and threw it open. Standing there, she felt a whisper in her mind. A grinding presence. Something familiar, but at a different tenor than before. She wobbled, the equilibrium in her ears thrown off. When she turned her head up, she saw Sean laying on the floor just inside the door, a puddle of blood pooling around the brown curls of his hair. His weapon was smoking and in his own hand. "No!" she screamed.

The preacher stood behind the bars in the small cell – his eyes wide with shock at the scene in front of him. With cold determination, she pointed her pistol at him and pulled the trigger, this time sure that the safety was off. Again, it did not fire.

INFERNO

Nova Turin

Sean Jackson had opened the cell and guided the preacher inside. He rushed his hand through his hair. It had been a wild night. He'd had his eye on Salla since she'd been back, unsure of exactly what to do with her. The remaining settlers on Nova Turin had been through enough. The last thing they needed was trouble from outside, but she was a Nova' girl, born and raised here. She had helped evacuate people during the War Fuel Uprising and her family had been killed under Gray. She was owed some protection.

But still, he was an inquisitive sort. He'd known she'd been on the Outpost and pretended to be surprised when she told him. She'd shown up on Nova Turin in an unregistered shuttle. That was curious, but people had lots of unusual journeys out here on the raggedy edges of human settlement. His question was, what happened in the two weeks between the destruction of the Outpost and when she had arrived on Nova Turin? He had his suspicions and decided to try them out on the man occupying the cell.

"Highland huh?" Sean asked the preacher. "You're from Highland, come here for that girl, haven't you?"

"That the place with all the dust? I woke up in the snow and the dust. I'd been in a box and there were tentacles around me, keeping me alive."

"I'm guessing you're not all plugged in, are you?"

"I'm learning fast," the preacher replied.

Sean scanned the man again with his smart-device. There were no personal identifiers on any factors, not even DNA. The only thing left to do was a retina scan. "Come up to the bars and open your eye wide."

The preacher complied; his hands still restrained behind him. The red light moved across the man's retina and to his surprise, the device dinged positively.

"Well, that's surprising!" Sean staggered backwards, drawing his weapon from its holster. "You can't be who this says you are!"

"I'm not sure who I am. Vincent said I wasn't a good man before I was born."

"No, you're not a good man at all. You're Emmanuel Gray!" Sean brushed the light that hung from the ceiling, making it sway back and forth. He could feel his heart pounding in his chest and a ball forming in his throat, but then there was something more.

It seemed like the room was spinning and a deep, gross purple haze came over his vision. The Preacher, Emmanuel Gray wearing another man's face, grew tall – his legs pushing him up to the top of the cell. The man's form fell to the ground now and writhed, breaking into snakes and sliding through the bars around Sean's feet.

A deep foreboding came over Sean, a sense of eternal suffering. In that moment, he simply knew that this small room would be his tomb. A dark oily substance crawled up the walls, covering the windows, blocking out everything that wasn't happening between these four walls. Before he even knew it, he was tearing at his eyes, trying to stop the horrors from reaching him. Then, almost with relief, he recalled he had a pistol, charged up and deadly. He allowed himself a relieved smile and then…

Salla stood outside the cell that held the preacher. She pulled the trigger on her plasma pistol again and again, but it still would not fire. "What the hell are you?!" she demanded of him. He stared at her, eyes wide and with no answers. That's when she heard the screaming coming from outside.

She backed away slowly to the door, not taking her pistol off him. A few houses down, a man was on fire in the middle of the street. Standing above him, a woman hacked at him with an axe. Turning the other way, she saw a half dozen people climbing the comms tower with unnatural speed, desperate to escape from invisible pursuers. They kicked and shoved each other from the structure, and Salla turned away before the bodies landed with sickening thuds.

In the cell, the preacher writhed, something unseen disturbing him. He screamed, as loud as Salla imagined someone could scream. He slammed his back against the bars of the cell and threw himself against the walls with unhinged violence. Back and forth, he drove himself into the walls, knocking plaster free. She turned away and at that moment, an explosion tore through the building across the square. She felt the sting of wood and stone hit her face, and a ringing instantly filled her ears. Then she was lying under a door blown off its hinges, the cold of the street against her cheek.

She laid there covered as the screams continued, and as the staccato rat-tat-tat of plasma fire joined the horrible cacophony. She dared not show herself, but desperately wanted to help someone, anyone. What the hell was happening? It was almost as if… and then the voice was there, deep and gravelly and coming from within her head, not from without.

I saw you and him together. So, I brought death, the voice came.

What is this?

I am the spider. You know me as Kizik. Timberwolf told you of me?

Why is this happening? she begged.

This is a peace offering. This is a demonstration. This is what I can bring to your worlds. From afar. You are a witness, and so is he.

Who? she asked.

There was a long silence. Kizik had assumed she knew Gray was nearby. To Kizik, there was something about Gray that seemed different, certainly still him but changed in some way.

I am sure you will find out very soon. Tell him not to wake the Symmetry. Keep him from that.

I don't understand!

And as swiftly as he had come, Kizik was gone.

PURGATORIO

Nova Turin

Salla laid there until it was quiet, until the screaming and the gunfire ceased. She pushed out from under the door that had hidden her in the street as the madness had exploded around her. Fires smoldered nearby, and a terrified dog rushed through the street, its leash dragging behind it. She realized she was horribly thirsty and found herself at the fountain in the square, lapping water into her mouth and rubbing the grit from her face. *These were people I knew!* What she'd seen rushed through her mind, while at the same time she tried to push the horrible images away.

She hung her head. She didn't know where to go. Smoke rose into the night sky everywhere she looked. A battered maintenance machine stumbled on spindly legs in the street. It was damaged but puffed extinguishing powder on the small fires it came across. Sean's thick sweater covered her, and she held it tight to hold in the heat. *Sean.* The man was dead, somehow killed by the preacher. He hadn't deserved that, none of them had.

It started as a tentative sound, a repetitive thumping. Then it became a clanging coming from inside the police station. Salla's shoulders sank; there was only one person that could be alive in there. She heard the creak of the old cell swinging open.

She turned slowly and she saw the preacher's lumbering form, supporting himself in the doorway with his hands free. Hoping beyond hope, she pulled the trigger on her pistol again and to her surprise, it actually fired, but the blast was way off, impacting on a wall at least ten feet from him.

She pulled the trigger again and again, and it only went off when the blast had no chance of hitting him. She dropped her weapon out of despair and the man began shuffling towards her. Before she could think about fleeing, he was standing before her. His eyes burned into her, and she saw something familiar in them, something that she prayed could not be true.

"It seems nothing made on Highland can hurt me," he said.

"Is that you?!" she demanded, and he nodded as a slight smile found its way to his lips. Then he faltered, falling backwards. He held his face, and she could see flames coming from between his fingers. He moaned, smoke rising from him. He fell to his knees, howling in pain and when he threw his hands wide, a puff of silver particles escaped into the night, twinkling under the streetlamps.

He knelt there quietly, with eyes closed and his arms at his side. Salla looked down the street and saw an axe lying there, one that had been recently used. She had it in her hands now and she approached him slowly. He was still and solemn like he was in deep meditation.

"I can see you, Salla," he said through closed eyes.

When he turned, she knew it was him, Emmanuel Gray. The man responsible for the death and destruction on Highland and the Outpost. The man that had ravaged this place just a few years ago. The man responsible for the death of her father and two sisters. His face was burned and bloated, but before her eyes, she could see it reverting to its familiar, awful form.

"I am going to swing this axe," she said, her shoulders tensing.

"I would," he replied, with a smile. With fluid grace, he stood, but instead of tending to her threat, he turned in the street showing his back to her. "I wish it wasn't you. I really do. You're a nice person who has been through enough."

She swung the axe at his back. Without even looking he ducked, and she fell into the street. Before she realized it, he had reached out and helped her to her feet, holding her wrist like a vice.

"Salla, Kizik knocked something free. Vincent hadn't planned for this."

"What are you talking about?"

He took the pistol from her, the one that had been useless against him. "We're not going to be here long. We've got a place to be." Then he had the pistol under her chin, its cell charged up to lethal. "Click," he said as he pulled the trigger.

He wasn't surprised that it didn't fire.

"I can't hurt you Salla, well not anymore. I've hurt you plenty."

She flinched, gritting her teeth. She was suddenly angry, her fear dropping away. "Fuck off," she grunted as she struck him across his face with her free hand. She hit the side of his head, his ears, his jaw. He took each blow, barely reacting, his grip growing tighter on her other wrist. She wound up for a haymaker and as she swung, he let her go and her momentum took her past him. She was free, standing in the street opposite him.

"Well, you can hurt me, it seems. Maybe a little," he massaged his jaw.

Once she was free, she wasted no time engaging him further. She was running along the cobblestone now, past burning structures, and unmoving bodies lying in the streets. She knew what she had to do, and she needed to do it before Gray found her again. She rounded a hill by Pan's Pub and saw the twinkling lights of the spaceport a few hundred yards away on the shore of the lake.

Behind her, she heard the clack of boots on stone. Adrenaline piqued in her and she ran harder, but there was something off about her pursuer that told her this *wasn't* Gray giving chase. She turned and saw a form bounding towards her, taking giant strides forward. The silhouette moved deftly but with an unnaturally jerky gait. In the seconds it took to reach her, she noted one thing.

It wasn't human, it was much, much larger.

PARADISO

Nova Turin

The form slowed when it approached her, and only when it got within ten feet could Salla tell what it was. A Phaelon, a seven-foot-tall reptilian warrior. Universally feared for their ferocity, and with aspirations to die in battle. Gray had bought a clan of them after Timberwolf had decimated his crew on the Outpost.

But this Phaelon wasn't going for her dagger or unslinging her highly powered chemical laser. She had her hands out as if to assure that she posed no threat. A long tongue slid in and out of her mouth. Salla could tell by her size that it was a female, the dominant gender of the species. She looked back, as if watching for someone following her.

"Droma!" she spoke and pounded her chest indicating she was saying her name. "Arnock…" she struggled to explain.

Salla's heart still raced but she didn't think she was in danger. "I felt the Arnock, in my mind. Did it leave you here?" Salla asked.

Droma tried for the words. Most survivors of the Phaelon race had picked up some English from the human guards in the labor camps.

"Clan Wessei was at Highland. Spider took! Spider took me!"

"You were on Highland! Fighting for Gray."

Droma nodded positively, huffing through her teeth. Then she pointed a claw at Salla. "Fight Dynata?" she growled.

"I… I don't understand."

"Fight. Dynata. Gray is Dynata!"

"Yes, yes! Fight Dynata. Fight Dynata! Do you know where his ship is?"

The Phaelon sniffed the air, searching the molecules for a threat. Sensing something, Droma suddenly took off through an alley, checking a computer on her wrist as she ran. Salla followed her and looked back to see a form slip across an intersection behind them, moving at incredible speed. *Was that Gray? How could it be him?* They came to the edge of the settlement, and then they were in the wet darkness, reeds and flora brushing past them.

An animal howl came from far behind them, like the high pitch of screeching metal. It echoed through town, seeming to move swiftly from one place to the next. It sounded familiar, but Salla didn't want to believe it. Droma looked back to her. "Sabatin!" she hissed as she ran.

Farther away, everything was quiet. The screeching had stopped now, and they moved swiftly through the trees. A green sliver of a moon peeked through the branches. The cold nipped at her ankles, and Salla wished she had put her boots on instead of her walking shoes. She knew these woods like the back of her hand though and guided Droma onto a path she knew was there. After just a minute or two of running, they came to a clearing. Nestled within the trees was a white sliver of a ship. A gorgeous, personal yacht with a long canopy. The moniker *Into the Mystic* was stenciled on its side.

"Light it," she said to Droma, bending over to catch her breath.

The warrior drew her chemical laser, and it took a moment to charge. The Phaelon motioned for Salla to cover her eyes. Then the laser tore through the ship's exterior with a crackling hiss as the pungent smell of seared plastisteel filled the air. In less than a minute, the starboard wing fell to the ground with a thump, making the vessel unflyable.

Droma slung her laser, and just then he appeared out of the trees. Gray just stood there for a moment, seeming to pose no immediate threat. When Droma turned her weapon to him, Gray moved with inhuman speed and crossed the distance to her in less than a second, grabbing the warrior by the throat and lifting her into the air. With an animal growl, he drove her into the side of *Mystic'* again and again until the Phaelon slumped limp, and he dropped her to the ground.

"Looks like we had the same damn idea," he said to Salla. While they had been destroying his ship, he had been destroying *Caravel,* the lifter Salla had flown here after Dr. Tier had let her go. "I didn't think you'd find my ship. I found yours."

"So, we're stuck here. Together?" she asked.

"That certainly puts a kink in my plan," he huffed, inhaling the night. "We can thank Kizik for her," he motioned to Droma, twitching on the ground. "Hey, aren't you still on my crew?" he barked to the Phaelon. "I did pay for you with the Clergy's money!" Gray kicked the prone form and Droma winced. "Kizik dropped you here like trash."

Salla took him in. He was Gray, but yet he was beyond Gray. There was something infused in him. Droma had said *Sabatin* when there had been the screeching. None of this made sense to her.

"I don't sleep," he said, sensing she was pondering him. "I don't have to eat. I can run for hours. I don't feel much pain." With that he punched the tail of *Mystic'*, and a deep dent appeared in its composite frame, "see?"

"You're a tough man. Always have been," she spat at him.

"I need you to come with me someplace. We're meant to be, Salla."

"I'm not going anywhere with you."

"Well of course you're not. We don't have a ride. Not right now."

"If I get the chance, I am ending you. Do you understand?"

"Yeah, yeah. Stop a second." He held his head for a moment, shaking something off. "There is a lot coming back to me now. I didn't know who I even was until Kizik's little flyby. Now I'm the man I was, plus a lot more."

"Sabatin?" she questioned, a chill reaching her.

He eyed her sideways. "Yeah, Sabatin," he agreed with a smirk.

A fireball erupted over the trees. Something back in town burning off. "He'll come for me. I know he will when he hears about this," Salla threatened.

"Timberwolf?" Gray grinned, a realization coming to him. "Don't you get it? If it wasn't for Timberwolf shoving me in that box, I would never be in the glorious state I am in now. Imprinted like a Sabatin! I can't wait to tell him. He'll laugh his ass off."

"What's all this for? What the hell are you doing?" she demanded.

"There is always an alpha predator. We're lucky right now it's us. It used to be somebody else."

"Who?!" she demanded.

"Don't shout," he shushed. "They're sleeping. That reminds me, I have to learn their language."

"Why are you playing games?" she questioned.

"The Symmetry have been asleep for two million years. They're going to wipe everything away! Start over. Vincent's asked me to wake them up and lead them back here."

Salla shuddered. When Kizik had touched her mind briefly, he had said the word *Symmetry* and that she must prevent Gray from waking them.

"You would do this?"

"You think I might have reservations, but it's the right thing to do. I am the Sword of God. This will test us beyond measure. Before I was talking a lot about God and faith and his plan, but now I see it. We're not a part of it yet. These are the times of will and you're going to help me shine the light."

"Wrong! You just want me alive to draw Timberwolf here."

"There's that too… but I need your strength when I meet the Symmetry. They'll need to see what we are. That's you."

She shook that last comment away, no time to deal with its layers of insanity. "And Vincent Dacha is who sent you? Can't you see he's using you for his own revenge? This is for what happened to his brothers."

Gray was silent as a broad smile came to his face. The smile of a man who had seen the truth and let it warm his heart. "Wrong. I'm using him. This is my war."

Droma stirred at his feet and Gray looked down for just a second. When he did, Salla was gone, running through the forest again. Running, just running away. She tore through the underbrush, trying to process everything that had happened tonight – everyone was dead on Nova Turin. Sean, her friends and neighbors – everyone. She pushed the thought away as she fled. Gray and his plan. Gray or a semblance of him twisted beyond measure. Gray and his need to burn everything down. *You're going to help me shine the light,* was what he had said to her.

"No!" she murmured, hearing brambles getting trampled behind her in the darkness. She ran up a bluff, leaping over the wall that separated the terraformed settlement from the alien wilds of the rest of the world. The forest of conical towers loomed above her now, thick purple vines wrapping around them. As she passed them, the towers exchanged arcs of electricity with one another and she saw her shadow jumping about on the purple, mossy ground.

Salla only had moments, but she had to get a message out. She spun in the darkness, a flash of electricity showing a place she could hide. She huddled under an arch of vines and pulled her smart-device from her pocket. She started a message to Timberwolf, and she selected audio, not text. She didn't care about the cost.

"Timberwolf, everyone is dead on Nova'. It happened so suddenly, some sort of attack. I don't know what. I managed to get away." And she proceeded to tell him all she could about Kizik, Gray, the Symmetry and everything else she could remember. When she was done, she hung her head. "I waited," she said, before hitting send.

I waited. She rested her head on the heel of her palm and exhaled. She closed her eyes for a moment, sensing that things were coming to an end for her. She scolded herself a little. She'd waited for Timberwolf to step back in and rescue her, but she was taking things into her own hands now. She wasn't afraid, she didn't have time to be.

Salla saw a silhouette in the darkness, crashing through the underbrush with incredible speed. Suddenly, it stopped and looked into the murk, sensing her nearby. When a crackle of electricity came, she saw Gray's muscular back, lashed, and scorched. He sniffed the air, trying to find her scent. From a dozen yards away, she could hear his breathing, he huffed like a racehorse.

She had her back up against a conical tower now, and began to circle away from him, careful not to make a sound. With the next flash of electricity, he was gone, and she heard a shrieking echo off the rock outcroppings. She knew she only had moments. *Run Salla!* She forced herself to move, and she was off again. She had to finish this right now.

She scrambled up a rock formation, not caring that the jagged flint was scratching her. *I have to do this, and I can't think.* She was done with this. She wasn't going to help wake the Symmetry and she certainly wasn't going to do Gray's bidding. At the top of the rock she leaped, not pausing to consider her actions and the jagged lethal spires below her. She closed her eyes and aimed herself into a dive. She fell, hearing the wind rush past her face.

She felt the vice catch her ankle. The cold hardness of her cheek striking the side of the rock. Above her, an electric arc flashed in the night and before she passed out, she saw his face, burned and burrowed.

She had not escaped Emmanuel Gray.

MONDAY

A.C. Challenger

"You know they left you here for dead," Captain Jephtah said as two doctors shuffled into the infirmary. Timberwolf could see that there were at least two guards outside, searching each visitor for something he might be able to acquire and use as a weapon. He was within a clear plastisteel medical pod, and most of his body was broken, but he felt slightly flattered they still considered him a threat. "There's a list you know, and you're at the top of it. You're one of the most dangerous people alive." Jephtah tapped the cover of the medical pod, reminding him that he was encased.

"Yeah, watch out." he coughed, and pain shook through him.

"We can't give you the best drugs, because you're conditioned to reject them."

"I noticed," he winced.

"But you're stabilized. Luckily there's no one to bill you for using that Sabatin as an airbag."

"It's dead huh?"

"Very, very dead," she paused, looking sideways at the doctors. They took the hint and left. "Everyone on this boat wants you dead too. I'm even sympathetic to that point of view."

"I don't blame you. What happened wasn't the plan. There was some deception." He licked his dry lips.

"The deceivers getting deceived!" she grinned. "There's a few things you can do to save your life."

"Shoot."

"Glad you're open to options. Where did Dr. Tier take *Archangel*?"

"I wasn't privy."

"What's her next strike?"

"I wasn't privy."

She paused, not hearing anything she hadn't expected. "I can see a pattern here. The good doctor seems to be a very compartmentalized gal."

"I guess there's nothing I can do," he shrugged.

She scrunched up her lips, "Guess not." Jephtah got up to leave. "Oh wait, there was a message intercepted from a…" she checked her smart-device for a name, "…Salla Birdwing. It's audio. Somebody splurged."

Timberwolf perked up, propping himself on his elbows.

She continued, "it's encrypted to your bios. We can't crack it." She held up the device, indicating that it was his if only he could reach it. "There's been an incident on Nova Turin. A lot of deaths. Nobody's in any position to get out there. We did pull a few seconds of audio from the signature, but not much. You're going to want to hear it though."

"Let me hear it," he said flatly, but Jephtah saw the hint of alarm on his face.

Jephtah smiled, reeling him in a little. "Ms. Birdwing sent the message *after* what happened there. So, she lived through whatever it was. Maybe think a little bit about where Dr. Tier might be headed. Let's talk on Thursday."

"What day is it?"

"Monday."

KRAKATOA

Forge Taika

The diamond-shaped hauler *Krakatoa* held back out of range of any plasma cannons. Captain Arnar Mallis assumed they were being targeted but hadn't detected any locks yet. This place wasn't the typical station or transport he and his crew of "unlicensed boarders" usually worked with. Forge Taika was an entire planet, a dwarf planet, but still a lot more than they usually bit off.

He sat in the second chair on the bridge. He spun a hologram of Forge Taika with his finger, not looking for anything specific, but to delay a few moments. He checked his smart-device and read the message from their unknown patron again.

```
Proceed to Forge Taika and retrieve my
property.
```

He had an idea what this place was, even if he hadn't been explicitly told. It was an off-grid 3D printing forge. The kind of place that made whatever you wanted, no-questions-asked.

"Trust," he said to Kai Mala, the petite and ferocious young woman who sat beside him. She was his pilot and doubled as his conscience.

"Trust," she echoed. She nodded her head, like she was trying to convince herself. "Does it really say to move *into* weapon's range before contacting him?"

"I keep reloading the message hoping for something new, but yeah," he huffed. "Trust?"

"So far so good, right?" she replied.

Over the last few weeks, they had been working for an unknown patron, receiving one task at a time but not the whole plan. Each stage was more difficult than the last and had a proportionally increasing payout. They hadn't received a lot of communication beyond instructions for completing the jobs, except for one thing.

```
Trust me. I am paying not only for your
efforts but for your trust. Follow my
instructions to the letter.
```

That hadn't seemed terribly important until now. Many of the parties that hired them sent veiled threats cloaked with expressions of partnership or fidelity, but this was different. Moving into range of the facility's guns could quickly get them blown out of the sky.

"There's enough zeroes in this payout?" Arnar asked for the fifth time.

"Plenty," she replied. "If she's buying trust, she's paying handsomely."

"OK, move us in to targeting range. This ought to be quick."

For a few minutes nothing happened. Their instructions were to hold until "recognized" by the facility buried in the dwarf planet. How that recognition was to occur was not specified. Once acknowledged, they were to make contact. There were no steps outlined beyond that.

A sensor sweep pinged them. That was enough for Arnar. He wanted to get this over with.

"This is Captain Arnar Mallis of the *Krakatoa*. You can call us the *Krak* if you're into the whole brevity thing."

There was no verbal response from the facility. Instead, dozens of orange dots began to glow on the holographic display of Forge Taika, indicating that every gun they had was charging to fire. Arnar exhaled deeply. An Assault Corps cruiser would be needed to take this place.

Arnar cleared his throat "Hey there, we're unarmed, technically. Just cool it and we'll tell you why we're here."

"How the hell did you find this location?" a high-pitched, gravelly voice finally came. Not only was this place heavily armed, but it didn't show up on any charts. Extraordinary measures had been taken to hide its location.

"Not sure. The lady that hired us said to come here and ask for Mr. Minue. That you?"

There was silence again on the other end of the commlink. Then the facility's targeting lasers locked on *Krakatoa*. When they did, a new message from their patron showed up on Arnar's device.

```
If targeted, use this countermeasure.
```

"Man, really?" Arnar's finger hovered over a glowing red icon on his device. He closed his eyes and pressed it.

Almost instantly, the containment cooler on each gun's plasma batteries reversed, driving heat back into the firing systems instead of venting it away. Within seconds they would be unfirable, in a few seconds more the heat would fuse them into molten, plastisteel bricks.

"So, we come in peace. But full disclosure, we're unlicensed boarders. We're here to pick up a package," Arnar said. "You want to shut off your targeting, Minue?"

On the display, the guns went from orange to green.

"Dirty pirates," Mr. Minue snapped.

"Hey, it's our job," Arnar replied. "We're coming down. Can you print me a nice bottle of Merlot?"

"Sending guidance, *Krak'*. Welcome to Forge Taika."

Mr. Minue led his "guests" through the facility. Arnar's long, red Phaelon-skin coat fell below his knees, and he swirled a glass of red wine. Kai walked alongside; hands close to her two side-arms. Humanoid ant-like Glox, peered out warily from behind boxy machines. Most of the cream-skinned aliens wore goggle computers over their eyes.

"So, we don't get visitors here. That's our whole point," Mr. Minue snipped. "This little planet is all mine."

"You're a dark operation." Arnar replied, putting his hand on the man's shoulder. "We saw when we scanned you. You've got tunnels and caverns down to the center of this rock. You bored out this whole world?"

Mr. Minue exhaled in irritation. "We're quite extensive. If you've seen it, you know. Here's how this works. We get the specs. We print. We ship. We don't ask questions." His forges took in the orders, assembled them behind four inches of unscannable lead and then deleted the instructions. "That was some exotic trick you pulled. You know I'll have to pull out of here."

"We won't tell anybody where you are. We don't care."

Mr. Minue huffed, "like I trust you. I'm still not convinced that you won't kill us all as soon as you're clear."

"Trust man, it's what makes the worlds go around. I've got no struggle with you."

"Then why the hell did you come down here? How's the wine?"

"It's good, hints of oak and maple," Arnar noted. "We got instructions to come here and pick something up. Beyond that, we don't ask a lot of questions. A lot like how you operate."

"You see friend," Mr. Minue pressed his lips together, "we have a *perfectly* good way to deliver product that doesn't involve almost getting everyone killed. Your naiveté is charming, but I bet…" Minue didn't finish, instead looking from Kai to Arnar with a look that told them he thought they were someone's disposable pawns.

They reached a cargo hold and two Glox maneuvered a container off a high shelf using a magnetic crane. "It took two weeks to make this. Ate up a ton of my capacity, but whoever you work for pays her bills. Hope you enjoy it."

"Arnar!" Kai whispered. "Please look." She showed him her smart-device. There was a new message from their patron.

```
Open the box. Make sure my property is
in there.
```

"It says we're to open it," Kai said. "We're going to open it here." She ran her finger along the plain, black container.

"Oh no," Mr. Minue said, his hands a negative flurry.

"Hey, that's what it says," Arnar said, indicating the device. "We're to check and make sure it's in there."

"That what's in there?" Mr. Minue looked from one of them to the other. "I don't know what 'it' is. You don't know what 'it' is."

"Well, I guess it's something marvelously impressive," Arnar replied, as unsure about all this as Mr. Minue. "Look man, we're operating on trust here, right?"

Mr. Minue shook his head and pinched the bridge of his nose. He gave a hand signal and the Glox scattered, leaving their distinct musk in the air. "I suppose you want me to open it?" Mr. Minue asked.

"No, she'll do it," Arnar said, and Kai looked at him sideways. "Hey, if it blows, we're all gonna die anyway."

"Fine, I've got the key." She approached the unscannable box and entered the code their patron had sent them onto a small panel. The container opened and a cloud of white vapor came out that instantly chilled the space.

"Holy shit," the three said in unison.

"I didn't think that was possible. This is from Highland. Someone got ahold of designs from Highland!" Mr. Minue said.

"Too bad you delete the plans as soon as you make the stuff, am I right?" Kai said.

"Well sometimes we…" Mr. Minue caught himself. "It's in the contract that we purge the record."

Inside, was what looked like a thin, purple-tinted window frame. Power cells were positioned up and down the sides and at every corner. Kai pulled a manual from the box with a yellow warning on it that read, "R&D – do not ship." The Matterhorn Highland logo was watermarked on the front of the packet. She flipped through the pages.

"Yeah, it's a portal," Kai said, her jaw agape. "These shouldn't exist. Put this against a wall and you can walk right through it."

"Huh, well this just brings us more questions," Arnar said. "Ain't life a roller coaster? I wonder what's coming next?" he mused.

Kai cleared her throat and pulled Arnar to the side, out of Mr. Minue's earshot. There was a new instruction on her smart-device.

```
Change   of   plans.   Proceed   to   A.C.
Challenger. Target T. Velez. Take alive.
More details soon.
```

"Change of plans?" Arnar shook his head, confused. He didn't know the plan to begin with, but it still bothered him that it was changing. "We have to grab somebody off of the *Challenger*? How much is this stage worth?"

"Enough!" Kai declared.

Arnar took the device from her and confirmed it; there were many, many zeroes in the payment column. "Hey Minue," he called. "Can you make us some guns?" Mr. Minue nodded positively, "and a case of this wine?" Arner added.

"And we're still safe right? Even after I saw…" Mr. Minue motioned to the object in the box, the piece of impossible technology that men would rightfully kill and die for.

"Yeah man. Trust," Arnar replied. But Mr. Minue's eyes were still narrow with doubt. Arnar lifted his glass as if to toast, "pirate promise."

SHUFFLING THE DEAD

Nova Turin

Salla woke to the chomp of a shovel hitting the dirt. She heard it coming rhythmically, then it would stop for a minute or so, and then it would begin again. She was in a bed, not her own, and not in her house. She could see out the window that it was a typical overcast Nova Turin day. Her head hurt, and for a moment she tricked herself into believing that last night had been an awful dream, then she heard the shoveling start again and knew that it had all been real. She had a notion of what it was.

She stumbled out to the day, shielding her eyes. In a field alongside the house, a knot of muscle and energy in the form of Emmanuel Gray drove a shovel into the ground. Bodies covered in sheets were lined up in a row. He stopped his work and picked up one of the forms. With surprising grace and care, he laid the bundle into the grave. When it was settled to the bottom, he turned to her, "I don't sleep, might as well dig graves."

"Thank you," was all she could say. Then she immediately hated herself for expressing gratitude, but she couldn't help but acknowledge that what he was doing felt respectful.

He turned away from her and began to dig another grave. "I'm glad you got to sleep that off. I was thinking. You have a lot of honor."

She wanted to run, but her head was pounding, "more than you."

"More than most people. You know what's right and you don't hesitate. You tried to kill me on Highland. You tried to kill me yesterday. You tried to kill yourself last night to put a stop to this."

"I've got to get better at killing."

He stopped shoveling for a moment, "never do that, Salla."

She stared at him for a long, silent moment. She willed herself to hold back any hopelessness that might suddenly give way to tears. "Do you know what that plaque over there means?" She pointed to a post in the square across the street, "it's dedicated to you."

"There's things that I don't know. Not everything came back." He pondered the plaque a moment, "I guess it's not for good deeds."

She walked up to him, her eyes slits of anger. "You know what happened here?"

He shrugged his shoulders, "you mean before? I know I just buried a lot of people."

"It wasn't the fucking first time. You don't remember the War Fuel Uprising?"

He shook his head. "I don't. Sorry." He paused, almost smiling. "I do remember saying 'what's this to do with war?' a lot. I would march around and look at what was being done here. 'what's this to do with war?' I would say. Funny."

"You were governor here. You had three hundred people shot. You had my dad shot. Your men burned half this place down. I'm an orphan. I'm more than an orphan. I lost two sisters. Eve and Mallie."

He tapped the side of his head. "That's not in here. Sorry. It's not."

"Eve and Mallie! Can you even say their names?"

"Eve and Mallie, Eve and Mallie, Eve and Mallie!" he repeated with anger in his voice, but somehow not mocking her.

"How do you feel?" she pried.

"I feel great all the time. Like I just had a long run and a cold beer."

"Must be heaven."

"What's heaven?" he asked as he turned away, dropping the shovel into the ground again and tossing several loads of dirt aside. "I'm a beast of the wilds. Instinct tells me things. I know which way that tree's going to sway. I knew where you were going to jump from last night."

"Do you know what's going to happen now? When do you get a grave of your own?"

He smiled and squinted as the sun peeked from behind the clouds. "It's time for us to find the answer. Where's the Rubicon cluster? Where are the Symmetry hiding?"

"And where's that all written down?" she asked incredulously.

"Half is around your neck," Gray smiled.

Gray placed another body into its final resting place, and when he looked up Salla was gone. Unconcerned, he trotted down the cobblestones of town, past the smoldering houses and faltering maintenance machines. He found her by the fountain across from the burned-out police station and blocked her way.

"This won't hurt," he winked at her as he brought his hand to her throat. The cufflinks Vincent gave him leaped to connect with the ones around her neck. She felt a glow at her templates, golden and warm, the telltale sign of your cerebral cortex connecting to a virtual reality.

But whatever was happening, she was locked out of it. Gray tensed for half a second, his gaze locking onto something she couldn't see. Then, before she could even react it was over, and a calm serenity came over his face.

"That felt like a real place," he said absently. "Penny…" he muttered but stopped before saying anything further. He stepped away from her. "I have what I need," he said with contentment. "Now I just wait in the jungle for whoever comes."

"Do you still need… me?" she asked, fearing he would simply dispose of her now.

"You? More than ever, Salla. More than ever."

THURSDAY

A.C. Challenger

Timberwolf could sit up by Thursday, thanks to the nano-menders and drugs that had been working overtime. Captain Jephtah had ordered double the normal safe level of treatments to heal him. He was free of the pod and his wrists were no longer restrained. He looked down at his hands, flexing his fingers. *Not bad for falling from space.*

His head spun and the drugs sent waves of heat up and down his back, though a monitor at the foot of his bed showed his temperature was actually a few degrees below normal. He tried to focus on the wall in front of him and keep his eyes on one place for a minute at a time. After a few seconds though, his concentration would wane, and he'd find an unbearable nausea building inside him.

He knew why Jephtah had made him wait; she wanted him ready to answer her questions. He was actually prepared to divulge a few guesses about where *Archangel* might have gone. Nothing but semi-educated suppositions though, as he really had no idea where Dr. Tier might be. He'd let them beat it out of him a little to make it look good. Timberwolf had no doubt that Dr. Tier had backup plans to her backup plans, but what they were was a mystery to him.

An hour ago, a team of six heavily armed troopers had transferred his bed to another room. They had moved him just down the hall with the precision of an ace breacher squad, yelling *clear!* and *hold!* and using hand signals as they turned each corner. Their precision wasn't bad. He thought he knew one of the guys from basic, but he was too hazy to be sure.

This new room was underneath the mess hall, and it was a supply hold. He heard crew right above him coming in for breakfast as the shift changed. The smell of eggs and lemons wafted down the vents to him. He sat at the edge of his bed and felt a rush of cold overtake him. Huffing, he cleared his throat of the nano-mender residue and coughed thick gray spit into a cup attached to the side of his bed.

After a few minutes, the alarm rang for the shift change, and he heard crew shuffling out above him. *OK, I get it Jephtah. You're making me wait.*

Seemingly on cue, a crewman entered with a smart-device and earbuds and left without acknowledging him. He placed the buds in his ears and found the message on the device. It indicated a preview of twelve seconds.

"Timberwolf, everyone is dead on Nova'. I'm fine. I'm safe."

When he heard Salla's voice, he gripped the bedsheet. He had been thinking about her every day since Highland, then came the part he knew was coming.

"It happened so suddenly, some sort of attack. I don't know what. I managed to get free, but wait, there's more though. Somebody is here. I'm not alone…"

And with that the preview ended. An icon flashed on the device, asking him to scan his thumbprint and enter his ID number to hear the full message. His head swam with drugs, and he could feel the conditioning in his body pushing back against their effect. He had been adjusted at the molecular level to resist pharmaceuticals designed to enhance interrogation. Timberwolf felt a wave of nausea as something new kicked in and part of him pushed back. Whatever the cocktail was that pulsed through his veins, he suddenly felt drunk and warm, and simultaneously chilled with paranoia.

He plugged in the first few entries of his twelve-character code and felt a joyful rush inside him, like a reward. He cancelled and the end of the message played again. *"Somebody is here. I'm not alone..."*

He started to enter his code again but stopped. He spied a crate filled with fruit. "Those oranges smell great," he huffed.

He rose from the bed and opened an emergency evac kit hanging from the door. He reached in and pulled a tool like a sharp-edged icepick from the bag. Just to be sure, he sniffed the crate of oranges reserved for the senior staff. The strong citrus scent filled his nostrils.

With that, he plunged the tool into his neck, pulling it sideways across his jugular as the blood spilled out.

Someone tore the VR goggles from his face, and they fell to the floor. He wasn't in the storage room or back in his medical pod. He sat in a straight back chair in a small, dark room filled with monitors, his hands secured to the arms of the chair. The virtual reality they had been running on him was displayed on monitors around the room. A swarm of med-techs unhooked IVs from his arms as he tried to blink the drugs away.

A man with short cropped black hair shined a light into both his eyes, checking his pupils. "Well, you figured that out way faster than I thought you would."

Behind him, Jephtah stood shaking her head, a slightly impressed smile on the edge of her lips.

"Yeah, I don't have a sense of smell."

"We fixed a lot of your damage. You didn't think we'd fix that?" the man asked.

"I've got waaaaaay more damage than you know," Timberwolf slurred his words. "And you don't have enough drugs to make me believe a setup like that. My hands are free? Are you nuts?" Timberwolf looked at the man's shirt. There was a patch that read *Sindar, Alexin*. "Hi Alex. You're wearing a fucking nametag? Have you done this before?" he asked with a sleepy grin.

Sindar began wrapping his knuckles with tape, not breaking eye contact. Timberwolf knew what was coming. "Don't," he warned, and to his surprise the man stopped what he was doing. "Don't, because I usually get out of fixes like this, and when I do, I come looking for the ones that hit me."

"You don't scare me."

"Huh," Timberwolf shook his head, feeling emboldened by the substances in his veins. "That's a first. Maybe you could give me some pointers? Lower my voice a little? Maybe I growl it out?" Timberwolf leveled his gaze and brought his voice from the back of his throat, "don't."

Then the man hit him over the eye with surprising force, knocking Timberwolf's head down. "You're immune to the best drugs, so I get to do this the old-fashioned way," Sindar grunted.

"You're graceless. You know, you're supposed to start with maybe just asking me where Tier took *Archangel*. Maybe I'm sick of that psycho's garbage and I'm ready to give her up."

"You'll just lie. That's what the D.P.E. does," Sindar said, and Timberwolf laughed aloud. "Where's *Archangel?!*" The interrogator demanded. "What was the plan in case Tach-Four went south?"

Timberwolf looked for a thought in the air. He had planned to throw them a bone, but decided he'd rather screw with this guy. "You know, forgot to ask, Alex." Slam. Sindar hit him with his other hand, the one he'd forgotten to wrap.

At the last instant, Timberwolf angled his head, and the blow struck the hardest part of his skull.

"Jesus!" Sindar yelped.

"You're awful at this. You remind me of this guy, Conrad but I somehow like you less."

"Enough!" Jephtah stepped from the shadows. "Get out, Mr. Sindar."

The man shuffled away, closing the door behind him.

"I'm going to put that dog down before I leave here," Timberwolf said casually, still slurring his words.

"You're not leaving here, Mr. Velez," Jephtah replied.

He shook his head; the intelligence operation here was rank amateur. "Can I give you some pointers?" she huffed but nodded positively. "Your play to use Salla to get my code wasn't bad," Timberwolf complimented.

"Well thanks."

"But was there really a message from her? You make that up?"

"Something awful really happened on Nova'. I can't promise you that Salla is still alive, but she sent you something. Shame you can't hear it," she said.

"I'll ask her when I see her. I was headed out there anyway."

Jephtah pulled a tablet computer from her jacket. "I need your thumb print. I'll just take it. You don't need to read all this."

"Really? I thought better of you." Timberwolf knew it was an execution order and a list of charges. She angled the tablet under his restrained wrist and pressed his thumb against it. A pleasant chime rang out from the device, and she turned it to him. A series of green checkmarks were next to the words…

Guilty of Treason.

Guilty of Murder.

Guilty of Using a Weapon of Mass Destruction…

The list went on past the bottom of the screen.

"You had your chance. The charming Mr. Sindar is an A.C. Intel officer. He'll be executing you here on *Challenger*. The regular procedure is to take you off ship and back to Tach-One but moving you out of my site is a horribly bad idea. Keeping you around? Also, a horribly bad idea. Most dangerous person alive and all."

"Oh, cease the flattery," Timberwolf grinned. "So, kill me, but maybe we've got one of yours. Some A.C. officer sitting in a cell on one of our cruisers."

"I doubt it," she said.

"We screwed up at Tach-Four, but who… who are the bad guys, Captain?" He was coming down from whatever they had given him, and he struggled to keep his thoughts straight. "I mean, the history might be written down by Doc Tier when all this is over."

"Again, I doubt it," she hissed softly, her patience very thin.

"Do you know who Dr. Tier is?" he grinned, locking eyes with her.

Jephtah remembered what Secretary Bozeman had told her. *Thea Tier can't be killed by order of the Chancellor.*

Timberwolf continued. "You have your rules of engagement. I. Am. Sure," he could hardly keep his head up now and his eyelids fluttered. "Bartender! Whiskey!"

"I think you need a rest. You've had a lot of action today." Jephtah signaled, and the med-techs returned and pushed his chair to the door.

"Captain," he said as he departed. "I know *exactly* who Dr. Tier is."

LAST CALL

A.C. Challenger

Timberwolf had four hours to live. He sat on the edge of his cot and turned over his knuckles. They were bruised and aching from pounding on the door. This was a separate layer of discomfort from the injuries sustained at Tach-Four. Despite the miracles of medical science bestowed on him, he still felt generally banged up – shooting aches and pains and a stiffness in his neck.

He knew he couldn't break through the door, but he wasn't just going to sit there. He was being held in a small compartment and even if he could get out, a burly guard wearing tactical reflective goggles watched him, his finger flirting with the trigger of his rifle.

He had tried to tear the cot from the floor, but all the parts of the room – the floor, the cot, the sink, and the toilet beside it – were all one continuous piece of plastisteel. The drugs were clearing from his head now. He had a disconcerting clarity about him, and the hairs stood up on his arms. There was no getting out of here. He searched his mind for Kizik again, still finding no sign of the Arnock's presence. No indication of rescue from afar via his old "friend."

He felt the snap and then the easy rocking of *Challenger* slipping into sub-light. Alexin Sindar appeared outside his cell.

"Mr. Velez, it's my solemn duty to advise that you will be executed, and your rig will be transported to Tach-One as evidence." Sindar wrapped on the clear door with his knuckle and turned to go.

"My last meal?"

"You want a chocolate and blueberry protein bar?" Sindar replied.

"No. They suck," Timberwolf replied.

"Suit yourself."

"Hey look. One last chance for you. We can be square if you just apologize for hitting me."

Sindar shook his head incredulously, "why would I care about that?"

"It's insurance in case I get out of here. All you have to say is 'I'm sorry.'"

"Mr. Velez, I have been waiting for the moment it's been legal to take out you D.P.E. traitors for a long time. I am not sorry. You are not getting out of here. You will be executed in four hours."

"Why wait?"

"It's your right as a citizen. Not my idea. I don't know, so you can talk to God?"

"He's never in."

Sindar left, leaving Timberwolf to stare at the guard. They nodded to each other, the courtesy of rough men. He sat back for a moment and tried to bring Salla to mind, but he couldn't think about her anymore. He had done what he could to help her, and it would not be enough.

"Nice shades," he said to the guard, starting to needle him a bit. A shudder went through the ship then, and the guard spoke into a commlink on his lapel. Relaxing, the man stood at ease.

A few moments later, the shudder came again, and the man looked towards the ceiling. "Switching streams again?" the guard wondered aloud. Above him then, a purple rectangle appeared in the ceiling with a sizzle, and he knocked his goggles off trying to unsling his rifle. Before he could get off a shot, a man impossibly fell through the ceiling, dropping boots on the guard's shoulders and flattening him.

The man was massive, rigged up in black and white space-camouflaged armor. After him, a small woman followed. As she landed, she pulled something off the ceiling, collapsing it under her arm. Timberwolf looked up and the ceiling was now completely solid. The woman covered the hallway while the man worked on the cell door. The small plasma saw he used muffled the sound of cutting.

"How are you doing?" the man's jovial voice came through his helmet. "I'm Arnar, and this is Kai." The door popped open with a shower of sparks and Arnar reached in and shook Timberwolf's hand vigorously. "Hey man, you want a gun?" he asked.

Before he could answer, Arnar had entrusted him with a plasma rifle. "Who sent you?" Timberwolf asked, not wanting to guess aloud that it was Dr. Tier.

"Don't know. Just know it's a woman. She tells us what to do one thing at a time."

Sounds like Tier, Timberwolf thought. "What's next?" he asked.

"Good question," Arnar responded. He read something projected in his helmet. "We need to find your rig. That's the next thing."

"I know the guy," Timberwolf replied.

Alexin Sindar was in his quarters and took in his weary face in the mirror. He held the blue Terecine pill up in front of his eye. "Special occasions only," he reassured himself. He had rules around taking the powerful opiate, and they had served him so far. It was just that he kept expanding those rules. *Executing a guy is a special occasion.*

A hand slapped the pill away and then there was a gun to his chin. "Those things will kill you," Timberwolf said. Kai and Arnar stepped through the portal in the wall behind him. "I need my rig."

"I'm sorry! Sindar cowered, "I'm sorry I hit you!"

"That's better!" Timberwolf said.

They shoved Sindar into the hall. It was two decks down and one compartment over to the secure storage area. "Turn 'em down," Arnar grunted, indicating that their weapons needed to be switched to the concussion setting. Firing off full-hot plasma on-ship was the best way to crack the hull and kill everybody. Arnar went first and Kai brought up the rear, shielding Timberwolf and Sindar between them. "We're going to try to do this quiet," Arnar assured.

From behind, the staccato chattering of concussion fire made Timberwolf's stomach jump. He looked back and Kai bounced on the balls of her feet, firing an arc of super-compressed air through the hall, as two crewmembers stumbled away. He pushed Sindar forward, his iron grip on the back of the man's neck. "Go left!" Timberwolf shouted above the din, knowing that the hall of the Apollo class cruiser would terminate around the bend. "Put that thing here!" he indicated to the wall.

Kai slapped the portal to the wall and Arnar went to step through. Timberwolf grabbed his arm. "Be shooting when you go through!"

"Ah shit!" Arnar stepped through the portrait-like aperture. He felt a static sizzle in his ears as the back of his skull left the hallway and entered the pure blackness of the folded space. With his senses taking in nothing, he dropped at least three steps before moving into what felt like a netting. Pushing through he found himself back in normal space.

A plasma burst zinged past him and he saw a holographic target dissolve right next to him. He was at the end of a target range and three crewmen stood pistols raised and jaws agape as the *very real* threat raised his rifle to them. Almost simultaneously, Timberwolf and Kai came through the portal, unleashing a wall of concussion blasts against the shooters, knocking them into the back wall.

"You were supposed to be firing!" Timberwolf scolded Arnar, still gripping Sindar's arm.

"You know, this is going to make a great story," Arnar remarked. "We just have to live through it!"

They turned corners, approaching the secure area of the ship, and running into no further crewman. They reached an empty cargo hold and Timberwolf fell to his knees, spinning Sindar off into Arnar's grip. He felt for something on the floor, and huffed his breath onto the slick surface, wiping the dust away. "Scan this!" he said to Kai.

"Getting nothing back."

"Perfect! That's the secure hold right below," he motioned for her to drop the portal to the ground. As she did, a piercing alarm rang out through the ship.

They dropped through the floor and landed in a compartment filled with black plastisteel containers.

Timberwolf knew what he was looking for and he dragged Sindar along. Within the secure hold, the shrill alarms were replaced with a gentle ticking and the repeating voice of the A.I., "boarders detected. All decks on lockdown."

Timberwolf dragged Sindar to a specific container. It was locked behind a plastisteel cage that would take an hour to burn through. "Open it!" Timberwolf demanded, shoving the intelligence officer's face up to the scanner. "Just open your eye." The intelligence officer resisted, wrenching away from Timberwolf.

"I've got something new!" Kai said, reading the latest message from their patron. She put a gloved fingertip up to their hostage's head. "This is going straight to your cranial nerve, is what it's saying." When she felt the electric tingle build in her suit, she tapped the man's temple, and his left eyelid flew open. The screen above the scanner glowed green, and the cage door unlocked with a click.

Timberwolf hauled out the container holding his rig as Kai placed the portal on the outer wall. "*Krakatoa* is coming around!" she announced.

"That wall is three feet thick. Can we get through?" Timberwolf asked.

"We'll find out!" Kai responded.

Sindar slumped to the deck, the right side of his face drooping from the shock. "I want my smart-device," Timberwolf demanded of him.

Arnar had his hand on Timberwolf's shoulder. "Let's go. That ain't on the list!"

"Alex, where is it?" Timberwolf grilled him.

Sindar grinned, "it's a message from his girl."

"Oh, there's no time and it ain't on the list!" Arnar growled.

Kai had the portal against the outer wall now. It was right then that Timberwolf realized something. Somehow, impossibly Kai and Arnar had boarded *Challenger* within sub-light. Two ships should never come within a million miles of each other in a stream, but apparently, they had managed to get within breaching distance. If their ship even brushed against *Challenger*, they would both convert to anti-matter, leaving debris no larger than dust. But Timberwolf had been hours from execution and had walked through walls today, he suspended his disbelief, turning his attention back to Sindar.

The man rubbed his shoulder, his arm crossing his chest. Timberwolf saw his tell. He reached inside Sindar's jacket, grabbing his smart-device. "So, this was your souvenir?" Timberwolf said, stowing his prize.

Kai stepped through the portal against the wall, dropping out of sight. "Hey, how am I going to…?" Timberwolf didn't have a chance to finish his question as the door to the compartment swung open.

Captain Jephtah stood there with two guards. She raised her hand, pointing at them, her mouth making the shape of the word *fire!* Plasma weapons flashed and then Arnar was pushing Timberwolf and the container with his rig through the portal. In the next moment, he was in blackness, falling backwards. He felt the resistance on the other side, the barrier back to normal space. He leaned into it, trying to push through, but it didn't give. Then he felt a shove from behind and the blackness gave way to every color he could imagine.

He was outside the ship now and a rainbow of light spiraled away behind them, brilliant and almost organic with texture. The arrowhead shape of *Krakatoa* was right above him. He connected with it and his bare fingers stung from cold when he touched the exterior. He felt his lungs burn as his chest bloated in the vacuum.

Next to him, through watering eyes, he saw Arnar shove the rig container through the portal and into *Krakatoa*. The man straddled the opening, pressing the last of it through. Then, he reached a hand over to Timberwolf and another hand reached through the portal to pull Arnar in. With a lurch the chain of grasps pulled them all inside, and out of the null of sub-light.

In a passageway on *Krakatoa*, Timberwolf gasped for breath, his face itching from the burn of vacuum. "Well, that was a first!" Arnar said, flipping up his visor.

"I've got too many firsts," Timberwolf managed.

Kai hovered over him, checking his eyes for vacuum damage. "Hey boss, I'm not sure how to treat him. That's not purely a vacuum."

"Some Visine? I don't know. Pour him a drink and check in the morning if his skin's turned to anti-matter!" Arnar shrugged. Timberwolf stood now, stretching out his lungs to take in air. Arnar threw his arm around him. "You are my favorite guy! You know how rich you just made me?"

With a mild jolt, *Krakatoa* dropped to another sub-light stream, peeling off from *Challenger.* "Maybe I'll make you richer. Where are we going?" Timberwolf asked.

"I don't get it," Kai read the incoming message from their patron with confusion.

"Nova Turin?" Timberwolf guessed.

"Yeah. How did you know?" she replied. "We have to kill somebody." Timberwolf's eyebrow arched up, asking *who?* "Emmanuel Gray," she answered.

"How much does it pay?" Arnar asked.

"I've never seen so much money," she responded, eyes wide.

Timberwolf slumped against the bulkhead, suddenly lightheaded. *Whatever Dr. Tier was paying them won't be enough,* he mused.

MOTLEY CREW

Krakatoa

"Do you know the reward for turning you in?" Timberwolf asked Arnar. He ducked his head as the pirate led him through the disorganized trap of *Krakatoa's* cargo bay. Arnar pushed a couple of hanging, tangled bicycles out of the way. "This is like my dad's garage."

"Yeah, you are in the company of honest to God stream pirates, my friend. Sorry about the disarray," Arnar said.

They pushed further through the mess. After a rack of old pressurized rigs, tinged red from the Phaelon war, the space opened up. "What the hell is that?" Timberwolf took in the large, featureless cube, twenty feet on each side.

Arnar knocked on the cube's exterior and it made no sound. "It's holding an incredible amount of energy. That's all I know, and it belongs to you, apparently."

"No instructions?"

"I'm showing you this to reduce the chances of it going 'boom.'"

"Well, you don't know me. I usually have the opposite effect. Where'd you get it?"

"We took it off a container ship in the Tiaski nebula. Those haulers ain't what they used to be. It was our first instruction."

Timberwolf was trying to piece this all together in his mind. Dr. Tier was clearly laying out a plan for them to follow, but it was impossible to surmise when this thing might come in handy. He noticed a bio scanner on the side of the box. He placed his palm on the panel, and it scanned him. For a moment, the container expanded, a series of glowing cracks appearing and then disappearing again. "Well, that's new!" Arnar exclaimed. "What do you think it does?"

"I have no idea," Timberwolf lied. He had a very good idea of its purpose. This object was most likely a weapon, much more powerful than any nuke. He looked to his smart-device again; his messages to Dr. Tier still not received or returned. That was certainly not a good sign. He wondered if Tirani had turned her over to Captain Jephtah or turfed her out an airlock for what happened at Tach-Four.

Timberwolf looked over at Arnar, the man had a curious naivete about him for being perhaps one of the most wanted criminals alive. Timberwolf had no allusions though, this man was garnering a huge paycheck and if Dr. Tier was backing him, he was undoubtedly highly skilled.

He was a stream pirate, a heretofore make-believe brand of thief, previously relegated to myth. Crews whose cargo went missing would often claim it had been "stolen in the stream." Usually, the real answer was that they sold it off to fencing operations and claims of stream piracy were treated with about as much veracity as mermaid sightings. But it was undeniable that Timberwolf had been pulled off a streaming A.C. cruiser, and he stood opposite a real-life stream pirate now.

"Where did you get the technology to board inside a stream?" The maneuver wasn't technically impossible, but so profoundly dangerous that it might as well be.

"Well, this ain't my ship, is all I'll give you. Crime finds a way." Arnar smiled and left it at that, but Timberwolf liked his answer, and appreciated the pirate's restraint. Arnar hadn't pried into anything beyond the job, but there were certainly things Timberwolf needed him to know. The first thing Timberwolf had done when he had a moment alone was to listen to Salla's message. There was a lot of danger on Nova Turin, more than he could have imagined. Timberwolf arranged a version of what he could tell Arnar.

"Look, Captain Mallis," Timberwolf said as the man shrugged off the formality. "'Nova' is not worth what you're being paid. I guarantee it."

"Yeah, it is. You see those zeroes?"

"How about this deal? You drop me off. I kill Gray and I pick up my friend. Your crew stays safe in orbit, gives us a ride out, you still get paid."

Arnar nodded, intrigued by the offer. "No danger, all paycheck?"

"Exactly," Timberwolf responded.

"Well, sounds too good to be true. That's why I'm going to have to say no to that."

"Some bad stuff happened on Nova'. It's a graveyard. Emmanuel Gray is a very dangerous man."

Arnar exhaled and leaned against the container. "Hey, this is nice and warm. Good for my back." Then his eyes became slits, and a menace came over his posture. "I'm dangerous too," and Timberwolf almost laughed. Arnar was crafty and smart but didn't strike Timberwolf as a killer.

Timberwolf considered Dr. Tier for a moment. She would certainly not think twice about getting this crew killed to further her agenda. He pulled out his smart-device and played the part of Salla's message about Gray. *"He's changed somehow. Been imprinted like a Sabatin. He's like an animal and I can't hurt him!"*

"Well, that sounds interesting," Arnar deadpanned.

"You sure you still want a part of this?"

"Why they hell do you want to do this yourself?" Arnar replied. Timberwolf didn't answer for a moment, and in that pause Arnar made him. "Oh, she's not part of the job. That woman there, she's not on my to-do list."

"I am not leaving Nova' without her."

"Oh man. Look, I'm a romantic at heart, but if push comes to shove, I'm not going out of my way for your girlfriend."

Timberwolf nodded. There was much more than his affection for Salla at stake here. "If we get Gray, then it doesn't matter. So, we will get Gray."

Two days later, Timberwolf and the crew of *Krakatoa* approached the freshly dug graves on the edge of town on Nova Turin. "Jeez, this was a bad scene," Arnar said. He gave a hand signal, and two twin brothers, Dennis and David took up tactical positions ahead of the group. Their flowing red hair hung in ponytails from under battered helmets and their armor bore insignia from the Phaelon war. They leveled their over-sized plasma rifles and scanned the town for movement.

A jittery intel-jockey named Nash released a swarm of micro-drones into the air. "I'm not reading anything yet, but I would be hiding too if I went through this," he observed.

"Getting nothing," Kai reported from *Krakatoa*. The ship was settled into a clearing a few hundred yards away.

"Eyes?" Arnar asked Echo, a tall and lanky firearms specialist with a long-barreled plasma sniper rifle slung over her shoulder.

"Nothing boss," she replied.

Timberwolf's head was on a swivel. He noted the burned-out buildings on both sides of the street, and the stony silence that covered the town.

Arnar took stock of the team and strode down the middle of the street. "Hey!" he shouted, his voice bellowing. "If you're here. Don't make us come looking!" Timberwolf eyed him disdainfully. "What?" Arnar shot back, "we're not exactly inconspicuous."

"I've got something ahead," Nash announced. "A human female in an alley eighty yards up."

Timberwolf trotted forward. When he turned a corner, she was simply there between two houses. "Salla!" Timberwolf exclaimed.

She didn't reply for a moment, and then her lip quivered. "Took you long enough," she said, relief coming to her face. She took a step forward and embraced him. Her grip was strong, and Timberwolf could tell she wasn't yet beaten by all of this. He hugged her back and exhaled with relief. She looked over his shoulder, to the motley assembly behind him. Arnar waved with a smile. "We have got to get out of here. Right now," she whispered urgently to Timberwolf.

IN FROM THE COLD

Nova Turin

"What do you mean we're not leaving?!" Salla demanded. "You know what's happened here? Gray can't go anywhere. Wait him out!" she paced in the aft cargo hold of *Krakatoa*. An invisible laser shield protected the lowered gangplank, and a light rain fell outside as dusk held on for a few more stubborn minutes.

Arnar was patient, but firm. "Our job says to kill Gray, and that's what we're here to do. Look, I'm sorry you've had a hard time."

She looked around at his crew. They seemed capable, but second tier. "Hard time? You reason what happened here was a hard time? If you think you've brought enough firepower to take out Gray, you are sorely mistaken. He's enhanced in some way, imprinted like a Sabatin."

"That's nonsense," Arnar huffed.

"Where is he?" Dennis and David asked in unison.

"He knew. He knows what's happening. He told me that whoever comes would hunt him and that they would die." They were silent, waiting for her to answer the big question. Salla continued, "He went outside the terraforming barrier. He's waiting in the jungle. He knows your plan!"

Timberwolf came back from outside. He had been trying to reach Dr. Tier on his smart-device. "Still nothing," he'd heard the argument. Had known Salla would react this way. She just wanted to get out of here. So did he.

"You support this idea?" she spat at Timberwolf.

"He doesn't have a choice, miss," Arnar replied. "You're the price he's paying for helping us. Only people I want on my ship, come on my ship. You're not on my list, so I made a deal with him. He helps kill Gray, and you've got passage." He clapped his hands like he was shaking dust from them, "end of transaction."

"Oh my God, you're all fucking kidding me?" she shook with anger. "He's an animal. He doesn't eat, or sleep or feel pain. You all think you can take him?" she paused for a moment, recalling something. She rubbed her temples. "You won't be able to shoot him!"

"What?" Arnar snorted.

"If those guns were made by Highland, they won't target him," Salla said.

They sat in silence for a moment. Arnar lifted a finger to speak when an alarm went off at the perimeter. "We've got something a hundred yards out," Nash advised. They raised their weapons to the outside.

"Kai, that you coming in?" Arnar urgently asked into the microphone on his collar.

A form appeared in the drizzle. Much larger than a human and draped in battered red armor. It was Droma, the Phaelon Kizik had dropped here and whom Gray had beaten mercilessly. She steadied herself, still recovering from her injuries. She clacked a green bladed sword on the barrel of her Phaelon-grade chemical laser, known to take out entire squads of A.C. troopers in the battle of the Red Forrest on Phaelon Prime. It was the pride-weapon of her race, and most critically *not* made by Highland.

"Kill Dynata!" she banged on her chest. "Kill Gray!" she bellowed.

"Well, there's our shooter!" Arnar remarked.

BAD GUYS

Nova Turin

As night fell on Nova Turin, the native ecology came alive. The terraforming system, damaged during Kizik's attack, had begun faltering and shutting down. The meadows and valleys on the inside of the settlement were now being encroached by dark, thick vines that grew several feet per day. Spores burrowed into the ground, soon to grow into conical towers. In a few months the settlement would be completely overrun and then lost to time.

The moss layer beyond the settlement exhaled its moisture into the air and a thick mist rolled into town. A loud creaking drew closer, and the arc of something huge broke through the soft ground. Arnar sat on the bridge of *Krakatoa* and watched the feed from the drones patrolling near the edge of the settlement. "What the hell is that?"

"That's just a moss whale. It's harmless, but it'll run you over," Salla replied.

Arnar had wanted to pursue Gray in the night, but he hadn't appreciated the nocturnal aggressiveness of Nova Turin's wilderness. Even without the natural hazards, Salla had warned that the darkness just gave Gray another advantage. "Attention everybody," Arnar said into his lapel microphone and his voice resonated through the ship. "We go in the morning. Bunk in for the night."

Salla slipped away, numb that she was safe for the moment, but unwilling to think about what might happen next. She felt bitter that she was so close to safety, only to have it snatched away because of greed, but what was safety really? If she did get off Nova Turin, what then?

She had scant choices. The D.P.E., if they still existed, would throw her in a cell or worse. The Clergy probably had agents hunting for her throughout all the outer worlds. Ask the Assault Corps for protection? Possibly an option, but after all she'd been involved in, they might consider her a criminal. Nova Turin had been her only refuge and now that was gone. She could only think of one option.

When she was a girl, she'd had daydreams about being whisked off on an adventure. Of being suddenly thrown into something bigger than herself. It was the romantic conceit of dime-store fiction, chock full of danger and excitement. In the center of that fantasy was the strong, silent hero - the protector. Someone who would keep her safe, guide the journey and take out the bad guys.

Bad guys. She considered that idea for a moment. If all this was just a story, Timberwolf would barely qualify as a good guy. He was more like a deadly weapon, momentarily sheathed. She knew coming for her was just one part of why he was here. There were the layers of killing Gray, the civil war, the Symmetry, and possibly other angles she wasn't aware of. Beyond him though, nobody in this story was even remotely the good guy. Was he her only option? *Maybe my best, bad option*, she thought. But still, he had come for her.

She reminded herself that her current company was here to kill someone; someone she had actually tried to kill – several times now. She shook her head, considering where her life had taken her in such a short time.

Krakatoa was a homey ship and felt lived in by the crew. She passed through the galley where Nash and Echo sat sharing a bowl of noodles. Dennis and David played cards on the steps leading down to the cargo hold. She found Timberwolf there in the cluttered space, his rig laid out on the deck like it had exploded off of him. He knelt, his shoulders hunched, and his jaw clenched in intense focus. He scanned each component with a diagnostic tool and manually directed nano-menders to perform maintenance.

"Thank you," she said to him, and he looked up, eyes heavy.

"Well, the bar is pretty damn low, but you're welcome. I'm sorry." He nodded up the stairs to the crew of *Krakatoa*. She knew that if it was up to him, they'd be leaving now and dealing with Gray later.

"Still, thank you. You didn't have to come for me."

He huffed, getting to his feet. "I didn't want to have to. I wanted to stay away."

"I wanted to stay away too," she smiled, touching his shoulder.

"What's our chance against Gray?" he asked.

"We have a better chance taking this ship and going," she said. He was pleasantly surprised by her suggestion.

He brought her close, voice low in case they were being listened to. He wrapped his arms around her back, and she pressed into him.

"You want me to kill these guys?" he asked.

"Could you?" she replied, more inquiring about the feasibility than about him actually doing the deed.

He took a moment to calculate, "yeah Vice, I could."

She smiled at him. Her title back on the Outpost had been *Vice* Governor. A grandiose label as she had been a glorified shipping clerk. He had latched onto it.

"No don't do that. I wasn't serious." She felt a flush go through her, partly from the excitement of being close to him and also at the awful possibilities she now considered so casually.

"There's some risk. They work for Doc Tier and these guys have some dangerous toys," he whispered in her ear, letting her off the hook.

"They're not as dangerous as you," she whispered back, her lips touching the side of his cheek. He turned his head and kissed her. It seemed like the thing to do. She sprung up on her toes to kiss him back and rubbed the side of his neck. She kissed him for a long time, not ready to go back to their circumstances. Finally, she let him go and he rested his forehead on hers.

"After you get Gray, where do we go?" she asked.

Timberwolf didn't try to hide the fact that he hadn't thought that far ahead, "I'm open to suggestions."

"Someplace warm would be nice," she replied.

"What, don't love all this frost and drizzle?"

She smiled for a moment and took the cufflinks on the chain out of her pocket. "You really need to keep these safe. I'll explain in the morning," she said, putting them around his neck. "Stay close to me tonight, OK?" she asked. "You can't be dangerous all the time."

OVERKILL

Nova Turin

The open-air skimmercraft knocked a trail through the shoots that covered the meadow. Arnar pulled up on the stick to clear the terraforming wall. "We're outside the wire," he said dryly, dark wraparound shades covering his eyes. The pale morning sun was just over the horizon now and the mist was quickly dissipating.

"Copy that. I see you." Kai replied from *Krakatoa*. The ship was airborne, and it would stay a few miles back and about a thousand feet up, providing logistical support. A drone swarm up ahead gathered data about anything moving that might be Gray. Herds of Nova Bison bounded through the thick vines and forests, causing hundreds of false leads. There had been a promising hit, about fifteen miles out. It was just three seconds of something that looked human, and it was from two hours ago.

Arnar cruised above the vines and was able to keep the skimmercraft above most of the conical towers, but he swerved to avoid the tallest of them. Timberwolf silenced an alarm in his helmet. This version of his Sabatin rig was self-repairing, but after the action at Tach-Four, it still creaked and sported multiple warning lights. He kept dismissing them as everything was in order, but he flipped up his helmet so they would be easier to ignore.

He leaned over the side of the open-air cabin and scanned the endless tangle of vines below him. Once he was committed to an operation, he thought it was bad luck to question the plan, but there was infinite cover down there to fire from. It was only Salla's insistence that Gray didn't have any weapons that gave him slight ease. That wasn't much though. He was part Sabatin now. Timberwolf didn't even know what the hell that meant or how it was possible. It seemed ridiculous. He tried to toss it from his mind, but the absurdity kept nagging him.

He looked to the back of the cabin. The whole mission had shifted to supporting Droma, their ace in the hole. Dennis and David sat opposite the Phaelon and watched her warily while fiddling with their weapons. She paid them no mind and focused on the blur of vegetation below. It was unusual but she clearly held a grudge against Gray. Phaelon typically let bygones be bygones, even with former enemies, but her gaze sliced through the tangle below in a manner that could only be interpreted as hatred. She snorted the air for scents and signals that might betray her quarry. "We're close to where we saw it," Nash remarked, checking the feedback stream from his drone swarm.

The bottom of the skimmercraft scraped against the vines, bouncing them all in their restraints. Suddenly keen to something, Droma unhooked from her seat and leaned over the side, then without warning, she was gone. For an instant, Timberwolf thought that Droma had fallen from the vehicle, but when she caught ahold of a vine and dropped to the ground, it was clear that she had jumped.

"The Phaelon's got something!" Nash remarked. Arnar cursed and slammed the skimmercraft into a turn to double back. "I see a heat signature. It's really hot. Way too hot to be a person. About a hundred and ten degrees."

"That's got to be him!" Timberwolf called. "Track Droma!" She snaked through the jungle, diving between the vines and around the conical towers. She disappeared for an instant and then showed up again running in the opposite direction. "She turned back, a hundred and eighty degrees!" Timberwolf announced.

"Something is flanking her!" Nash had a bead on the heat signature again and it was coming around behind Droma.

Dennis and David leaned over the railings now, powering up their oversized weapons to fire blasts that would leave craters. They might not be able to hit Gray, but they could lay some fire down to keep him within a perimeter. "Got 'em!" David barked, and the brothers let loose with barrages that left ten-foot clearings with every blast. Echo angled for a position, jumping from one side of the vehicle to the other. She fired off blasts from her sniper rifle with a single crack, before leaping to the other side.

Then a flash as bright as the sun tore through the jungle below as Droma's chemical laser vaporized the undergrowth. "Damn it! I can't see," Arnar complained.

"I lost him!" Nash announced. "There was something there, but it's gone."

"Did we get him?" Timberwolf demanded.

"No, I saw it trail off, then I lost it," Nash replied.

Below, Droma stood in one of the blast clearings. The Phaelon held something above her head. Arnar settled the skimmercraft next to her and the crew scrambled out. She tossed a small, mangled machine to Timberwolf.

"It's one of your drones," Timberwolf barked at Nash.

"I've got my whole inventory accounted for. I didn't lose any!" Nash countered.

"He reprogrammed that one and had us shooting at it." Timberwolf threw the smoldering drone into the jungle. "Gray was a drill instructor, which means he likes to remind you he's an ass. Make no mistake, he is planning to school us."

"So, what do we do?" Echo asked.

"I'd use a little fire discipline. Maybe don't shoot everything we have at once."

"Hey, this is my crew you're ordering around!" Arnar retorted. Timberwolf drilled through him with his eyes. "But yeah, don't you all blow through your stashes."

"This thing is useless." Timberwolf kicked the skimmercraft. "If we're hunting, we need to hunt. Droma had a scent on him." He turned to the Phaelon. "Dynata? Gray?"

She sniffed the air, turning slowly. She had something, and she hissed, the red scales on her back fluttering. She growled and indicated that the humans follow her.

"Thataway," Timberwolf said, trailing Droma into the jungle.

"So, you're taking charge?" Dennis said, his voice naturally hoarse.

"Hey, I'm following the seven-foot lizard warrior like the rest of you," Timberwolf replied, and the party fell in line behind Droma.

ALPHA

Nova Turin

They're following the Phaelon. Gray watched them from almost four hundred yards away. He clearly made out seven of them. The Phaelon, and six humans. He didn't have binoculars or a smart-contact over his eye, he was simply able to see the details like he was looking at the hairs on his own arm. The sniper woman was left-handed. The two big shooters had Red Forrest patches on their armor. Timberwolf's rig, the new one Penny had given him on Highland, looked like shit. *You never did take care of your gear!* He smirked.

"This is good," he said to himself. He'd lead them in, let them chase him a while, then he'd strike. He could tell that the short one who jockeyed the drones was the designated medic and the sniper's lover. He'd use that. That would help him get what he needed. This was going to be some good hunting.

Gray felt something on the top of his forearms, an itching that had been getting more intense. He had an idea of what it might be, but when he lifted his arm to be sure, he still couldn't believe it. Under his skin, he sensed it was now fully grown. He threw his arm forward, almost as if he was cocking a shotgun. He felt the sharpness almost breaking his skin. He threw the other arm forward and the blade came through. It was a retractable biological bayonet, like what a Sabatin wielded. The other one came through easily now, and he swung his arms, the residual blood spraying off in a pinwheel of red mist.

He brought one of the blades to his face and took in the scent of this new part of him. It didn't smell human, but musty and metallic, and profoundly alien. Knowing it wouldn't break, he swung the blade down, effortlessly slicing through a thick black vine at its widest part. He stood, grinning. He pulled the blades back into his forearm and then threw them out painlessly, the aperture on top of his forearm now permanent.

Gray barged through the undergrowth beside a winding brook. He was uncareful on purpose, leaving a clear trail for the party to follow. He looked back and the Phaelon took almost every step he had. *Wow, she hates me.* He observed the muscles in Droma's face, contorted and straining. Her breath came quick and from her diaphragm. *A Phaelon that holds a grudge. That's a new thing.*

He had discovered that he could control his scent, the particular musk that was his olfactory signature. He focused on his skin and made his flesh dry, then watched with amusement how the Phaelon sniffed the air in confusion a few moments later.

This part of the wilds was less dense. Gray put a bit of soil on his tongue. Nitrogen with a hint of sulfur. He discerned that a fire had swept through here in the last year and cleared the undergrowth. He put his ear to the forest floor, "two hundred, two-fifty-five." He sensed a rhythmic clatter a few miles away and approaching fast. A river of muscle was headed this way. He estimated two hundred and fifty-five distinct animals – a herd of Nova Bison. He took off away from the brook, leaping and diving past the husks of singed trees. He saw the herd rounding a curve in a minor valley below him. They were four-eyed and bulky, but with the effortless dexterity of deer.

The animals bounded between the blackened vines. Gray saw an open spot in front of a slower animal and dropped down into the herd. He disregarded the hooves that struck his shins and ankles and pushed past the cows and young ones, finally reaching the front. Gray was eyeball to eyeball with the massive alpha male now and grabbed the beast by the thick shag under its neck. He wrenched it to the left, and it followed his lead, snarling and biting at him, but to no avail.

He ran beside and held onto the animal, crashing it through trees and hanging on as it leaped over outcroppings. At a blackened conical tower, he forced the alpha male to make a tight left turn. Looking back, the rest of the herd flowed after the leader, some leaping up out of the crowded curve of the gulley and then back down again. *I can't wait to see the look on Timber's face!* Gray relished. He was circling behind the party now and they were a half-mile up.

When he saw the seven of them directly ahead, he released the lead beast and leaped up to a flat rock. He watched as the bundles of muscle and power bore down on his targets. They were almost on top of them before Timberwolf started running, the others following him. He saw someone flip in the air and the staccato sound of panicked plasma fire rang out. *This will be good hunting indeed.*

HUNTED

Nova Turin

Arnar saw the sky and the ground and then the sky again. He landed on his stomach with a hard bounce that took the wind out of him. Before he had time to understand what had happened, Dennis and David grabbed him, one taking each of his massive arms. They pulled him behind a conical tower, and the herd of Nova Bison channeled around them. Huddling behind a stump not far away, Echo dodged left and right as the animals leaped by one side and then the other. Dennis stepped out, firing his weapon into the air. His massive plasma cannon chattered deafeningly, and the animals sharply bounded away from him. He methodically crossed the distance to Echo and brought her back behind the cover of the conical tower.

Timberwolf saw hundreds of dots in his heads-up. He stood amid the oncoming horde, unable to find a space to run through. A massive bull came right at him, and he used the thrusters in his rig to leap upwards, landing a dozen feet away in the same circumstance as before. Then, Droma was at his back, shrieking and fierce with her chemical laser unslung. They dodged and weaved, as antlers and hooves clanged into them. Timberwolf watched the beasts' faces to guess which way they'd go, their bodies moved so fast he could track nothing else about them. In the blur, he saw a man's face pass him, mocking him with a wide grin. "I've got Gray!" he declared. "Dynata just passed me!"

Timberwolf and Droma turned the way he had gone, their backs towards the tide of the herd. A single Nova Bison cleared them from behind, landing in front and then bounding to the left. As soon as it disappeared, Gray was there, running directly at them. Something gleamed on his wrists as he passed them, his arms pinwheeling. Timberwolf felt the smash against his faceplate and a blade driving under his ribs. Droma hissed, her finger itching on the trigger of her chemical laser. She fired short, quick bursts at Gray, shrieking as she took shots.

Then Gray was gone, and Timberwolf found himself tangled up with hooves, a massive Nova Bison shoving him against a rock. He lit the molten sickles at the end of his gauntlets and slashed at the beast, singeing through its thick coat and driving it away. He saw Gray rushing from Droma's flank, his eyes inflamed and the muscles pulsing in his neck. Gray hit the massive Phaelon from the side, driving her to the ground as the herd of Nova Bison thickened around them. Timberwolf slashed through the animals to reach them - wails and grunts coming as he struck the beasts.

Timberwolf caught glimpses in momentary gaps between the charging animals. Droma on the ground and Gray thrusting a blade down at her, the Phaelon dodging to the side and snapping up at Gray. When he had a clear path, Timberwolf rushed at them and dropped his shoulder, knocking Gray away, but he was up an instant later.

A look of satisfaction came over Gray and he cocked his head. He had Droma's chemical laser. Gray leveled the rifle at Timberwolf; the thick reddish-purple blood of the Phaelon trickled from his blades. On the ground, Droma held a wound on her neck and grunted, her jaw gritted in pain.

Gray fired the laser from just ten feet away, but a cluster of Nova Bison blocked his shot and were incinerated as they passed between them. Timberwolf was on him then, swinging at him with his gleaming sickles. That's when he noticed something about the blades, *are those coming out of his arms?!*

They smashed again, armored elbows and weapons crashing. One of Timberwolf's white-hot sickles slashed across Gray's shoulder but drew no blood. His flesh was hardening, taking on the biological armored properties of Sabatin skin. "You think that hurt?" Gray mocked him. "You think anything hurts?" Sensing the danger of these two men, the bison channeled around them, giving them a pocket of clear space.

Timberwolf stayed locked up with him, knowing that giving Gray any space at all would allow him to fire that obscenely powerful laser. Gray lunged at him, and Timberwolf held back his arm, the blade in Gray's wrist drawing close to Timberwolf's visor. As strong as the servos in his rig were, Gray's strength was overpowering. Timberwolf felt the pressure of the blade up by his eye. He dropped to his knees to gain a few precious inches and crossed both of his white-hot sickles in front of him, catching Gray's arm between them and knocking him away.

Timberwolf backed away to catch his bearings and the animal that was Gray panted, his shoulders hunched up like a gargoyle. Droma got to her feet, dropping a canister of nano-menders to the ground. She pushed in front of Timberwolf, unfazed by the obscene mixture of man and Sabatin standing before her. She pulled the green ceremonial blade from its sheath. Grunting and chanting, she clacked it against her helmet in a challenge of one-on-one combat. She tossed a second blade to Gray, and it stuck up from the ground at his feet.

Gray picked up the blade, the signal for the challenge having been accepted. She tensed for combat, claws digging into the ground. He checked the weapon's balance, casually turning it one way and then the next as if he was considering its purchase. She growled and took a step forward and he raised his other arm, the one still holding her chemical laser.

He smiled, as if to say *fuck you* and pulled the trigger. The stock glowed, but the energy didn't exit the barrel. Instead, a brilliant flash engulfed Gray, throwing him back into a tangle of vines. Droma had shielded her eyes, having rigged the weapon to explode, knowing Gray wouldn't play fair. He gave an ungodly shriek from the undergrowth, like a lifter grinding on its belly. With that, the Nova Bison turned like a school of fish, fleeing from the noise and the sound of their gallop faded off into the forest.

Farther away now, Gray's shrieking came again and Timberwolf and Droma gave chase, coming to the top of a small ridge.

"That thing almost blinded me!" Arnar scrambled up to them trailed by Dennis and David. Droma snarled in greeting.

"We hurt him, but we lost the laser," Timberwolf told him.

"How bad did we hurt him?" David asked.

"He should be in bits and pieces, but he's running out there." Timberwolf flipped up his damaged visor. "A Phaelon grade chemical laser just blew up in his hands." He paused a moment to let that sink in and scanned the tangled vegetation for surprises. "Look," Timberwolf continued. "We quarantine him down here. I can get us some old Tiaski belly busters and we nuke him."

"Hell, no. That'll take weeks. I need to get paid. There's seven of us, one of him," Arnar countered.

Two quick plasma bursts came from a tangle of vines behind them, and a pained yelp followed. "Echo?" Arnar called.

"We're here," they heard Echo reply. "Get over here!"

They found her in a crux between two conical towers. She had Nash in her arms, and he held his belly, moaning lowly. His breath came in short huffs and he barely exhaled, and seemed to struggle to hold his life in. He raised his head and tried to talk, but blood spilled from his mouth. "I've jacked him with menders," Echo said desperately. She wiped her face with her hand, and it left a long slick of his blood on her forehead.

In his heads-up, Timberwolf could see the man's vitals fading. He knelt next to him, touching his arm to get a better reading. "Blood pressure is really low. He's going to die if we don't get him…"

Before he could finish, Arnar was calling to Kai on *Krakatoa,* "get down here and drop the med line. Nash is injured."

"Copy that," Kai replied over the commlink.

Echo shook her head, "he came out of nowhere. Nash was right behind me. It was just a blur and then he was gone."

"Oh shit," Timberwolf muttered.

"Three minutes in-bound," Kai reported.

"Call her off," Timberwolf said, rising from Nash's side.

"The fuck?" Arnar challenged.

"He's schooling us. Don't bring your ship down here," Timberwolf warned.

"I've got a member of my crew bleeding out!" Arnar growled and Nash moaned at the suggestion of his fate, "I take care of my own!"

"Gray did this on purpose," Timberwolf countered.

"No kidding. We try to kill him. He tries to kill us, that's how this works!" Arnar barked.

"No, he cut Nash, so you'd bring the ship down."

"That man's not dying today! It's not in his contract." Arnar stepped to Timberwolf, anger flaring at his nostrils. Timberwolf considered putting a blast into Nash and taking him out of the equation, but that would only solve their problems for a moment. Gray would still be out there and Salla would no doubt be tossed out the side of *Krakatoa*.

"Don't bring your ship down here. I'm warning you," Timberwolf said.

Arnar narrowed his eyes, decision made. "Dennis and David, make us a hole we can drop the med line through. We'll do this quick."

The two brothers nodded and headed off. A few moments later, the chatter of their plasma rifles rang out as they cleared the forest canopy above.

"Droma!" Timberwolf called, "defend." He motioned to the blackened tangled vines and trees, where Gray might come from any second. He turned to Arnar. "I know there's no good options here, but last chance. Call off the ship."

"Brother, I'm going to put my foot up your ass later, but right now we fight, got it?" Arnar spat back, and he locked a new charge into his plasma shotgun.

Echo rested Nash against the conical tower and rolled out a canvas that instantly stiffened into a combat stretcher. She eased Nash onto it, but when she did, he moaned, and more blood spilled from his wound. She jammed a syringe of menders into his chest over his stomach, but the blood kept flowing out of him. "I'm not going to make it," he managed. "Don't bring the ship down. That guy is right."

"Shut-up Nashin!"

"I did two years of med school. He cut an artery," he replied.

She fumbled for another syringe of menders but dropped it. "Why isn't this shit working?"

Nash shivered, "there was an anti-coagulant on what cut me. Don't bring the ship down."

"Let's bring him!" Dennis called as he picked up the other end of the stretcher. He and Echo maneuvered their load around the stumps and vines. The hawk-like triangle of Krakatoa was coming over the makeshift clearing, smoldering tendrils of vegetation dropped down from above.

Droma's screech rang out as she sensed something on the perimeter. "Movement!' Timberwolf called. David planted a mortar into the ground and hit the plunger. The team ducked as a dozen balls of white-hot plasma thumped out of the canister and arched overhead.

An expectant silence hung over them as they waited for the mortars to hit. "Ten seconds," David murmured, and then he mouthed the countdown *nine, eight, seven, six, five, four, three, two…*

All at once, the mortars burst, and mushroom-shaped plumes of fire erupted a half mile out, a channel of flame creating a ring of devastation. The shockwave hit them, and the team shielded Nash as debris rained down around them.

"Maybe try underkill?" Timberwolf suggested as he turned away from the smoking flora. *Krakatoa* hovered just above the trees, its thrust blasting downward on them, and a gurney descended to the forest floor. Echo and Dennis clipped the stretcher on the gurney, securing Nash to be hauled back up to the ship. The man was chalky now and shook his head negatively as Echo rubbed his face.

Arnar saw the movement streak through the settling dust. "Get him up Kai!" he ordered. Then a form came right at them, a human shape moving obscenely fast, blades flashing on the ends of his arms. The team unleashed a wall of plasma on Gray, their faces illuminated in the bright flashes. But their weapons, all made by Highland, would not fire when the blast would hit Gray. Any shots by luck bounced off his thickening skin. He dodged and weaved, almost mockingly, and drew closer. He raised his blade to strike Echo but turned at the last moment.

Gray leaped at the rising gurney, making a vertical bound of at least eight feet as *Krakatoa* pulled away. The rig swung as Gray's elbows gained purchase on the gurney and he came face to face with Nash. The man knew he had to act now. Sitting up, Nash used the last of his strength to put a flare gun to Gray's face and pull the trigger. Gray howled as the awful white-hot phosphorus filled his eye socket. He slipped, holding on by one hand as the gurney spun but he managed to swing his weight forward and haul himself up past Nash.

He stood on the platform rising up to the belly of the ship, his face smoking from the flare. He grimaced, digging the smoldering embers from where his right eye had been. He sliced the restraints holding Nash on the gurney and kicked the nearly lifeless man to the forest floor below.

"Kai, stop the line!" Arnar ordered, but it was too late. Gray disappeared into the bottom of Krakatoa. The ship hung there for a moment and then it happened. A form came hurling out from where the gurney had gone, a lock of dark brown hair trailing it. "Kai!" Arnar called, racing to where she was falling.

Timberwolf rushed as well, diving to break her fall. She was just inches above him, her fingers reaching out to the end of his gauntlet and her eyes wide, but he knew it wouldn't be enough. Sliding in out of the corner of his eye though, was the bulk of Arnar. The man flattened himself out and Kai landed on him, and he grasped her with his bear-like bulk.

Kai coughed and rolled off him, and Arnar sat up, trying to gain back his wind. *Krakatoa* turned and disappeared over the forest. Then they saw it rising, its glowing thrusters angled to the ground to blast up to orbit.

"Here," Arnar tossed Timberwolf his smart-device. On it, a large red button glowed, "sorry to give you this choice."

Timberwolf looked at the device, the button was labeled *a very bad day*. It was *Krakatoa's* self-destruct. He looked to the white and blue blast of the ship's thrusters trailing off towards space. He knew there was no choice. For a moment, he put himself in Salla's place. He took her strength and did what she would not have hesitated to do had their situations were reversed.

He pressed the button.

EXIT MUSIC

Nova Turin

Kai had rounded the corner ready to haul Nash into the belly of *Krakatoa*. She came face to face with a demon instead. Gray stood there, his eye burned away, and the awful scent of smoking flesh filled the space. He brushed smoldering phosphorus from his cheek like it was dust. "Don't worry. I'll be fine," he said. "Half my face is rebuilt from my time on Ceres anyway," he grinned. Before Kai could react, he had grabbed her, putting a blade to her neck. "Tell her to hit it. I know Birdwing is flying."

Kai tapped an intercom. "Hit it," she said and instantly the ship began to pivot. Without a second thought, Gray tossed Kai out the way he came in, extra baggage discarded.

When he got up to the bridge, Salla turned, expecting to see Kai. At the site of Gray, she simply closed her eyes and exhaled, not jumping to fight him or making any aggressive moves. "Where's Kai?" she asked, swallowing hard as she already knew the answer.

"She doesn't need to meet the Symmetry," Gray said, as the panels around the front windscreen all suddenly glowed red. "Looks like our vessel's primed to blow."

"Good, let's get this done," she snapped.

"I think you're forgetting something," he said, approaching her. He slipped a blade from his wrist and her eyes went wide. He didn't bring the edge to her neck though but used it like a pointer and indicated a countdown on one of the panels. "We're here. I'm betting this is a Highland ship. You know the rest."

She turned to the panel, where the countdown dwindled - *three, two, one...* When it reached its terminus, Gray mouthed the word "boom!" but nothing happened. "Yeah, Highland ship. Highland bomb. Looks like I found us a ride!"

WORST WICKED FRIEND

Arnock Prime

Kizik had to talk to someone. What he had learned over Nova Turin about the Symmetry had chilled his bones. It unnerved him even more so than the slaughter he had committed there. He had forgotten what the individual screams of humans felt like. He thought he would be inured to it, but he'd seen the horror through their eyes. The device he had used to amplify himself didn't permit him to look away. Still, what he had discovered and carried inside of him...

Gray wants to wake up the Symmetry!

The Symmetry, ancient boogeymen of the night. Their unmoored megacity of destruction. Perfect killers trapped forever. Where were they hidden? Were they even real? Kizik had felt such certainty when touching Gray's mind that he simply knew it to be true at the core of his being.

He had to talk to someone, and only one name came to mind. He descended through the thin atmosphere of Arnock

Prime in his shuttle. He'd been told that he would be killed if he came here, but that was a risk he was comfortable with.

When he landed, he opened the box holding the Amp and the cube glowed when he grasped it. Instead of projecting himself outward though, he took his thoughts inward. He made himself a void to become undetectable to all here who had promised him death. He stepped out onto his world, shaking and buzzing as his claws touched the surface. The ground was cold, and the wind smelled of ash. Not far away, a small fire burned.

Far? He whispered with his mind.

Far! He called louder. A form covered in rags stirred by the fire, and with a twist of its shoulders it turned to hobble towards him. Far's windswept face came into view, cragged and cracked from the elements. They stared at each other, neither sure where to start.

Finally, Far broke the silence, *Kizik, everyone hates you.*

Hello Far, Kizik replied.

I've been asked to hate you. I told them I wouldn't give you refuge with the Farhallen if you came here.

Would you keep that promise?

I kill because I enjoy it. I might do anything. Far made the Arnock equivalent of a shrug.

I'll look forward to a warm nest then, Kizik snickered.

We're not your kind. There's no order here. It's nice to talk to you, but what do you want?

There's grave danger.

Again? Kizik tried to explain but Far stopped him. *Let's go inside. This weather is bad for the bones.*

Far turned and hobbled away. He led Kizik along a path further down the plain. They rounded an outcropping of rocks. *This seems familiar…* Kizik considered.

Remember? Far asked. Past the outcropping was the skeleton of the blocky, building-sized human command base they had forced to crash here during the invasion. Far approached the massive wreck and pulled open a makeshift door. A cockeyed placard read *A.C. Alhambra,* in the human language.

Oh Radem, you live in this? Far didn't answer but shuffled inside. He had indeed converted the ruin into a makeshift home. They continued to an inner chamber of the wreckage, to a clearing among twisted girders.

Get out! Far bellowed, hurling curses. Three rummaging Farhallen screeched and fled into the darkness, hiding behind debris. They looked out at him with darting red eyes. He spat and hissed at them until they shuffled away. When they were gone, he cranked a wheel attached to a generator. An adjacent stove began to warm, and a dull glow illuminated Kizik's face. *You look awful,* Far observed.

Kizik noticed skeletons around them arranged on rocks and debris. Human forms, the flesh picked clean but their uniforms still hanging off them. They were arranged in a sort of council, surrounding Far's living space in a semi-circle. Some were supported by their old rifles, tucked under their arms or chins. Kizik paid the macabre display no mind. It was well within the realm of what he expected from Far.

Is he awful? Far asked the assembled bones around him. He pretended to wait for a response. *They say no. They say that you're just muddled in circumstance.*

Talking to the dead?

I'm not talking to anyone among the living here. They're insane. Far flung a rock out at a Farhallen still skulking in the darkness, causing him to flee. He touched a pot hanging over the stove and pulled back from the heat. Then he gingerly poured the steaming liquid into two cups. Kizik took a sip, and the mildly intoxicating nectar sent a warm shiver down his spine.

You mentioned grave danger? Far continued, with mock casualness.

The Symmetry.

Far shrugged, *who?*

The humans call them that, try 'Strallokahna.'

Far laughed, *you risked death to come tell me ghost stories? Legends of a galactic menace frozen in time?*

They are coming. I am sure of it.

Huh, maybe you do belong here. There was a long pause, *So, why did you come to me?*

I visited here not long ago. I have a device that allows me to amplify my voice.

Your voice. You're the wind of doom, Far chuckled. *Yes, our friends below are NOT happy at all about that. I was extremely amused, but I truly like you. You hate that I like you?*

Kizik ignored the question, *I need to think outside of my current boundaries.*

You need someone with no morals. Well, I'm a good choice! I heard of some ghastly trouble on a human world. Everyone dying horribly. Seemed familiar.

That was me. I needed to send a message, Kizik admitted.

Oh, I love it. I've rubbed off on you!

You showed me the depths I was capable of, Kizik spat back.

You're welcome! Now what would I do if I believed in the Symmetry? I'd tell the humans. They enjoy fighting them. They'll fight anyone. We sit back with our nectar and watch them all burn. Far gave the Arnock equivalent of a smile, mandibles turned to the side and all six eyes wide.

Kizik was silent, holding his thoughts in. He shivered from the cold. *I have another idea.*

What's that? Far asked.

I bring them here. To this ash heap that is our world.

Huh, Far was uncharacteristically wordless. Kizik could sense that Far didn't know how to respond. He took uncommon satisfaction from the fact that he was making the psychopath uncomfortable.

Kizik stared through Far, *I know about them. The ones buried on the sunward side. I saw them when my mind came here before, but I didn't realize what they were.*

Far released one of his bellicose laughs, but it was tinged with the unease of being caught. *Do you want a prize?*

I want you to explain! Kizik demanded.

When the humans attacked and we lost the Southern Nursery, we mourned. ALL OF US mourned. Even me and the perverts and the maniacs. It tore our hearts out. These were our young.

Hundreds died trying to retrieve them, all for nothing, Kizik added.

Far drained his cup. *Well, there's where you're wrong.* He lowered his tenor and whispered with conspiracy, *I saved most of the nursery. That's what's in the sunward caves!*

I'm supposed to believe this?

Use that toy of yours and look. Not along the north/south axis but look sunward, where no one looks.

Kizik grasped the Amp and shifted his thoughts, careful not to dwell on any Arnock settlements. His mind borrowed through the rocks, through the horrific heat under the mantle and towards the sunward side of the world. There, many miles below ground, he found a chamber, hot from the shifting of nearby tectonic plates. He saw them there, millions of Arnock, large and hulking, colored every hue of the rainbow, jostling and living together in a crude city.

Far, there are millions here?! Kizik gasped.

Yes, I didn't wait until there were preparations like Arnock usually do. Fitting them into this role or that. I just let them all hatch at once. They're raising themselves. They fight a lot. Kill each other, but they're not of the collective mind. That's why our friends below can't sense them! They don't even have a caste system. They're individuals.

Kizik was staggered, unable to fully process what he was experiencing.

How did you do this? How did you recover them?

You would be disgusted if I told you, but look closer.

Among the Arnock, were other creatures, walking on two legs and wrapped in environment rigs. There was no doubt as to what they were.

Yes, those are humans. Puppets on strings. Us Farhallen collected up what was left on the surface after the attack. They were useful, but most were destroyed recovering the eggs. These leftovers can do simple tasks. Don't worry, most are without higher function.

Far? Kizik asked when he finally could muster the question, *all those that were born, are they all Arnock Masters?*

Oh! I wanted to tell you that but you're too smart.

These revelations were almost too much to bear. Kizik felt some joy that there was a whole new civilization of Arnock, arising different than the old, but also horrified at what that meant. This was a world of millions of individuals. His kind was obsolete. They were a ticking bomb that would destroy what was left of Arnock society. If they decided to, they could sweep through the Arnock cities and simply take them. They were young, undisciplined, and probably poisoned with fanaticism.

Far exhaled with satisfaction. *They have no idea where they came from! They have no history. They've just, become. I call them the 'Lost Ones' but I think they're more found than lost.*

What Far had done was unfathomable to Kizik. Birthing thousands of generations at once without planning on their integration into Arnock society. It was the antithesis of the order the Masters had maintained for millennia. It was downright human.

I know what you're thinking, and you're right, Far said.

That these Arnock are a grave danger to our kind?

My kind as well, Far responded. *But I don't really care about my kind. I accept your offer. If the Symmetry are real, lead them here.*

Why agree to this? Kizik asked, hating that he longed to know what was driving Far's thinking.

Why? Far gave a long sigh. *Because that war we had last time was loads of fun. I want to do it again. I want to make the humans beg us to help. I want to wreck their place in the universe, not out of revenge, but just because.*

Kizik considered the magnitude of Far's deeds. He could have returned the eggs and become exalted, but no. He'd set in motion events that would render Arnock society unrecognizable. Kizik wanted to throttle him, to force his brains out of his skull, but what good could that do? These Lost Ones might be their only hope.

Who are you going to contact now? Far asked.

I know who. Goodbye.

Don't I get a thank you? Far grinned.

Go see Radem, Far.

PERCHANCE TO DREAM

D.P.E. Archangel

Dr. Tier usually rested easily; despite the types of dark decisions she made on a daily basis. She had the ability to compartmentalize, and push things into drawers where she rarely looked again. Recently though, interloping dreams had begun to encroach on her resting hours. Dreams that seemed wholly unconnected to her subconscious.

The Spiders.

They began as dreams of small, terrestrial spiders. Harmless arachnids inconspicuously near her. Spiders infused into banal imaginings, like trying to make dinner and being unable to find the pots and pans, but there on the counter was a spider simply minding its business. Soon though, the interlopers became larger, and more present. Before long, their six glowing eyes made it clear to her that these were Arnock she was dreaming of.

She rested fitfully after an evening of arguing with Captain Tirani. She dreamed she was walking through the empty corridors of *Archangel*. She passed by the infirmary. The only person present was Relaund Velez, Timberwolf's brother. Previously paralyzed, the Arnock had abducted him and later returned him with his vertebrae healed. It had been interpreted as a sort of macabre peace offering. Even in a dream, his presence was out of place. They had transferred him to Purity Hospital weeks ago. He waved to her pleasantly from his medical bed. She pressed on, knowing she was looking for something.

She turned a corner and found she wasn't on *Archangel* anymore, but in a wide and dusty cavern on Highland. She had never been there, but her dream logic told her she knew the place. She reached down and took some of the dust in her hand. It was gritty and sticky like crushed regolith, and it reminded her of the surface of earth's moon.

A few people shuffled around her, lethargic workers dressed in red or yellow jumpsuits. She turned and suddenly the place was bustling. Racks and racks of armored fighting rigs were being loaded onto massive, bulbous haulers. One transport behemoth floated into the air and hummed by just overhead, its running lights pulsing and bright. A worker came close and inside her yellow hood, Dr. Tier saw dead eyes on her vacant face.

As she turned and backed away, she found the space suddenly glistening. A silver web covered the cavern from top to bottom. The workers shuffled away, leaving quickly. At the height of the cavern, something spread the web aside and clambered down. She could tell that it was Kizik. His face was covered with its signature red mark.

He beckoned her forward. For some reason she didn't dread Kizik, but simply felt impatient. The situation had a sense of administrative burden. "Name?" the spider asked, its voice a deep growl. It spoke aloud, not mind-to-mind, and rumbled in a low octave through its grotesque mandibles.

"Thea Tier."

"Title?"

"Secretary of the D.P.E., cabinet level position."

"I am sorry this has taken so long. I did not wish to kill you."

"I appreciate that," she said sharply. A web grew below her into the shape of a chair, and she let it support her. She was moving into a state of lucid dreaming, when the dreamer realizes they are dreaming and wakes without waking.

"I've come to your subconscious so I could get to know your mind, without destroying it."

"Again, appreciated," she replied.

"This is different than with Timberwolf. He was blunt." Dr. Tier nodded at the assessment and Kizik continued. "I have a way to amplify myself." He held up a small cube. She saw that it was the same type of device that Vincent had used to amplify the power of the cyberwar package in Timberwolf's rig when they had escaped Highland. "It can be a tool of death."

"You killed everyone on Nova Turin?"

"Not everyone. That's why I am here."

The web that formed the chair started to tingle up Dr. Tier's side, metallic and alive. "Gray was on Nova Turin?" she asked.

"With Salla Birdwing."

Dr. Tier felt a chill down her spine. "We're en route there now. You're telling me this for peace? You wish for peace?"

She felt an overwhelming *"yes"* come from the creature. He stopped there, and she knew he was hesitant to share anything further until she offered something.

She felt her mind making connections in the dream, jumping several moves ahead. "Arnock are capable of horrible things. Also, great compassion. The deaths on Nova Turin and the healing of Relaund Velez. These are opposites of each other, which is your point." The web supporting her climbed up her torso and began to circle her waist.

"I know Gray's purpose," Kizik said bitterly.

Again, she felt the connections coming. Maybe it was Kizik helping her make them or maybe it was just her mind making leaps. "You're in danger. Are we in danger?" she asked.

"He plans to wake the Symmetry and lead them back to our space."

"What are the Symmetry?" she asked.

"Start over. Wipe everything away," Kizik murmured.

The webbing reached up to her neck now, but she paid it no mind. "What are the Symmetry?!" she demanded.

Kizik was silent for a long time, and as the silence sustained, the spider began to get smaller. Dr. Tier pulled the webbing from her body and tossed it aside. She stood over him now. Kizik was tiny and still diminishing. Then right before her eyes, the Arnock squeezed down into nothingness and Dr. Tier was suddenly alone.

Look in the mirror, she heard in her mind, not sure if Kizik was answering her question. *"What are the Symmetry?"* she had asked.

She didn't get a direct response, but instead realized a deep understanding. *If Kizik has to contact me again, it will be because things have gone very, very bad.*

She sensed someone next to her and turned to see Vincent Dacha's cherubic, grinning face. He kissed her on the cheek, before slowly backing away.

"Killing you all will be hilarious!" she heard as she woke. Her feet found the floor and she made her way to the door in the dark. She reached for the handle, forgetting that she wasn't in her quarters any longer.

She rapped on the transparent plastisteel. "Capote, I need to see the captain." The lights came on in her tiny confinement cell and the man looked in at her with unsympathetic eyes. Dr. Tier and her analysts had been in "protective custody" since Tach-Four. She considered it the right move. She had no doubt if any D.P.E. people moved among the crew, they would quickly succumb to "accidents."

"That's good. He wants to see you too," Capote said.

THE ENEMY

Krakatoa

"What's next?" Gray asked Salla. They had been traveling together in utter silence for the last two days on a direct route to the Rubicon Cluster. During their travels, they had barely occupied the same deck. When he would come near, she would depart as if the air had been filled with a rancid odor. Now she pulled a container of noodles from the ship's stores beside the galley. She cracked the seal and the ramen cooked instantly. She sat at a table and tucked into her lunch, not making eye contact with him.

He had fashioned a patch to cover his wound, but he had lost all sight in his right eye. His body may have been altered to be nearly indestructible, but a burned-out eye wasn't going to heal. Salla ate her noodles numbly, ignoring him completely. After she was done, she placed the container in the disposal. "I said, what's next?" Gray repeated.

She gripped the counter, her shoulders stiffening with tension. "What do you mean?" she finally responded. She glanced at him sideways. His skin was covered in splotches from blood vessels bursting under his skin. In some places his flesh was ridged and hued purple.

"To be honest, I have been waiting for you to leave," he replied.

"You mean off myself? Step out the airlock or inhale a plasma rifle?"

"Uh huh," he responded hesitantly, taken aback by her directness.

"What's the point?" she asked, climbing the stairs to the small gym above the galley. She flipped on the treadmill and began to run.

"I thought you wanted no part in this? Or helping me?"

"I don't, but what do I accomplish by killing myself? You still wake the Symmetry. I didn't stop you from getting their location. Timberwolf didn't stop you on Nova'. If you want me 'to leave,' you'll have to show me the door."

She pumped her arms, running faster on the treadmill. He positioned himself in front of her. "You think I'm a monster?"

"Yes, you're literally a monster!"

He shook his head. "You are one of the bravest people I have ever met."

She slapped the safety button and the treadmill wheezed to a halt. She panted, her hands on her hips. "I look at you, and I see a thing that can't keep his pain to himself."

"I'm sorry you see me that way," he responded.

"I was planning on doing some reading, so if you're going to kill me, just do it before I start my book, OK?"

"You have my word; I will not kill you tonight Salla."

"OK, good to hear. How far are we out from wherever the hell we are going?"

"You'll see tomorrow."

Salla leaned back on the treadmill, and it started again. She stumbled and he instinctively caught her. She pushed him away, her jaw contorted with disgust.

"Just let me fall," she hissed. "Got it?"

He showed his hands, offering a smile that told her he understood. Gray backed away, leaving her alone. She listened to him climb the ladder up to the bridge and heard him close the heavy door that separated it from the rest of the ship. He had been living in there, presumably to make sure she didn't try to mess with the controls.

Satisfied that he wasn't coming back down, she looked in her palm for what she had taken from him. When she'd fallen, she'd slipped her hand into his pocket. The cufflinks were in the shape a *D* and a *V.*

"I'll take those back, Salla." Her heart jumped and she looked back to Gray standing there. He snatched her prize away, and her back stiffened. "I can be very loud and very quiet. These are mine. You have yours."

He backed away, slipping into the darkness of the corridor and then up to the bridge. "Get some rest. You'll need it," he called before entering his area, this time for real.

Salla slipped back to her bunk pod and slid the privacy door closed. She splashed some water on her face from the tiny sink and sat on the edge of the commode. With a clank, the door locked magnetically from the outside. "Get lots of rest," Gray repeated over the intercom.

Salla thought about what he said. *You have yours,* referring to the cufflinks, but she didn't have her pair, she had given those to Timberwolf. She kicked herself for making it incumbent that he rescue her again. She was getting sick of needing rescue.

She pulled the book she had been reading from under her pillow. Arnar had last read it and he'd written observations in the margins. It was an old story about earth's Second World War. Its logic was simple and from an older time, but it intrigued her. She flipped to her last page, *"the enemy is anybody who's going to get you killed, no matter which side he's on,"* she read aloud. Arnar had circled this line and double underlined it. "Can't argue with that," she muttered.

INTO TEMPTATION

Krakatoa

Gray had a complicated relationship with God, and after a torturous progression, he was now considering it a give and take of equals. Just a few years ago, he hadn't believed in God at all. Then he'd had his downfall on Nova Turin and had fallen into the orbit of Cardinal Jacob. He had begun to believe as a bare necessity. Then Jacob had beckoned him into his inner circle. Gray had twisted that circle inside out, outshining the good Cardinal and then stepping on the clergyman's neck in order to elevate himself.

On Highland, he'd felt an unbearable confidence rising within him. He'd experienced so many incredible things that the word of God seemed to just fit into the story perfectly. The intoxication of being on hallowed ground. The adulation of the crew. The beasts of all sorts fighting before him.

During the battle with the Arnock deep within the hollowed shell of Highland, he had felt that he had actually heard the almighty's voice. He had asked if God was there, and he swore he got an answer. *"This is not my concern,"* God had replied to Gray's infinite disappointment. God had told him to fuck off, that none of the violence and folly that had led to the disaster on Highland even mattered.

He sat on the bridge of *Krakatoa*, flexing his forearms, watching the blades within brush against the underside of his skin. *So, what am I now, 'holy father?'* he sneered. *I am certainly not made in your image any longer.*

He steadied himself, waiting until his breathing calmed and his heart dropped to a few dozen beats per minute. "Are you there?" he breathed. "Are you there?"

For a moment, he heard nothing but then the voice came, like he had heard before on Highland. "Be at peace," it told him.

"I'd rather not," Gray replied through gritted teeth. He realized then that he had fallen to his knees and his hands were clasped into a hammer of prayer. He rested his head against the panel in front of him. He looked up to the windscreen, to the infinite blackness that always hovered before you in the sub-light stream.

"This kingdom is not for you." He heard the voice again, this time with so much finality that he felt his heart stop for a long second before it began its patter again. As to put a point on it, the walls of sub-light fell away, and *Krakatoa* shuddered as it dropped into normal space again.

Gray was greeted by a monstrous scene – a purgatory of twenty-four singularities torturing a red giant. The massive star had squeezed itself into an almost oblong shape, with solar refuse arching from both poles like the horns of the devil. The matter collected into a ring of swirling copper-red plasma around the singularity cluster.

He recalled the formula to calculate the Rubicon Cluster's location, and this was all very wrong. It was off by sixty-two light minutes from where it should be. He checked the readings on the interface in front of him and the melee of gravity was tearing at the delicate balance of singularities. The cluster would not remain stable much longer. He needed to wake the Symmetry very soon.

"Oh no," he said, shaking his head with a smile. "This *is* my kingdom." Feeling the light of faith filling him, he closed his eyes in invocation. "You push my kingdom away, but you only draw me closer." He felt heat within him, the pulse of the alien life force that now ran infinitely faster than his own. "So be it."

THE STILL WORLD

Symmetry Lifeship – 60 years ago

Joseph sensed the eyes on him and slowly reached for the plasma pistol he had in an inside pocket of his overalls. He charged it up to its highest non-lethal setting, but he didn't dare turn. He had jerry-rigged the null-shield bubble that surrounded him, and he monitored it closely for collapse. Maybe whoever was back there hadn't seen him?

He hurried off across the plaza, moving towards the miniature sun. It looked huge as he approached it, a glowing hot ball fifty yards across. As he got closer though, it appeared to move further away. Directly underneath, it seemed as distant as earth's sun at noon. He looked down at his smart-device and incredible amounts of data were streaming in. And still at his periphery, *something* was following him.

He began to hurry, brushing past the Symmetry frozen everywhere like mannequins. His breath came fast to him now and looking back, he saw something weaving through the motionless crowds just like he was. He was definitely being pursued. "Only one other thing on this entire world is moving, and it's chasing me!" he muttered.

He found himself near a fountain, water stilled in mid-arc. He took three deep breaths to center himself, and then parried and turned, raising his pistol to face the threat. He found a female Symmetry opposite him, an adolescent he surmised. She had orange fur striped with rich brown, and she held her hands out, as if to assure she posed no threat. She spoke, but he couldn't understand her. The automatic translator, unfamiliar with her language, jangled in his ear like a set of keys.

Quickly enough though, discernable words came to him via his earbud. "Frozen, all frozen!" she repeated. "You? Did you?" she demanded. Her eyes filled with fear. She raised an accusing hand to him. He saw her claws were painted in bright colors.

"Slow down," Joseph said gently, and he sat on the edge of the fountain. Not sure what to do, she sat on the ground opposite him. He wiped his brow. He had no idea how this one individual had become unfrozen, but he assumed his presence had something to do with it. "I didn't do this." He motioned to the greater circumstance around them, in which her entire civilization was stuck in a single moment. "You're alone?" he asked her, but she didn't answer his question, and simply repeated the same phrase over and over.

The translator had a rudimentary sense of her language now, and her voice came out tinny and broken, but more comprehensible than before. She had one simple question. "Can you fix it? Can you fix it?"

He walked and she followed. Joseph had introduced himself and she had made it known her name was Pisen, daughter of Gane and Draja. He feigned interest when she told him that she had been with two friends, but they were gone now. After a half hour, he had stopped trying to answer her questions and focused on pushing on to his destination.

They crossed a bridge, heading towards a pink hued spire looming in the sky. "Destination?" she asked and kept repeating, clearly uncomfortable with where he was heading. He crossed over a red stripe in the street that seemed to ring the district under the spire. Warrior Symmetry stood behind the demarcation. Gleaming silver and blue armor covered them, and large imposing rifles were slung over their shoulders.

"Where are you going? Destination?" Pisen demanded again, this time grabbing Joseph by the wrist. He spun away, her claw drawing blood.

"Ow!" he yelped, and she shied away, clearly not having intended to hurt him. He looked for the words, waving his pistol about to help him think. "Take me to your leader," he finally blurted, feeling ridiculous.

The spiral staircase seemed endless, but they went downward, not up. Joseph had been right, the massive, beautiful needle of a structure was indeed the Symmetry's seat of government, but the command area was buried deep within the structure, not brushing the clouds above. There were pneumatic elevators, but he was concerned that the movement might be too disruptive to his null-shield bubble.

Eventually, they came to a massive underground cavity. Black marble formed arches and caverns. She led him further, consulting wayfinding diagrams on the wall. "I visited once. In school," she told him.

He suddenly felt a kinship for these creatures. She had visited this place like a human child on earth might have visited the White House. Indeed, the Symmetry seemed very much like humans. *That's probably why they're locked in a prison guarded by black holes,* Joseph thought. He considered for a moment what he would find when he reached their command area. If what he suspected was true, then this place and this species could serve a purpose more meaningful than he could have possibly imagined.

They reached an area that was protected by a shield of red security lasers crisscrossing an entryway. They stepped deftly between the unmoving beams and into an ornate white hallway adorned with fixtures of obsidian black. Heavily armed soldiers and functionaries were dense here and Pisen led him cautiously through a warren of corridors, sometimes unsure and doubling back. Everywhere, guards were frozen in mid-stride, or urgently motioning for others to follow. Beyond the plasma cannons charging to fire, there must have been something alarming occurring right before everything stopped. They found half-a-dozen guards in front of a set of black double doors, poised to enter and silently shouting.

Joseph maneuvered around them, noting their vicious fangs. He made sure not to catch them in the null-shield bubble, for fear of un-freezing them for even a moment and catching a claw across the throat. Once past them, he came to the locked doors. He projected the null-shield bubble onto the lock and a red light above the handle began to blink. He cracked the entry code in a few moments and the door clicked open.

"Oh my God!" he exhaled when he saw the scene within, and Pisen exclaimed something that surely meant the same. Before them, half-a-dozen guards plunged knives into a Symmetry wearing a long, ceremonial cloak. Thick purple blood slicked the floor, and Joseph was careful to avoid it for fear of slipping. Around the room, monitors showed the surrounding space in the moment they were frozen. There was nothing but an oily blackness soaking up the light.

"This is very bad," Pisen was able to get out.

"You think?" Joseph responded, bringing a computer terminal to life. He quickly cracked into it, pulling up historical data about the Symmetry. His smart contact translated the ornate script for him, and he was quickly able to understand what had happened. His assumptions were certainly proving to be right, about the nature of this species and why they were imprisoned here. He pitied Pisen, for what he was about to do to her, but he pitied all the Symmetry as well, even as he was disquieted by their familiar nature.

"You," he indicated the collective society around them. "Are a horrific species." Her expressive face became stony, unsure how to respond. "You are very much like us!" he smiled, relaxing her a bit. "You're trapped here because you were wiping out others."

"It's to protect us…"

He silenced her with his hand. "Twenty-two entire civilizations! I certainly do not judge." He forced himself to look at the pained expression of the Symmetry being murdered on the floor. The data from the computer said his name was Tanqar Tenock. "But I need you to help me. The next thing you see will be a creature like me, standing right here in front of you. They will be my messenger. If he or she is harmed, then your people will stay trapped here forever. It's a simple test."

She nodded affirmatively. *Nodding of the head to indicate agreement!*

"And you will do exactly as my messenger asks," he added.

"And what if they don't?" she asked, motioning to a large, portly Symmetry in the front of the room. The one being stabbed grasped at his tunic.

"You will tell them my messenger has awoken them after two million years." She took that in, unknowing until this moment the length of their imprisonment. "And if they still don't, I will simply…" he snapped his fingers suddenly, "wish you away!" He smiled, turning from her. "Thank you Pisen, but it's time to go," he said.

He entered a command on his smart-device, and she froze before him, joining the rest of her species in suspended animation. He may not have understood exactly how he had unfrozen her, but he had figured out how to withdraw his null-field bubble from enveloping her. Her face was beautiful in its balance, now perfectly still like porcelain.

He took in the room one more time. Project Voodoo had done more than gather a scientific bonanza, it had earned Highland an insurance policy. Someday, for some reason, he might send someone here to wake the Symmetry up. Let them tear through the galaxy like a wildfire. *Who knows when we might need to clear everything away!*

FOOTFALLS

Symmetry Lifeship

Gray simply knew how to descend *Krakatoa* through the Rubicon Cluster. It was information that came to him right when he needed it. He weaved through the gravitational eddies between the singularities and slipped into the clear space beyond them. A gleaming white sliver showed on his scope. From far away, the Symmetry Lifeship looked inconsequential – a little over forty miles long and two miles across.

As he got closer, the ship's A.I. gave up trying to interpret the readings it was receiving. Scans showed that time was losing its meaning at the locus of the singularities, and not a single molecule vibrated in the mini world before him. The Symmetry were still locked in their time prison. He entered a sequence into the panel in front of him and a null-field wrapped the ship, which would allow Salla and him to experience time normally and avoid the Symmetry's fate.

As he got closer to the Lifeship, a hazy skyline of towers became visible on its topside. He was focused on managing the approach and maintaining the null-field and only when he began his descent through the pink-hued atmosphere did he begin to appreciate the Lifeship's utter majesty. An entire civilization lived under an atmosphere that clung to the tablet-shaped object. He glided over a vast megalopolis interspersed with green and red natural spaces, and even meandering rivers. Glowing yellow orbs floated equidistantly along the structure's length and width, giving off heat and light. The reflection off the mostly white structures made the whole place blindingly bright, like the way sunlight reflects against snow. He saw scans of the lifeforms below appear on the screen in front of him. As anticipated, the Symmetry were a striking species. Massive, bipedal felines with coats of countless hues. A wave of satisfaction washed over him when he saw a readout of their numbers, five billion.

He landed on the Lifeship and released Salla from her bunk. Before they stepped out onto the surface, he generated a null-field to envelop them and allow them to experience time normally. Again – this was knowledge and capability that became available just when he needed it. He assumed there was some sort of transmitter buried within his body, and this information wasn't being delivered miraculously. "Thank you, Vincent," he muttered, as they stepped onto the surface.

They both donned sunglasses and made their way through the squares and boulevards. They passed thousands of Symmetry frozen in place. There were old and young with vibrantly colored coats - some solid and others with stripes and patterns. They passed familiar urban trappings at every turn – buildings, fountains, bridges, etc., all roughly a half size larger than their human equivalents, and all gleaming brightly. These aliens were so much like humanity – they rode in vehicles through towns and neighborhoods. They built towers and railed transports. Their faces even seemed familiar to human eyes – wide and feline with a reptilian touch. They were unmistakably beautiful – like leathery bipedal tigers and panthers from Africa's savannah plains.

They had been walking for half an hour, and Salla hadn't resisted or even complained. In fact, she spun about in awe of the Lifeship, taking in the alien megalopolis that was so much grander than anything she had ever experienced. Billions of beings were stuck in a single moment here and she had never lived among more than a few hundred people. It felt alien, but not unlike the kind of place humans would live. It reminded her of vids she'd seen set in New York, Victory Mons, or London.

They moved across a walkway that stretched over a thoroughfare. On both sides, a wall of flowers of every color intertwined and rose over ten feet tall. Between the flora, they could see the city stretched out in the distance. Gleaming white structures blessed with a pink hue. Salla was especially captivated by the spheres of light hovering over plazas. Gray noted her wonder and was about to explain that they were actually artificial suns but didn't think it worthwhile.

"I feel this is wasted on us, the splendor here. Hey, you know what the Symmetry call species that live on the surface of worlds?" Gray asked her. They maneuvered between beings frozen before them.

"What?" Salla responded, peering closely at one of the still, young females. She noted leathery flesh beneath her coat.

"Suckers, or something like that. I've been learning their language. They lived in a time when the galaxy was riven by war. This species was like a swarm of locusts, driving everything in their path to flee."

"I assume you're a big fan?" she turned to ask him.

"They'll do," he responded, with a grin. He slipped the blade out of his forearm and casually sliced a flower off at its stem. He took in the rich cherry-mint aroma, released after two million years of stillness. "Us, them. This game is a lot bigger than one piece. Children's blocks that come together or fall apart."

"Or you know, get devoured by locusts," she said.

"If all goes well."

Gray hadn't told her about the deterioration of the system, but she had caught unsettling signs that things here were not completely stable. Fissures sliced across boulevards. A thin tower was cracked at its midpoint. If time started again, it looked like it would slide apart. He surmised that the balance that maintained this place had broken down for brief moments, allowing monstrous gravitational forces to rip through the structures.

She leaped over a crevasse and Gray followed after her. "I know why you're still here, tagging along with me."

"Why is that?" she spat back.

"You think that you can stop this. Maybe if you're here, things won't be so bad."

"Maybe."

"Well, I think you're here to test me," he said. She didn't respond but continued down the walkway that now wound through a garden. Large orange plants reached a dozen feet high. At their tops, heavy black bulbs hung down waiting to open. Gray continued. "You tested me on the Outpost, on Highland, and you tested me on Nova'. Now you're testing me here."

"You must love tests."

"These bulbs." He pointed to the dark bundles above. "They're not black. They appear black, but they're not."

"They look black to me."

"You would not believe the colors I am seeing. Way into ultraviolet. You can't comprehend."

She watched him moving through the garden, his shoulders hunched, and his gait was like that of a stalking animal. A pit filled her stomach, and she measured his humanity against what he was becoming. She decided that he was not yet done changing.

"So, I get it. I'm not 'aware' enough to understand any of this? Are you going to write this part down into some new, New Testament?" she asked.

"You can do that, if you like." She was about to respond, but he cut her off. "Salla, there are things accelerating here. Clearly beyond what I had expected. You think you are testing me? God is testing me. God is trying to deny me my kingdom."

"Best of luck to him."

He laughed, "you don't get it. I'm done taking tests." He stopped walking and turned to face her. She could hear the squish of the blades slowly exiting his forearms. "Why the hell are you challenging me?"

"You said you wouldn't kill me."

"I won't, but I have to ask you who you think you are?" He stared through her with his one good eye. It had begun taking on a yellow hue flecked with red. She stepped backwards, truly afraid of Gray for the first time since he'd taken her from Nova Turin.

"You're right," she admitted. "I'm going to stop you if I can." She began walking again, turning her back and unwilling to look at him. She forced herself to take measured breaths.

"Oh, I know about that," he said. She was relieved to hear the blades sliding back into his arms.

"Then how am I testing you?" she finally managed.

"Where's your cufflinks?" he demanded calmly, pulling his pair from his pocket.

She didn't look back but answered matter of fact. "I gave them to Timberwolf."

"Really? Did you think that through, Salla? I'm sure Dr. Tier has come for him. Now she's got them. Did you want that?" he spoke to her like a patronizing instructor who already knew the answers to his questions. In his current state, his manner seemed disconcertingly human, and unbearably hostile. She expected to look down and see a blade sticking through her chest any moment, but nothing came. They walked in silence for a few more moments.

"I don't want to do this to you Salla," he said. She stopped and turned to face him. He stood about a dozen feet from behind her.

"You said you weren't going to kill me," she said again, this time with fear cracking her voice. She took in the stunning pink clouds and the haze from the pale curtain of atmosphere that wrapped this place.

"Goodbye Salla," but instead of lunging towards her to spill her blood, Emmanuel Gray simply stepped backwards, taking the null-field with him. She raised her hand at the last second, realizing what he was doing.

In the next instant, she became a statue like the rest, still in time and unmoving. Gray moved past her, taking in the gentle contours of her face. In a moment, from her perception, she would spring back to life and so would all of the Symmetry. She would be emerging into instant chaos. Billions of hostile aliens all around her. "Now I'm testing you," he said.

LAST CALL

D.P.E. Archangel

"We're not going to Nova Turin," Captain Tirani began.

"Les, please explain." Dr. Tier had already surmised that the circuitous route and the switchbacks through sub-light had not been to avoid pursuers after all, but rather to rendezvous with Captain Jephtah.

Tirani rose from his desk. Capote tensed behind Dr. Tier, but the captain waved the security man off. He looked out the porthole. It wasn't a real window, but a composite visual from exterior sensors. This ready room was an interior chamber, protected by crew areas. "Thea, I have made the call. I am turning you over to Captain Jephtah," Tirani finally said.

"Jesus Les!" she thundered.

"Can you blame me?" he responded. "I made a deal. I am not going to be executed for what happened at Tach-Four. I am going to jail, so good for me! The war is over. You lost."

She shuddered for a moment, wondering if she should hide her reason for asking to see him. But no, there was only one way she could possibly get him to change his mind. She needed to tell him as much of the truth as she could.

"I want to go to Nova' because Gray is there, and Vincent Dacha sent him there. There are dangers larger than the conflict with the Assault Corps."

"What dangers?"

"The Symmetry," she responded to his blank stare. "We must continue to Nova'."

"What are 'The Symmetry?'" he asked, his face lined with impatience.

"An unknown force. Vincent has set something in motion to wipe us all out. Kill everyone because 'it will be hilarious.'"

"What you just told me makes me think you need a long, long time by yourself somewhere."

"Les, I'm warning you."

"Thea! You're lying. You lie so much you don't even know when you're lying. You didn't mention 'The Symmetry' before, so when did you find out about them? In some dream?"

She paused, almost telling him he was right. "If you needed to pick a time to believe me, make it now. Turn this ship."

"I'm handing all of you over. I'm sorry it's come to this but… you're toxic."

She couldn't blame him after everything that happened, but she was still nominally in charge. "I want Conrad

Stonefield released before we get to the rendezvous point. Otherwise, I won't go quietly."

"Thea, really?"

"It's not a big price. He slipped your net. So, what?"

Out the porthole, the sub-light spectrum began to fade, and the ship settled back into normal space. "We're here?" she asked, and Tirani nodded positively.

"Hey, at least Timberwolf Velez is still out there."

"What?" she questioned. She had heard he had been captured back at Tach-Four.

"Someone snatched him off *Challenger*," he said to her, knowingly. She looked at him quizzically, and then nodded before he realized she didn't know what he was talking about.

"Well, of course he slipped away. Comes natural," she responded.

"So, now that all of this is done. What was plan B? I know you had one."

"There was no plan B, Les," she said, and he smirked, clearly not buying it.

They steadied themselves as *Archangel* slowed. Out the porthole, *Challenger* was coming alongside. With its defensive armor deployed and plasma cannons swiveled towards them, the flagship looked like a massive, jagged piece of tin foil.

Tirani nodded. "Goodbye Thea," he said, as Capote led her out. She left without argument, but her mind spun. The use of nuclear weapons had technically been within her purview, even if she hadn't intended it. She considered her defense, and what her next move might be once she was turned over to Jephtah. It was about time to call in big favors, but in the next hour, she had scant time for scheming.

She was taken to the infirmary and examined for bioweapons and data storage devices she might be trying to smuggle off *Archangel*. The med-tech was good and found most of them. Capote then took her to her cell and watched as she stuffed a few personal items into a small sack he gave her. She had barely enough room for a change of clothes and a toothbrush. After she was done, he escorted her towards the starboard airlock. The halls were full of other D.P.E. personnel being prepared for transfer to *Challenger.* Everyone had a security person accompanying them.

"I tried to get him to let you slip away," she said as Conrad was marched beside her.

"I did the same," he looked at her sideways and she smiled at the young analyst.

"No talking, Dr. Tier," Capote said, as he guided her around a corner, keeping a safe distance from her.

"You had my back at Tach-Nine, Mr. Capote," she said. "Thanks for that."

"After this? I'll probably do five years just for standing outside your cell," he replied. He was a man of few words, and she knew this was as close as he'd come to telling her off.

When they got to the junction near the airlock, the rest of the D.P.E. personnel were there. Tirani sidled up not far from her. He had a security man escorting him as well, and he was surrendering with the rest of them. After a few minutes, the bulk of *Challenger* grew closer, and a boarding corridor extended from the side of the ship. Small fighter pods circled outside, flying in pairs, and swinging in close to show they meant business.

The airlock spread open and a four-man team quick-boarded, rigged up in black-and-white space camo. They pointed their gauntlet rifles to every corner of the space, the laser sites dancing over those collected there. "Everyone show hands!" the lead man demanded, and Tier and the others raised their palms. When he was satisfied there were no threats, the D.P.E. people, and Tirani and his senior staff, were cuffed with zip ties and led over one at a time.

Dr. Tier found herself headed over right after Tirani. The man hung his head, his feet flopping along in the connecting corridor between the two ships. For a moment, she regretted what she'd done to him, then tried to push the guilt away, as was her habit. It came back up though, sour in the back of her throat. This morning Les Tirani was the captain of a beast of a cruiser, this afternoon he was just happy not to be executed.

Dr. Tier missed a step as she passed the midpoint and moved into *Challenger's* gravity field. Timberwolf? She considered. Who had gotten him off *Challenger?* Tirani had thought it had been her, and that was certainly her M.O., but she really had no idea. She assumed she would have a lot of time to think about it.

"Oh shit," she said to herself. Hanging from the top of the corridor, a single strand of silk held a tiny spider. It turned as she got closer, and she saw that it had six red eyes. She felt slightly held back, like something was catching on her. She shrugged as she felt the irritation on her face and brushed a web away that wasn't there. *Am I awake?* she wasn't sure if she was talking or thinking.

You're asleep, but I'm waking you. This is very, very bad, she heard the deep warble of Kizik in her head.

That didn't take long, she replied.

Kizik was taking control of her. It was instant and felt like a someone opened the back door on a frigid day. An icy wave came over her, sharpened her, focused her.

This is happening, she thought. She knew her life was about to change, and these last few moments were a precipice. These would be her last, few steps before the spider. *Oh shit, I forget to call Cammie.* She bit her lip. She'd forgotten to tell her daughter about her dad. That he had died. What had been the most important thing in the world had become a task that slipped her mind. Cammie had grown up so fast, it seemed like just weeks ago she had cooed over her crib.

"The itsy-bitsy spider went up the waterspout..."

She must have been talking aloud because the Assault Corps trooper escorting her turned towards her. Even though he had his black visor down, she swore she could see his left eyeball. It was a hazel ring and the pupil inside suddenly grew wide with alarm.

She felt the outside of her palm strike the man along the side of his neck right under his helmet. Suddenly, there was the sizzle of troopers wielding stinger sticks coming towards her. She knew which way they were coming before they did and parried, sending them into walls and putting their heads into the floor.

Seconds felt like minutes, and she was close to *Challenger's* airlock now. There she was, Jephtah standing with a phalanx of guards. Jephtah pulled a sidearm from her hip and Dr. Tier felt the sting of plasma against her shoulder. But it was too late, and Dr. Tier was too close. She clasped her zip-tied hands into a hammer and leaped at her rival. Time seemed to almost stop as her fists smashed into Jephtah's face and then…

A white haze took over her vision. There was so much noise and then no noise at all. Her fists striking. Her heels crushing knees. The warm splash of what could only be blood. Screaming, muffled and also clear as a bell. Then even time was gone. She barely knew her limbs were moving and suddenly it was over.

How the hell did I get up to Challenger's bridge?! Why am I weightless?

Gravity came back as Dr. Tier dropped into the command chair and flotsam fell to the deck. A man dropped out of the air and landed on his belly, his head thumping hard. As she got her bearings, she saw the readout on the armchair display.

A.C. Challenger underway.

Destination Nova Turin.

CHALLENGER MINE

"What the hell happened, Dr. Tier?!" Conrad demanded. He spun the command chair Dr. Tier sat in to face him. At the front of *Challenger's* bridge, Alexin Sindar, *Challenger's* intelligence officer, struggled upright. He held a bloody wound on his head and rested against the bulkhead.

"Secure that man!" she ordered, instead of answering.

"I think he's secured!" Conrad retorted as Sindar groaned. Conrad pulled a pistol from the wounded man's hip. "What happened?!" he demanded again. A half-dozen other D.P.E. people circled Dr. Tier on the bridge.

"Evac bags have been launched," Audra Cheng, a slim lipped young woman read from a status panel. "Atmo's been purged and it's coming back now. The A.I. is finding eighteen bodies between here and the lock."

"Is *Archangel* pursuing?" Dr. Tier asked.

"How could they be?" Conrad answered, leaving that response hanging in the air. A pit grew in her stomach as Dr. Tier realized she had no idea what he meant.

"I need to be as honest as I can," she said, rising from the chair. "There is no denying what you saw. Kizik is responsible for what happened," she admitted. "He's been in touch with me, mind-to-mind like he was with Timberwolf Velez. I have no memory from the airlock until now."

"So, do we kill you?" Conrad fiddled with the safety on the pistol. "Like how I was supposed to kill Timberwolf Velez if he appeared compromised again?"

"I'd prefer you didn't and that you put that weapon away right now for your own safety." She put her hand on the barrel of the pistol, gently brushing Conrad's wrist. "Please Conrad. Please, I can't guarantee what I'll do." She pleaded with her eyes, and he handed her the pistol. "There's a lot more at play here. Vincent has got us fighting each other so we're not ready for what's coming."

"What's coming?" Sindar asked from the floor.

Dr. Tier knelt next to the wounded man, her medical training coming back like instinct. "What happened?" she asked, as she pulled a med-kit from under a workstation.

"You kicked me!" he said, incredulously.

She sprayed a coagulant on a nasty gash on his forehead and nudged a tender egg-shaped bump that was getting bigger by the second. "Stay still and rest. You probably have a concussion."

"Conrad," she called as she turned away from tending to the wounded man. "Secure all systems on this ship and find Jephtah's codes."

"You already did that," he deadpanned.

"Of course," she looked over her team, all young and scared. She had no way to reassure them, and she had just demonstrated that she was compromised by a malevolent alien presence that could work through her to kill them all at any moment.

She surmised it was best to just give them the bottom line. "I would not pull a weapon on me or attempt to usurp my authority in any way, is that clear?" she said. There were nods from the assembled. "Not simply for my safety, but for yours. If you move on me, I will straight up murder you and I won't remember doing it. Is that clear?" Again, more nods, and dropped jaws. "No discussion amongst yourselves of anything related to this matter. Specifically, I am referring to Kizik." She turned to Conrad, "I understand this is strange, but you simply have to trust me."

Conrad exhaled. "Dr. Tier, there is NO WAY we can trust you after what we just saw. As your aide, I have to be clear with you."

She took a moment to be impressed by Conrad's balls. Especially considering the utterly shocking nature of what they had just seen her do. She wondered if she could bring herself to watch the security footage of her rampage. Her fists were bloodied, and her elbows and knees felt scraped raw – wounds typical of hand-to-hand striking.

"That's a good instinct, Conrad, but you must continue to obey my orders."

"What's coming?" Cheng asked, recalling the question that had not been answered. "What has Vincent Dacha set in motion?"

"Vincent has sent Gray to awaken something called the Symmetry. I don't know if that's a weapon or a species we haven't met. We'll find out when we get to Nova'. We'll assess and diffuse the threat. In case you've forgotten, we enforce the peace." She was barely able to get that last part out without choking.

"We've got a live one!" Cheng announced. "Airlock one!"

"Keep the bridge secured!" Dr. Tier ordered as she rushed into the hall. She turned through corridors and was surprised by the amount of blood on the walls and decks. She leaped over a body, its hands up by its neck as if trying to keep from suffocating. *Jesus.*

At the airlock, she could see someone moving within. She placed her palm on the reader and prepped the exterior door to open. Yellow lights spun as a countdown began. *Ten... nine...* "Who is that?" Dr. Tier demanded.

The form within wore an emergency pressure suit. They brought their face to the window, but their reflective helmet hid their identity. "Take off your helmet!" Tier ordered as the countdown slowly continued *six... five... four...*

The helmet came off with a click and Dr. Tier exhaled. It was Captain Jephtah, with a crusted and bloodied gash under her eye. Dr. Tier halted the countdown and the two women stared at each other, equally unforgiving.

"I wasn't about to abandon my ship," Jephtah said.

"Looks like I connected," Dr. Tier indicated the cut on Jephtah's face and opened the airlock. "Welcome aboard *Challenger.* You're going to Nova Turin."

THE GRINDING

D.P.E. Challenger

Dr. Tier roved the ship, moving through the gleaming white and blue decks of *Challenger*. No one would meet her gaze. She had ordered the dead removed and the blood scrubbed from the walls and floors. Her team, analysts by trade, typically looked at streams of data and wrote reports. Now, they worked in pairs, taking bodies down to the morgue, one holding the feet and the other taking the arms.

Over the past few months, they had been hardened by the stress of space combat aboard *Archangel,* but they had experienced nothing like this. Nothing like the rawness of dead and bloodied corpses. Cheng and another analyst hauled the heavy bulk of a black clad security officer, his arm flopping down and crusted with blood. When they noticed that Dr. Tier was nearby, they quickly shuffled their load away, not wanting to be in her presence.

Dr. Tier knelt on the deck and dipped a sponge into a warm bucket of soapy water. The blotch of a bloodstain marked the wall, and she swirled it into a pink spiral. The residue of nano-menders made the stain gritty and gelatinous. She knew from prior experience that it would leave a tell-tale grey halo no matter how much she scrubbed. Still, she worked her arm into a frenzy trying to remove it.

"Timber, I had no idea," she said through gritted teeth. She had gotten over the shock of Kizik's uninvited presence in her mind. Now she was pissed off.

She wondered for a moment what she would be doing if she had been taken into Jephtah's custody. Would she be in a better position than now? Might she be working her diplomatic channels to maneuver for her release? It would be a political game and outside of her usual operating procedure – and certainly not one she liked, but Kizik had pushed her into a situation that was not her choice. She could not shake the fact that she was a marionette, doing the

Arnock's bidding. She scrubbed the sponge almost dry and bit her lip.

"Kizik?" she asked aloud, casting her eyes to the ceiling, and not getting any response. "Kizik?!" she repeated. Two analysts appeared at the end of the hall and then swiftly backtracked. She focused, searching for the spider in her mind, imagining the gross pulsing of his mandibles as he communicated with her. She suddenly felt the shiver of violation, recalling what it had been like right before he had taken her over.

"This is not the way this works, you bastard," she breathed, holding her head against the cold, white wall. "You answer me when I call."

She looked down and saw a nametag on the floor. The man she had killed at this spot had been *P. Isiah,* clearly the name of a Believer. "At least you believed in something," she muttered.

"Dr. Tier," she turned to find Conrad standing at a safe distance. "We're six hours out from Nova'. Scans show nothing going on in the main settlement. I'm getting sub-light particle residue. A mid-sized craft departed for parts unknown." He shuffled, clearly not wanting to be near her one instant longer than necessary.

"Something got away. Maybe we're too late," she said.

He didn't respond to her speculation. "*Challenger* is secured. I'm sure we'll have company coming in from all over. I'd give us two hours at Nova Turin."

"When I'm down there, I'm confining everyone to the brig except you. Separate cells for Jephtah and her intel officer. I need to know you'll be here when I get back."

"You trust me? I don't trust you," Conrad admitted. "I'm scared out of my mind just talking to you."

"I watched the footage, Conrad. I stabbed a breacher named Paul Isiah here through the chest, then I shot him through the neck with his own sidearm. Same story through four decks. For good measure I blew the atmo and cut the grav. Kizik made me a monster, but I don't *feel* it, Conrad. I don't feel it."

"I don't understand."

"It's gone. If I felt guilty for even a moment about what I did, it's no longer in here." She was almost shaking, and her eyes were slits. "I can't even explain how that feels. We have to move on. I don't know what the next steps hold but you have to buy into this."

"You're perfect," he said after pausing a long time.

"Excuse me?"

"We thought Timberwolf had the toughest mind, but no. You're who we should have sent down to meet Kizik for project Jackhammer."

Anger swirled inside her at his bitter words, and she was about to argue with him, but she couldn't think of any rebuttals that made sense. A sickening realization came over her – he was right. A small part of her, something that she didn't even want to look at, acknowledged that she could work *with* Kizik. Even as she detested every nuance of the alien's presence, she felt she might even be able to get the better of him.

"Get everybody into the brigs when I go down there. Make them understand why. Give them my thanks." Conrad nodded, and she saw him picking at a red smudge on his sleeve. "Whose blood is that?" she asked.

"I don't know," he said, backing away.

When he went, she realized she wasn't alone. She sensed something that felt like a pebble in her mind, turning over and over. It seemed abrasive and close, but it became fleeting when she focused on it. *The grinding.* Timberwolf had described it to her, and she had never believed him, but here it was, the ever-present reminder that Kizik was with her. The spider didn't communicate with her, but she sensed a profound *satisfaction*, a feeling much deeper than the human understanding of the emotion.

Don't get too close, she warned, but instead of fading away, the presence grew warmer. The pebble even seemed to glow.

RETRIEVAL

Nova Turin

Timberwolf held the bundle over the grave on the edge of town. He bent on a knee and added Nash to a grave Gray had dug earlier. Arnar paced and swore to himself. "I thought we could save him," he said for the thousandth time. Timberwolf didn't want to tell them the crude details, but Gray's wrist blades were coated with an anti-coagulant compound. There was no way they could have saved Nash.

"Put some dirt over him," Arnar said. Dennis and David grabbed shovels and began to cover the form. "Echo, have you got any words?"

The woman brushed her cheek. Her eyes betrayed that there should have been a tear there, but her face was dry. Instead of eulogizing him though, she simply turned to Arnar. "Thanks for trying," she said.

"I thought we could save him," Arnar said again, by now that line seemed no longer mournful, but rote and factual.

Timberwolf backed away from the crew of *Krakatoa*, not wanting to interlope. He found himself watching them. Soon, he could hear them telling stories about Nash and laughing uneasily, like what happened at most funerals.

He looked to the sky. It was clear that Gray had gotten away on *Krakatoa*. He had schooled them, and he'd made it hurt. He had a ship. He'd drawn blood. He had Salla and he was probably on his way to wherever the Symmetry might be, if he hadn't found them already. "This is in fact, a very bad day," Timberwolf muttered to himself.

"Timberwolf!" he heard an impossibly familiar voice over his commlink.

He paused for a moment, unsure how to reply. "Who may I ask is calling?" he answered.

Dr. Tier huffed. "It's Thea. I've come a long way to get you. I see you on the edge of town. I'm six miles out. You've got company. I want them neutralized."

"Negative, these are your people."

"My people?" she replied incredulously.

"The ones who broke me off Challenger. They think they work for you."

"So, you're with friends. I'll be there in two minutes."

Dr. Tier's shuttle emerged from the mist at the edge of town and settled into a clearing on creaking gimbals. She quickly exited down the gangplank. As she descended the gangplank, she drew a bead on each of Arnar's people with a gauntlet rifle.

"Hey, it's cool," Arnar said easily, his arms raised. "We've had a bad day, but we get it. We all get it. Our man knew the risks. I'll just need you to cash out his 'death bonus,' if you please."

"Timberwolf, are these people a threat?" Dr. Tier asked.

"Not to me," he replied.

Dr. Tier turned to Arnar and his crew. "Look, I didn't hire you. I don't know who did, but the job is over," she said. "Let's go Timber." She motioned with her weapon for Timberwolf to board her ship and made it clear that Arnar and his people were not to follow.

"We don't have a ride. Hey, can you not leave us here?" Arnar appealed.

"Sorry, I can't have any complications."

Arnar shook his head. "Look, we may not have been working for you, but I know who you are. We can be helpful."

"Not where we're going," she replied.

"Where are we going?" Timberwolf asked.

"We're obviously in pursuit of the man you could not kill." Her remark stung Timberwolf, and Arnar stepped back out of the space between them.

"Yeah, but what's your next move?" Arnar cut the tension after a beat. "You don't have access to Station Corps refuge. Everyone knows about that."

Dr. Tier bit her lip. "We'll restock *Challenger* at…"

"*Challenger?!*" Timberwolf and Arnar responded in unison.

"It's not a story for now," Dr. Tier snipped.

Arnar interrupted, "listen, I know your plan. Just hear me out. You think you're going to head to Saavas or a place like that and you'll pay off folks like me to give you sanctuary. But thing is, you can't trust folks like me."

"Your point, sir?" Dr. Tier demanded impatiently, but she had to admit, her plan was something like what he described. Arnar's smart-device buzzed and he looked down at it.

"Sorry, I need to read this," Arnar said, as Dr. Tier looked at him sideways. Arnar took in what he was reading on his device and after a few moments continued. "I know a guy who owes me for not destroying his little moon," Arnar said.

"No thanks," she huffed, and backed up the gangplank.

"Look, take us with you and I'll take you there. I'll be breaking a pirate promise, but I'd do it for you. I may be an outlaw, technically, but I want to see you win this war. Gotta pick a side. It's more than a dock on a rock, I'm telling you."

"Nice try," she said, and the gangplank began to pull in.

"It's a 3D printing forge. Hidden. I know how to approach undetected. Best operation I've ever seen. You could do a lot more than replenish your synthcafe machine. I assume you have a fleet to look after?"

She took in what he was offering. Access to a facility to keep her fleet fighting while she hunted down Gray would be invaluable. It seemed too good to be true, but she had heard of off-the-grid printing operations like what he was describing. She looked Arnar over and then shifted her gaze to Timberwolf. "Can I trust these people?"

Timberwolf nodded positively, just wanting to be out of his rig for a while.

"That's a hell of an offer, just for a ride, Mr. ...?"

"Captain Arnar Mallis, formerly of the *Krakatoa*. We operate in the streams. The *Krak'* wasn't my ship, but I treated her so. I had her in my possession for a bit. Nine tenths of the law and all. Long story. This is Kai, Dennis and David, and Echo. Our friend in the ditch was Nash."

Dr. Tier nodded, "condolences, and who are you taking me to see?"

"He goes by Mr. Minue," Arnar answered.

THE DARKNESS

D.P.E. Challenger, Over Nova Turin

Timberwolf had almost convinced himself that he had misheard Dr. Tier down on Nova Turin. Had she really said, "*Challenger?*" He watched through a porthole as the crescent of the world receded below them.

He sat in the shuttle opposite Arnar. Seeming to read his mind, the man winked and turned over a buckle on his harness and showed the 'AC-Chall' insignia. Dr. Tier worked at the flight controls in the cockpit, though she didn't need to. She looked in a mirror over the dash and Timberwolf saw her clenched jaw and determined face. She seemed intermittingly to be elsewhere and then suddenly focused on her passengers. She made eye contact with him for just a moment, and then got back to watching the telemetry again.

In a few minutes, the bulk of the Assault Corps flagship came into view. *Challenger* appeared to be undamaged, at least on the outside. Timberwolf surmised that Dr. Tier must have acquired this ship by the use of non-traditional force. Seemed typical. "So, anything I need to know?" Timberwolf motioned to the massive cruiser hanging several thousand yards away, "about that?"

He hadn't expected much information, and her eyes said, *don't ask now.*

Arnar shrugged contentedly, and they sat in silence as the shuttle sidled alongside the ship. Timberwolf noted that the docking bay doors were open and glowing with light. This could only mean one thing – there was nobody aboard *Challenger* with authorization to open them.

The airlock hissed open, and they found Conrad on the other side with a plasma pistol levelled on them. "It's fine," Dr. Tier advised him, and he lowered his weapon. He noted Arnar and his crew. The motley assortment loomed behind Dr. Tier and Timberwolf.

"It's fine?" Conrad questioned.

"Yes, it's all copacetic." She stepped aside and Arnar and his people came aboard. "I need you to bring Captain Mallis and his crew to the mess. Show them to coffee."

Conrad came close to her, so only she and Timberwolf could hear.

"Should I free the crew?" he asked awkwardly.

"Yes, but Jephtah and Sindar first," Dr. Tier replied.

At Captain Jephtah's name, Timberwolf's eyes went wide. *What?!* he mouthed.

"You need to come with me. I need your help breaking orbit." Dr. Tier turned to go, and Timberwolf followed her.

"You don't seem yourself," he said as they turned corners. To Timberwolf, she looked exhausted, but she also exuded energy, like someone who had been running for a long time but was steeled and committed for the miles to go.

"You and I have a lot in common," she replied, after considering her response.

"That is 100% not true. What the hell are you talking about?" he asked.

She got into the lift that went to the command deck. Timberwolf noted a dull red stain on the wall. She didn't reply until the doors opened and they stepped out onto the bridge.

"We need to get out of here and hide in the streams for a bit, until and if I decide to trust your new friends. That's a hell of an offer, a 3D printing operation." Dr. Tier strapped into the pilot's chair. She flicked on displays showing *Challenger's* position in orbit over Nova Turin.

"You've got a lot going on, huh?" Timberwolf said dryly. She didn't respond but motioned for him to review the departure checklist that scrolled down via a hologram in the middle of the room. "Looks like the shuttle bay door is still open. That would have killed us all." He closed the door and resolved a few other issues before turning to her. "Thea, just jump to the end. What is going on?"

Her face tried a few emotions, starting with bitter conviction and ending with her lip nearly trembling. "I never believed you, Timber." He nodded; knowing more was coming. "You carried something in your head for years."

Oh shit, he gripped a railing near the pilot's chair. He counted the moves it might take to kill her. "Have you not been sleeping well, for any specific reason?" he asked, trying to remain steely calm.

"I sleep fine. I take melatonin."

"How about a grinding, in the back of your mind, all the time?"

"It's like having a passenger," she said, leaving the rest to him.

"Kizik?" he asked. He looked over her face for the same creases and twitches he'd seen in the mirror when the alien spider had been in his own head. Timberwolf kneaded the intelligence together. "He helped you take *Challenger!* Why?"

She stared at him. Her eyes were cold, but her voice was as soft as he had ever heard it. "We have fucked up. There is something a lot bigger than our little war with the

Assault Corps, Timber. Highland was a bigger disaster than we knew."

"Where is Vincent?" Timberwolf asked.

She shrugged her shoulders. "He's dead, or not, or in a new body. But he's got us fighting each other while Gray wakes the Symmetry."

"Gray took Salla with him," he responded.

She let that hang in the air. "Timber, I was very stupid when I threatened you aboard *Archangel* before Highland. I said I was considering throwing you out the airlock. If I had tried that, you would have killed every one of us."

"Oh, so he's given you that too?" He imagined her fighting through *Challenger*, viciously killing anyone that got in her way. "And you sleep fine!?"

She nodded in reply.

"What do you want?" Timberwolf paced, finding himself looking at a cracked display panel. He surmised that her violence had taken her all the way to the bridge.

"As usual, you're critical. We *have* to find Gray before he wakes the Symmetry. There must have been some clue as to where he was going. Did Salla give you any idea?"

Timberwolf pulled the cufflinks Salla had given him from his pocket. "She gave me these. She said she would explain later."

"It's past later."

He clicked them together, clumsily connecting them but to no avail. "If I knew what these did, I would tell you."

"No, you wouldn't."

"What's the difference now?" he spat back.

She engaged *Challenger's* engines, committing him to at least taking the next part of this journey with her. He steadied himself as the ship rocked forward. Its acceleration was smooth, and terrifically powerful. He took Dr. Tier in as a singular element for a moment, harnessing this powerhouse of a vessel as an extension of herself. She looked at him, and instead of looking through him like she usually did, she peered *into* him. As if with one gaze she knew what every molecule in his body was doing.

A smile came from the corner of her bottom lip. A chill went through him and stayed at the back of his neck. She wasn't pushing Kizik away, she was drawing him in. Gray may have been a monster but at least he didn't choose the path. "I'm scared of you, Thea," he said to her.

She shuddered, as if suddenly exposed. "Of all the people, that feels like a compliment coming from you."

"I've been there, and I wanted to blow Kizik out of my head." He pulled his pistol from his hip and handed the charged weapon to her.

She turned it over, like it was a tool she'd never seen before. "Why would I want to do that?"

"Yeah, I'm scared of you," he said, snatching the pistol away.

"There's no way out for you. Not now," she told him.

"Don't tempt me."

"Gray has Salla. We're going to where they *both* are. Stick with me a little longer." In that moment he considered if he even had the moves to kill her. Would Kizik take her over and murder him if he stepped out of line? He considered blowing the reactor. He knew four different ways to do that.

"Timber, I know what you're thinking. You've got a streak in you. Beyond all the times you've pulled the trigger, you think you're a boy scout. I just want you to know something, we *are* still the good guys."

He considered a dozen rants and counters to that argument but could surface none of them. He threw up his hands, literally and figuratively. "Can I go? Maybe find something to eat?"

"Dismissed," she replied, with unnerving calm.

He took the lift from the bridge and buried his head in his hands. "Peace," he muttered. The door opened and he found himself face to face with Jephtah, escorted by Conrad. She nodded, acknowledging him. "She's at peace," Timberwolf said to her.

Jephtah looked to the bridge, to where she had been summoned. "That good?" she asked.

"No," he replied. "It is very, very bad."

EVERYTHING IS ILLUMINATED

Symmetry Lifeship

Gray knew where to go and even though he had nearly infinite time, he rushed through the still city to his destination. He descended into the administrative command area, through corridors alternately carved from gleaming white and obsidian black marble. He reduced the size of his entropy bubble and nimbly avoided stirring the ferocious soldiers he passed in the halls. He soon found himself exactly where he needed to be, at a door left slightly ajar.

Vincent left the door open, how nice.

He slipped inside. He found everything covered in blood.

Even as he had prepared himself for the next step in his story, Gray was shocked by what he found. For a moment, he considered stepping back and departing this place entirely. Blood covered the floor. Blood slicked the railings. Footprints of wine-colored blood tracked about the room. All of it stilled down to the molecule, this pivotal moment frozen like a diorama. A purple mist hung in the air before a figure that grasped upward at another in agony.

Tanqar and his brother Raif.

The details of what had happened here came to Gray. There had been an argument over the pursuit of the Srathi Lifeship. Srathi, a mortal enemy the Symmetry had been fighting for generations. It had been Raif's Semi – his half-day of command. Tanqar had seen the danger and knew they were walking into a trap. Raif's guards had done their duty and drew their knives on Tanqar. If time hadn't stopped in this moment, Tanqar would surely be lying here dead.

Gray knelt down next to Tanqar, careful not to allow his entropy bubble to touch him just yet. He pulled a cylinder from his pocket and looked at the inscription on the side. It was Tanqar's name in the swirling Symmetrian language. A billion nano-menders swam inside it, specially calibrated by Vincent for Tanqar's injuries and physiology. Still, Gray took stock of his wounds and doubted how anything could help him survive when time began to flow again. "OK, here's the first miracle."

Across the room, standing in the corner was someone who did not look like she should be here. A young, female Symmetry – an adolescent – stood wide-eyed with her hands to her sides. *When my brother came, he left her here, so she could help tell your story. She's Pisen Gane.* Gray heard Vincent's voice in his mind. "At least someone knew what was going on," Gray remarked.

Gray took his breaths in short huffs and readied the cylinder in his hand. He popped open the cap, exposing a dozen short needles. Tanqar had his neck exposed and his head craned up at his brother. Gray would inject using an underhand thrust. *Strike as hard and fast as you can!* He felt the instruction from Vincent come to him.

With that, Gray swung upward to where a jugular vein should be. In that instant, Gray's entropy bubble enveloped Tanqar and the tiny healing devices surged into his bloodstream. Tanqar writhed and fell to the floor and Gray pulled him into his lap. He jabbed another cylinder of nano-menders over his heart that were simple coagulants.

Blood gushed from between Tanqar's teeth and the Symmetry locked eyes with Gray. An expression of disbelief appeared on Tanqar's face at the sight of this alien, suddenly here and helping him. The Symmetry stiffened and arched his back. Gray wrapped his arms around him, holding him as still as possible while the nano-menders did their work.

He kicked like a beast and Gray felt like he was squeezing the life from Tanqar instead of trying to infuse it back in. A few minutes later though, he relaxed and Gray released him from his grip. He lay breathing heavily on the floor, rolling his head from side to side. Gray opened Tanqar's tunic and covered his wounds with battlefield patches, to help keep the blood and menders inside him.

Gray sat and caught his breath, even with his enhanced strength; it had taken everything he had to hold Tanqar down. Now he took in the scene around him, this place filled with so much chaos. He wondered how the hell he was supposed to explain who he was and convince everyone here not to kill him. He stood and waited for the information from Vincent to arrive, but nothing came. He didn't think any revelations would be forthcoming from God either, and he was right on that account. He reached for his smart-device and on its screen, a red button blinked. He knew it could only do one thing.

"The tests keep coming," he said to himself. He pressed the button and waited, unsure what the next moments might bring. At first, he thought nothing had happened, but then he felt the buzz. An energy field emanated from his device, at first moving just inches at a time, but then accelerating exponentially.

As the energy field went through the walls of the room, everything came to life again. Raif, the Symmetry that Tanqar had been prostrate before, noticed Gray first. "Hello." Gray purred to him, trying the Symmetrian language. "I have a story to tell you. You've had a long day."

For more news about Tom Julian, subscribe
to our newsletter at *wbp.bz/newsletter*.

Word-of-mouth is critical to an author's long-term
success. If you appreciated this book, please leave a
review on the Amazon sales page at *wbp.bz/rubicon*.

To learn more about the Timberwolf series,
visit *facebook.com/Timberwolf*.